REFLECTIONS
More Tales from Tipperary

Edward Forde Hickey

Grosvenor House
Publishing Limited

This book is published by
Grosvenor House Publishing Ltd
Link House
140 The Broadway, Tolworth, Surrey, KT6 7HT.
www.grosvenorhousepublishing.co.uk

This book is a work of fiction. Any resemblance to
people or events, past or present, is purely coincidental.

A CIP record for this book
is available from the British Library

ISBN 978-1-83975-289-6

CONTENTS

FOREWORD

I first came to know Edward Forde Hickey (the author of these tales) in 2015 when his debut novel – 'The Early Morning Light' – was published. Edward spent his early years living with his grandmother in a post-war hillside community not too far from Keeper Hill in north Tipperary. His first foray into writing captured wonderfully his many reminisces of growing up, and he successfully continued that theme in each of his follow-ups ('A New Day Dawning', 'Footsteps in the Dew' and 'A Bunch of Wild Roses'). All of the books were inspired by the people, places and happenings of a rural part of Tipperary similar to the book's fictitious arena.

These days, Edward lives in Kent but keeps a small farm in Dolla, not far from the town of Nenagh. He has always felt that the rural lives of previous generations were inspiring enough to captivate those readers who have an interest in Ancestry itself and the particular way in which the past social landscape, unchanged over the centuries, has contrasted with our own busy and impersonal world – a time in our history when country folk had to make do with very little and form their own amusements.

His tales were compiled during the recent pandemic lockdown and they authentically mirror the vibrancy of a closely-knit group of people, each story dealing with the complex daily emotions of love and hatred. They include colourful incidents in the lives of bonesetters, matchmakers, youthful lovers, newcomers from beyond the mountains, and a reformed villain's wedding - which was celebrated by the whole community for days thereafter - and much more besides!

Edwards writes with an eloquent prose that celebrates the colloquial tongue of the times he depicts. This small volume has been written in a lyrical language similar to that of past storytellers, and I am sure you will find his tales enthralling, even unbelievable at times. They should certainly appeal to those not only with an interest in Ireland's social history but to fans of his earlier novels.

Simon O'Duffy, Nenagh Guardian, Tipperary

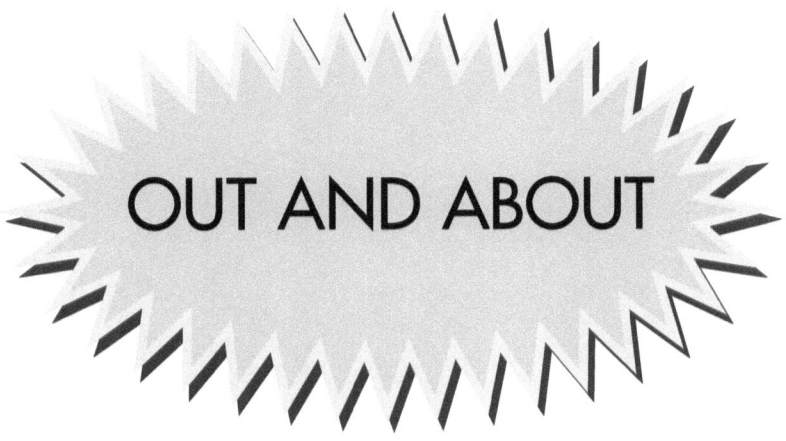

OUT AND ABOUT

1

One Saturday of late we saw two of Moll-the-Man's children (Lippy and Philly) heading down towards the orchard for their usual afternoon ritual ('twas the same with all her older children) - the joy of lighting up the fag-butts stolen from their grandmother's tobacco-jar and trying to put the smoke out through their ears and noses. They were sitting as contented as you like on the fallen fir tree at the lower end of the orchard near the well-hole and had just started their smoke, when the rain from far-off Kerry came down suddenly, the way it always did from beyond Corcoran's well. Soon it was hopping off of the road and turning it from bone-white to deep blue. From their half-hidden hidey-hole in the ditch, they could see the huge spatters making music off of the puddles.

Then they heard the flapping wellingtons of Leggins (the son of Leppalong) stamping down the road. The rain was beating off of his black beardy face and his ashplant was bouncing gallantly on his shoulder. Strutting along behind him were his three important-looking piggies (named A, B, and C), their snouts pointing pompously up in the air. Lippy and Philly had to laugh at the sight of these charming little creatures dancing a tippy-tappy rhythm in the middle of the downpour and their curly tails shivering along behind them. They were spaced out in a line like obedient little school children and following Leggins towards Echo Bridge and Gret's Kill and then on to Curl 'n' Stripes' shop door for Leggins' daily package of biscuits and his pint of stout. Rain or shine, nothing ever stopped this quaint little scenario. Leggins would ring the silver door-bell, enter the shop, sit on the barrel-planks, munch and crunch his biscuits, scrape his lips deliciously across the pint-glass, and rub the froth delicately onto his coat-sleeve.

From outside the shop door, his little piggies could be heard setting up an almighty racket that would have suited the Abbey Theatre above in Dublin.

'Come on out, Leggins — come on out to hell, blasht ye!' they seemed to cry. 'Can't ye see we're awfully lonesome out here, standing around in the rain.' It was clear there'd be no knife-of-death to pierce the throats of these princely little creatures. Leggins (the big softy that he always was) would rather die than let anyone put a hand on his petty-petty piglets. Oh, Leggins! Leggins! From where on earth did your mother get you? Was it from under some foreign gooseberry-bush that she dropped you? In heaven's name, piglets and pets, I ask you.

2

It was a fine spring day, and Clever Jack got down on one knee and held Caruso close to his side.

He whispered into the ear of his brave little dog, 'Caruso, mee noble friend, what good fortune has brought the two of us here this blessed day?' He turned the little hound's nose to where he was looking across at a carefree hare, sunning itself some distance away.

The little dog was already following his master's eye, looking at the gently sloping bank and the little stream that flowed in between themselves and the hare. What a mighty challenge a gap of a hundred paces would prove for a masterful dog like Caruso and the speed of his gifted feet. His instincts were already aflame for chasing the hare, aflame for its blood, aflame for the killing of this mysterious creature.

He emitted a faint humming whine, scraping his paws at the ground. Then away he flew, faster than an eye could blink, zipping through the ferns and leaving terror behind him midst the fluttering hearts of small birds and their chicks. In days to come, the cardplayers round the fire would compare him to the Limerick train, to the streak of blue lightning — even to the new electricity, whose unknown force flew magically through time and space. And when the legend of Caruso became a part of their everyday life, our children would rise to the heights of poetry. Caruso (they'd tell you) outshone the shimmering sun that day before it plunged into the silvery sea. What a flame (said they) there was in Caruso's red-hot paws! Was it wings (said they) that sprouted from his wiry legs?

The little dog leapt the stream and raced up the slope that led to Clashing River. Nearer and nearer he drew to the terrified hare. Two desperate animals lost to everything else in the world. For one of them, the gloomy fates were now waiting, accompanied by their sad-eyed mother (Lady Luck herself), who had hurtled down from the sky. She wrapped her arms round the hare and pointed to a small hole in the stone-wall ditch.

'A last desperate chance for you, my little friend,' she whispered.

There followed an agonizing dash — just an inch between the hare and Caruso — an Olympian leap out of the hare's body and a supernatural lunge from Caruso as he dived against the stonewall ditch. With a push and a shove from Lady Luck, the hare flew through the hole.

No-one but Clever Jack was there to witness the hare's great leap or to marvel at the brave lunge of Caruso. In years to come, he'd wear our ears off by comparing the leaps of both creatures to those of the noble cheetah herself.

Caruso! Oh, Caruso! How can we ever forget what hap-pened to you that terrible day — how you drove your bared teeth at the retreating heels of the hare and how the hare (bewitched, said some) hurled her palpitating mass those last six feet at the chasm that lay between her life and death.

Caruso! — most wretched of all dogs — you wouldn't stop. You couldn't stop. And in that fierce trajectory of speed (a race too great even for so fleet and famed a hound as yourself), you struck your miserable head off of the stonewall ditch.

From where he was standing, a sobbing Clever Jack saw Caruso turn somersaults in the air and knew for certain that death had snatched his dearest friend from him. He hauled his wellingtons over the stream and tramped over to the ditch. The fur on Caruso's back was tinged with the lovely pink light of the sun, but that was all. For there the little hound lay — no better than a broken twig, his dog-soul now far out over the clouds and on its journey into everlasting darkness.

It seemed as if Clever Jack's own heartstrings had flown out of his body like a bird from a gunshot. He picked up Caruso's body, and the tears started flowing down the sides of his nose. The dog's blood was on his hands, and he kept asking himself what unimaginable harm had he ever done to any man (or beast for that matter) to deserve so hateful a punishment as this? He hadn't stolen an ass or a calf like the tinkers. He hadn't (God forbid) run off with another man's wife. And this was his reward — the death of the finest dog that ever warmed a man's blankets during the night.

He began making cat-like noises like some crazed banshee: 'Mee fine friend-of-a-dog, why on earth couldn't I have died in yeer place?' It was Caruso's unstoppable speed that had crushed his skull off of the stone wall. He knew it. And yet, so close to victory had the little dog been (would you believe it!), that his teeth still held the white smoky trails of fur from the hare's tail.

Poor Caruso. In future days when hares and rabbits shake the dew from their hind legs, you'll never be there to taste the freezing air of the early morning, never stand at the stream to let the cows drink their fill as you eyeball your master with your soul-kiss, never feel the crispness of the fragrant ferns near Red Scissors' ditch.

Clever Jack hobbled out the gap to his mare (Red Baggy), but how he got there he'd never be able to tell you. The mare too seemed to be full of her own animal sadness at the sight of Caruso hanging down the length of Clever Jack's back.

3

Moll-the-Man's children ran down the hill and saw Caruso lying dead on Red Baggy's saddle. They couldn't help noticing the tears in the dead dog's eyes. Nor had they ever seen a grown man crying, and yet here was Clever Jack, and he was bawling like a sick ass.

A day later, their father (By-Jiggery) told them that the big man (to quote Dowager's scholarly words) had turned himself into an indolent recluse and had taken to his bed with neither a bite of food nor a drop of drink inside him. By-Jiggery had gone up there to milk the poor man's cows for him. Little did he know that for the first time in his life, Clever Jack had felt his blood about to stop pumping round his body, that he'd never again be able to move a muscle or get up out of bed.

A day or two passed by in this way, and still no-one heard a scrap of news about the poor man — not even from the old gossips at the well. None of the children were sure what they should do. They couldn't ask the grown-ups about it for not one of them helped them a bit these days or gave them an ounce of praise. Instead, they were forever making them the daily butt of their wrathful reprimands. This had been especially true during these last sunny days when we had witnessed the children's youthful restlessness and playfulness. We referred to them as scallywags or ragamuffins — even scoundrels — depending on what particular crime they were charged with — like kicking Old Stroller's dog around the yard while he was inside in the cowshed milking his cows or bellowing out his rosary in front of the Sacred Heart picture inside in his welcoming room.

The question for them now was, what should they do about Clever Jack? They couldn't stay sitting on their hands doing nothing about a sadness as great as this — one that their old friend had never experienced before, could they? If they did, there'd be no dark evenings when they could go visit him and listen to him prattling off one of his lying tales.

A change had now come over them, and they couldn't explain it — as though an unknown force had taken hold of them - an impulse to do something completely out of the ordinary, and they promised themselves that the woes of Clever Jack would become their own woes from now on. Indeed, they would.

On Friday morning, the three older ones (Lippy, Philly, and Gallantry) were awake - even before the sunrise - and they took the three-mile trek to Copperstone Hollow where it was rumoured that Black Sal's whippet (Rosy-Nose) was about to bring forth her litter of puppies. She had made her little bitch as comfortable as possible behind the bikes and mangolds-pulper abroad in the turf-shed with heaps of straw under her belly to keep her snug and calm. Rosy-Nose whined contentedly and, an hour later, delivered her four puppies without too much traces of blood out of her. However the weakest of these tiny specks was unable to feed off of her milk, and Black Sal took him into the house and placed him in a cardboard box near the fire where she fed him with a heated bottle of milk.

It was getting on for mid-morning before the children were able to reach the village and walk into Black Sal's yard. They flattened their noses up against the window and peeped in longingly at the newly-born puppy. Black Sal saw them, and she called them in. She had to smile at their tongue-tied shyness but soon began to realise the depths of their pity for Clever Jack over the death of his young hound.

She gave them each a slice of currant cake and a mug of milk and then handed them the cardboard box with the bewildered little puppy inside it. She made sure there was plenty of straw under it and a few holes for it to breathe. The merry smiles and joyful eyes of the children — they couldn't get out the door fast enough and they each took turns to carry their tiny gift the long trek home. For the next few days (together with By-Jiggery), they nursed the infant dog into something like a fit state of health.

The following Wednesday saw the daylight creeping up the sky and sharpening the trees' outline in Clever Jack's haggart. Not that he'd ever notice. The children tiptoed across his yard and peeped in the window at the sleeping huntsman. They beckoned their little sister (Battlin' Sal) inside the half-door, and, together with her, they tiptoed across the floor to his bedroom door. The little girl now had the honour of laying the puppy in some hay on the floor beside Clever Jack's bed together with a bowl of bran-mash and milk, and they all waited outside the half-closed bedroom door and peeped in to see what would happen next.

Clever Jack lifted his head from the pillow and glanced towards the window. A tide of bright sunlight flooded across the room and rested, not just on his own weary face, but on the face of something else. He turned in the bed and blinked back the sleep from his eyes. And then he saw a small watery-eyed puppy lying beside his bed and looking up at him. Was he drunk or was he dreaming? The bedroom seemed hotter than usual, as though one of the angels was passing by. Even the flies seemed to be happily singing in the shafts of light and the back wall to be glowing.

He staggered out of bed and his heart, which had been almost dead, began to shake fiercely inside him, and his blood started rumbling round his body once more so that he felt he'd break asunder with joy.

'Yoong bones! Yoong bones!' he kept crying, as he gazed down at the puppy. He knelt beside his bed and he thanked his Saviour again and again for this wonderful gift. The mystery of how a tiny dog came to be lying in the middle of his room was never revealed to this simple soul, and from that day to this, he has never found out from which part of the universe such a heavenly gift was delivered to him.

'I will call ye Lightning — yes, Lightning will be yeer name,' he cried, picking up the shivering puppy and holding it to his heart.

And each day after that, seeing that it was still unable to drink or eat too well, he guided it with an almost motherly patience to its scraps of bread and milk.

The following morning, Moll-the-Man's children were out in the Rishy Field, the little ones trying to catch a storm of white petals that were blowing down from the overhanging branches of Old Stroller's apple tree and they all laughing hysterically. At the other end of the field and with their usual wild war-cries (hoolah! hoolah!), the older ones were encouraging their sheepdog, Shark (the very same dog into whose eyes they had spat their tobacco juice only the week before) to go off and catch some imaginary rabbits from inside Old Stroller's ditch.

Suddenly, they all stopped playing, and they listened. They could hear the mechanical sound of Clever Jack's axe chopping his logs outside his cabin and then they heard the stamp of his boots as he came down the side of his pig house with an armful of logs. Inside in his welcoming room, he threw a few bits of broken candles and a half-jar of paraffin amongst the kindling and brown paper. He put a match to the burning twigs and listened to them crackling. After a smoky start, the fire began flickering and then feathery rivers of firelight shone on him and vomited cheerfully up the chimney. Smoke was soon belching its way up out of the thatch.

The children ran out onto the road and stood there, fascinated on seeing the smoke. They smiled, and they laughed and kept on doing so. They knew it — by-jakish, they knew it! The daylight had come back into their old friend's life, and from now on, his life would be nothing but a load of smiles and dimples. They jumped over the singletree into Old Stroller's orchard and sat on the fallen pine tree. The older boys lit up a few celebratory fag-butts (the ones they'd again stolen from their grandmother's tobacco-jar) and once more put streams of smoke out through their ears and noses. Battlin' Sal watched the way her big brothers smoked — like men — with her usual awe and admiration. Yes, it had turned out to be a blissful bit of a day, and they purred like a group of wise old cats in front of a big bowl of cream.

Later on, Clever Jack was sitting by his fire. He cupped his hands and lit himself his first Woodbine fag in ages, inhaling mouthfuls of smoke and puffing it out deliciously. He lolled back in his chair and watched the wreaths of firelight in front of him. Suddenly, he looked down and saw that the little puppy was again squinting up at him.

'Ye'll be a great big hunter, mee young friend,' said he, 'a great big hunter like the mighty Caruso before yeer time,' and shafts of softness sped from his eyes and down into the puppy's eyes.

He lifted the bemused little fellow in his arms and hurried up from the fireside, almost swallowing him with affection. He brought him over to the holy water font at the half-door where he made the sign-of-the-cross on his nose, blessing him ceremoniously as though he were baptizing him. He took his cap from the nail and put it on. Then he rushed down the haggart towards the laurels behind the reek. It was as if he was showing his new gift to the ghost of Caruso, who was now lying buried beneath the sod at that end of the haggart. For the first time in an eternity, he could sense the murmuring melodies in the trees and see the flickering leaf-shadows dancing in his yard stream.

4

What with all the ribbons and bits of string, the floor of Moll-the-Man's welcoming room was as cluttered as a fair day. From some unknown treasure box, she had managed to find a number of black jerseys and some dark skirts and trousers for her would-be child actors on this great day — Hunting-the-Wren. The first thing she did was put several bottle-corks into the fire to blacken them and then smudge her children's arms and legs with them. As if that wasn't enough, she scraped the soot from the back of the hob till she had a canister full of it.

The children lined up in a row and held out their arms and cheeks for her to blacken till they looked like a bunch of black natives out of Africa. Moll's niece (Pudge) arranged rows of masks on the table, and the children (even little Battlin' Sal) chose a mask apiece. Their mother tied them fussily round their jaws with a bit of twine.

To see the excitement when they were all dressed up! And then, like a herd of charging bulls, they made a few wild runs at one another till they almost toppled into the fire. The noise of them must surely have alarmed Clever Jack and his puppy in the nearby haggart. Their appearance frightened the daylights out of the inquisitive cat (Hen-chaser), who was peering in the half-door. It was a wonder Moll-the-Man didn't spend the rest of the day in bed with a splitting headache, but she was determined to put some semblance of order on their childish playfulness and at last she managed to line them up outside in the yard.

There followed a solemn procession, which must have frightened to death the hens, ducks and geese (and the bemused Hen-chaser all over again) as the little masquerade marched round the dung heap, over by the pig house, in under the haggart trees, down by the hen house and back into the welcoming room.

At this stage of their lives, they could all sing and dance a bit — skills acquired from By-Jiggery rather than Moll-the-Man for she, like her mother (Ducks-and-Drakes), hadn't a stem of music in her head. However, she reminded her young actors that as soon as they reached a stranger's yard and began their entertainment, they must trot out only their very best songs like *Banbury-Fair and Little-brown-jug-don't I love thee* and recite only their best poems like *The gypsy rover came over the hill*, which their schoolmaster (Dang-the-skin-of-it) had drummed into their skulls whilst marching them up and down among the carrots and lettuces in his garden to keep the weeds down.

By this time, it was nine o'clock, and By-Jiggery had already taken the cows back to the Rishy Field. The excitement had increased to an intolerable level. An hour or two later, every child round the slopes would be vying with each other in giving their best artistic performance. The efforts of By-Jiggery's children would have to match those they had rehearsed with him the previous week if the old folk in the hills were to reward them with a few coppers for the traditional wren's capture (the wren that had betrayed Jesus in the garden of Gethsemane).

They stood at the half-door and blessed themselves at the holy water font. The journey was going to take them at least an hour. The older children (crafty beggars) had searched the place upside-down so as to steal their mother or father's old boots from whatever press or cupboard they could and fill them with brown paper. The younger ones were not so quick off the mark and would have to go shoeless. Their feet, however, were as hard as a shovel from rarely having seen a shoe — except for the special pair they had for Sunday Mass or when entering the school gate. Not to worry, their big brothers would carry them on their sympathetic backs for much of the way.

The band of masked entertainers made their way first of all to Ducks-and-Drakes' yard where they'd be joined by a number of other children at the side of her hayshed. She and her excited flocks of turkeys and geese were already waiting for them out in the road. It was the same thing every year, flocks of children with their sparkling costumes arriving more or less at the same time — a sight that regularly delighted old Ducks-and-Drakes. They'd place their masks on the lower bench of hay so that everyone could get a proper look at them and see the way each house had cleverly invented its own set of frightening masks.

Ducks-and-Drakes quietened the noisy children and lined them up for the parade. She marched them round the side of the hayshed and down by the cowshed. The turkeys and geese (her hens were far too startled to offer so much as a croak) made their own stately procession behind the masked visitors. It wasn't every day they had the privilege of witnessing so fine a spectacle as this, and they looked well-pleased with it all. The geese clapped their wings, and the turkeys gobbled in a manner that only a priest could surpass during his Sunday sermon.

Ducks-and-Drakes would now be the judge and jury of all the masks and black outfits. She brought her rocking-chair out into the yard and rocked herself back and forth in front of the strutting children. She laughed her two sides silly at the sight of them and the way they twisted and turned in front of her. The inspection of the masks then took place, and she (cute lady) heaped praises on the individual features of each and every mask. The children were well satisfied when she said she was sure they'd all get a great collection of coppers for their singing and reciting before the day was out. She hoped so, for the money they collected was to be brought back to her so that she and the rest of the women could run down to Curl 'n' Stripes shop and bring back a list as long as your arm for the evening feast: the sugar and tea, the two types of lemonade (the red and the clear), the jellies and iced cakes and the various jams so that the children could have the treat of their lives.

But where on earth were they all going to fit in for this evening's festivities? There was only one house big enough to prepare itself for such merriment — the long-house of Din-Din-Dinny, whose welcoming room was as long and wide as a barn.

For the second time that day, the children waved goodbye and set sail for the hills, each group finding the route that Ducks-and-Drakes had mapped out for them. In their fanciful masks, they felt grander than Bishop High-Hat with his colourful red-and-purple rig-out when he came for the sacrament of confirmation. This was the one day in the year when they'd outshine even their mothers and fathers.

Their journey would take them out past the forge before turning for the house of the tin-whistle player (Gentleman Jim), who had half a dozen beggars sleeping with him every year, each competing in singing their unique songs, the likes of which were never heard before or since.

So as not to get their throats too hoarse, they kept their singing voices soft and low when marching towards the first of the strangers' houses — that is until they were within earshot of the yard. Then they set up such an unholy din that the sow and the cockerel ran for their lives, in over the ditch. The masks were so heavily disguised - their mimicking voices too - that they knew they'd never get recognized. And besides, they were much too far from Ducks-and-Drakes' yard, and nobody up here had a chance in hell of knowing who were these children hiding behind their masks.

The old men and women, however, were always a suspicious and inquisitive lot and in each of the houses they would heave a sigh and put their fingers on their lips and drop their heads to one side.

'Who have we in it at all, at all?' they'd say. 'Who's hiding behind this fierce-looking mask? Let me have a little peep at ye — g'wan, do!' This was part and parcel of the day's entertainment, and the children were expected to turn their heads away and pretend they were anybody other than who they really were, giving out any lying name other than their own (I'm Jonjo Gleeson from Knockahopple), to make sure the old schemers didn't recognize the face behind the mask. Otherwise, they'd go home without a copper to their name.

They started off by bowing their heads.

'We are the Wran-byze,' they said, as though the old people were blind fools altogether and hadn't been able to work this bit out for themselves! Then they commenced their traditional song of the wren (the little bird caught in a furze-bush) followed by their own practised songs and recitations, which they hoped would dazzle the old-timers and get them a pile of money.

By late afternoon, they'd sung a good few songs and recited all their school-day poems. All they had to do now was sit on the ditch, empty their pockets, and count the jingling coins. It didn't need much imagination to picture the sparkling glasses of lemonade and the iced buns that'd be laid out for them that evening at Din-Din-Dinny's place.

At last, worn to a thread, it was time to say farewell and go home and get ready for the evening. They trudged down the hill and, as soon as they were home and with whatever strength they had left, they began polishing the pewter and scrubbing the crockery that they'd be taking up to Din-Din-Dinny's.

An hour later — and before the grown-ups brought back the fine food and drink from the shop — they had put such a shine on Din-Din-Dinny's table and press-cupboard, that both sparkled like jewels. It'd put young and old alike in the best possible humour for the evening's festivities.

It was now evening, and the grown-up guests came in (there were so many of them) to join with the giggling children and share in the celebrations. The tables were heaped high with Ducks-and-Drakes' currant-cakes, and Moll-the-Man had brought up her famed doorstep sandwiches (you couldn't get your jaws round them) with plenty of butter and layers of sugar and jam on the top.

And now we could see that the crows in the treetops were never going to get a wink of sleep. For one or two of the older children were handy with the concertina, and they seated themselves underneath the hob in case a roguish dancer with his almighty dance-steps should knock off one of their musical fingers. Everybody (even the shy little ones) joined in the polka set-tunes with their own paper-and-comb instruments, their rattle-slates or spoons tearing into the rhythm of the dance. The entire gathering was full of good cheer, and the children were enjoying the swish and the grace of their parents' half-sets and siege-dances. Some had already worked their way out beneath the rising stars and round the shaded yard. You would think the blaze from the turf-fire was underneath their feet.

What a time we were all having until a sudden bit of sad news came in and hit us like a rock. Larry from Cureeny had lost his arm in the mineworks, catching it between the sidewall and the cage. It happened at four o'clock — just as he was coming up to the surface and when the children were cleaning the soot from their arms and legs. Our joy in the music and dance was completely gone from us, and Din-Din-Dinny's floor was as cold as the grave. Poor, misfortunate Larry!

The younger children sat huddled round the fire, a wave of darkness hugging them and their little hearts wobbling in their chests. They'd never felt anything like this before. It was like the pity they'd recently felt for Clever Jack, only much stronger — a feeling of the utmost sorrow.

The older children could picture Larry as he once was, he and his rosy face and his blue shirt and his stylish Sunday boots and his new brown suit and his Woodbine fag dangling from the corner of his mouth. Would he ever again be able to strike a match to light a fag for himself? They remembered the time he'd cast the smoke mischievously out through his ears so that all of them were left squealing with delight. They recalled his rubbery lips, which never showed a tooth in his head while he was speaking and yet, when he was laughing, showed a truly beautiful set of white teeth. And now old and young alike reached for their coats and with bowed heads all of us disappeared off into the night.

SAMMY

1

In Merrymouth's drinking-shop, Saturday evening was always the same. The drinkers knew what was coming when Sammy started throwing out his hatred against the British above in what he called the black north. The nudges and jokey laughter of one or two young rascals only added to his rage. They couldn't get enough of his hobnail boots stamping in temper across the floor. They could see him marching up to the black north. They could see him marching twice as quickly back home with his britches very wet. Oh yes, they could!

As they goaded him further, Sammy worked himself up into an even grander head of steam, drilling his military goose-steps round the floor and making sharp wheeling turns with an imaginary rifle on his brave shoulder — up to the door and back to the counter.

'Which of ye little whipping-boys is man enough to come with me,' said he 'and put up a bit of a fight in the north?' The young men left down their pints of stout and slapped him on the back.

'We're behind ye, Sammy — every man-jack of us!' There followed another bout of laughter. 'More power to yeer elbow, Sammy,' they said and filled his glass once more for him. But Sammy knew they were merely laughing at him — that it was simply a way of passing the time for them.

'By-jakish, if none of ye basthards will go with me, I'll go meeself and set fire to the bleddy heathens.' And once more, the shop resounded with laughter at the picture of Sammy putting up a bit of a fight for the freedom of the black north.

And that's when the Yellow-Boy came into our tale. He lived a mile from the drinking-shop and was a bit of a rogue.

He was known to be a dasher after the ladies and was seen wearing the best of clothes ever since his return from tunnel work in the hills of Bonny Scotland. Like his father before him, he was known as something of a rebel and a man with dark and bloodthirsty intentions against those he called the foreign settlers above in the north. He had got hold of a starting-pistol from somewhere across the Irish Sea. Such an item was something that none of us had ever seen before or had even heard tell of. The reason he had it (he said) was to frighten away the fox and the weasel from his hen house. This pistol would make an unholy racket when fired.

A Saturday night came on and our thoughts were bent as usual on next day's Mass and trying to fathom out what Father Laudable's sermon might be urging us to do with our lives. The evening light began to grow dark, and Sammy was again strutting about like a young turkeycock inside the drinking-shop. He'd been drinking like a fish and had his hurley-stick strapped to his shoulder. He was making little runs and dashes here and there and again pointing his so-called gun fiercely at one or two of the shyer drinkers. Once more, he saw himself as the leader in the burning of the black north.

There came a sudden tap on his shoulder. It was the Yellow-Boy. He leaned in close to Sammy and whispered conspiratorially in his ear.

'Don't turn around or look behind, Sammy. We have a miserable traitor in our midst this very evening.' He let this bit of dreadful news sink into Sammy's bleary head before he went on. 'We've got orders from the commandant to get rid of the basthard before we take ourselves off home tonight. Sammy, my noble friend, this is what the rest of us were thinking when we held our meeting last night above in the Rebels' Den — that we could depend on yeer good self to give us a bit of a hand in the killing of this bleddy article. Ye're the very man for the job. It's yeer one great chance to make a bit of fighting history for yeerself.' The Yellow-Boy (the rascally hound that he always was) could hardly hold back the laughter that was bubbling up inside in his throat. 'Sammy, will ye listen to me for once in yeer life and stop fiddling with that old hurley-stick. Believe me, yeer job is of the utmost importance — vital to our fighting cause. Once we have him outside, ye're to keep a sharp look-out for the Guards in case they come running down the road and spot us when we're dragging the little fecker down the yard to put a bullet in him.' The Yellow-Boy stopped speaking. He gripped Sammy by the shoulders and glared into his eyes with a look of almost brotherly love. He had said enough to convince our hero of the murderous deed about to take place — a deed that would put Sammy and his hurley-stick firmly on Tipperary's role of honour.

He led the dazed Sammy out from the shop-door and stationed him next to the window. By this time, the poor fellow was as sober as he'd ever been in all his life — terrified out of his wits.

'Remember, Sammy,' warned the Yellow-Boy, 'keep a look-out for the Guards, the sound man that ye are.' Then he went back in the door with a determined soldierly stride on him. A minute later, he brought out the supposed informant (Handy-Sandy), dragging him roughly by the scruff of his neck and out across the yard to the end of the shop-wall where men usually went to splash their poolie.

Suddenly, and with a merciless roar out of him, he held Handy-Sandy by the throat up against the wall. Like the rest of the merry rogues, this wily rascal was himself well into the trickery that was being played out to test the nerves of our brave Sammy and his so-called fighting spirit against the north. The Yellow-Boy removed his cap, and then he reverently blessed himself and asked Handy-Sandy had he any last request to send home to his beloved mother before he met his death. The brief silence was agonising to behold. The Yellow-Boy slowly traced the sign-of-the-cross on Handy-Sandy's chest, and after that, he pressed the starting-pistol into his chest and fired a single bullet into him. The explosion shook the shop windows, and Handy-Sandy (the finely-tuned actor that he was) slumped to the ground — stone dead and in a heap.

Sammy (God spare him the health) let an ungodly shriek out of him that you could have heard above in the hills — a roar far worse than a dying pig.

'Oh, mercy-on-us! Poor, poor Handy-Sandy, what have ye done to him?' With a speed that nobody knew he had in his boots, Sammy flew towards home, his feet scarcely touching the ground — back to his one and only hope of safety, his mother.

The drinkers came out and stood in a row outside the shop-door. All they could hear were the repeated screams of Sammy (the little driveller). All they could see were his two heels speeding round the bend and running like a demented leprechaun with the fire coming out of his arse.

'The Yellow-Boy has killed poor Handy-Sandy,' he kept bawling at anyone who could see him in his flight. 'He has shot poor Handy-Sandy stone dead.' The old gossips reported that Sammy and his fighting spirit passed out at least two motorcars (including the Bearded Vet's) on his homeward retreat. These old harridans said (although none of us ever believed a word from them) that his poor mother had to come to the rescue and wash out his stained britches as soon as he got home to throw himself in the door. There would be no more talk of going to the north to fight for its freedom, and from that day onwards, our hero was far less stalwart and even became known for a while as *Captain Shun-the-battle*. But when he found out that the entire escapade had been nothing more than a terrible hoax, he was too ashamed to darken the drinking-shop — at least till the ribaldry and laughter of us all should cease and give him a chance to redeem himself.

2

It was a year or two later that there came a night when an angry blue-black storm started howling at us from somewhere out west. All night long it hung over us. Older men and women remembered no previous wind with which to compare it — at least not since the Year of the Deluge and the loss of our wooden bridge a decade previously. We first heard its eerie ghost sizzling and prowling round the back of Shy Dennis's shack and after that it travelled with the speed of a bullet towards Corcoran's well. It must have terrified all our cattle, sheep and horses. The little hearts of the crows in their nests in Old Sam's grove were left speechless and children closed their ears from the thunder of it and shut their eyes tight from the lightning of it.

Next morning, when this mighty hurricane had drained itself out and gone on its merry way, we ran out to inspect the damage. Trees were left smashed in splinters along the creamery road, and the glass had been knocked out from some of our windows. Sadly, it had brought down a sturdy old elm tree and left it straddled across the thatch of Sammy's house, its branches crashing across the top of his chimney. It had cut its way in through the rotten rafters.

With his mother now dead and with no one to guide and nourish him, the rest of us were worried about the poor fellow. We rushed up and in along the lane to see what on earth had happened. We crowded into Sammy's yard (the children now as ever leading the way) to see the huge tree on top of the poor man's broken-down roof. Nobody had ever before seen a house looking like this. It seemed a miracle that the walls of Sammy's bedroom were still left standing.

Red Scissors and Rambling Jack rushed across the yard and broke in through the front door. The rest of us followed them into the welcoming room. The roof had tumbled down behind the fireplace. The tree's branches had fallen straight down on top of Sammy, landing across his bed and piercing him in the chest. There he lay — in front of our eyes — stretched out on the bed underneath the suspended rafters.

The children ran around the back of the house and peeped in from outside the back window. They saw the huge tree on top of the fluttering remnants of Sammy's roof. Through the great hole, they saw the sun streaming in on his dead face, tingeing it smooth and soft. It was all so quiet and strange and not even a cricket stirring. Though young, they had once seen a man with only one arm and a man with only one leg and now they had seen a man stone dead, as lifeless as the rabbits hanging on the back of their door from time to time. He looked just like Saint Francis in the prayer-book (said the older ones) with his dark hair and his skin the colour of cream. They knew, of course, that the ghost-of-him was gone far away from them, sailing high above the clouds.

The men had gathered together in the room. In spite of themselves, they had to smile, realizing that their good friend was free from the constraints of his life on Earth and that he'd never be lacing his boots and stamping them down the road to drink his pints of stout, that he'd never be going to the black north to burn it but going to keep his mother and father company instead in the Beyond. The women looked at Sammy's remains and heaved a sigh. There was none of the blue-jaw look of old about the poor misfortunate man and not an ugly bruise or scar on him. In death, he was at peace and without a wrinkle.

'Doesn't he look beautiful with his jetty Spanishy hair and his innocent cheeks like the smooth face of a newly-born child,' said Moll-the-Man.

'I never saw him looking better,' sighed By-Jiggery. 'He looks good enough for a church mortuary-card.'

RENARDINE

1

It was the middle of winter and, by now, every farmer's wife (especially Galloping Gret) was as jittery as hell and hoping that the lives of their faint-hearted hens would be spared. It had been the same the previous year. During the first days of February, the foxes were giving birth to their playful cubs all around the hills above us.

That's when the hill-folk saw Renardine and Prowler hunting every blessed minute of the day and night. The hungry faces of their cubs turned them into the most urgent of killers and every hen, duck, and goose redoubled their fears (unlike our own silly hens, and the likes of Moll-the-Man's Speckles and Little Ruby). It was Prowler they feared the most (she being a mother) — even more so than Renardine — and as the days went on, these two fierce foxes didn't wait till the midnight hour to come down hunting.

And now, with winter still suffocating us here on the slopes, we began to have the same fears as our friends above in the hills. Time after time, you'd hear the high-pitched screams of Prowler as she gave out her orders to Renardine. Sometimes she herself (the cheek of her) would come marching into Galloping Gret's yard as early as mid-morning and even come back a second time when poor Gret was abroad at the afternoon milking her cows. It was time to send the pair of them down into the bowels of Hell (said Dowager).

These days our women had become holier than ever before, down on their knees and wearing their beads away in the hope that God would help them murder Renardine and Prowler.

'Dear God, please let our men put one or two bullets into their cubs as well,' cried Moll-the-Man. For, though these little animals might be running around playfully at the mouth of their den, the day was surely coming when they'd grow up to start butchering our fowl all over again just like their parents were doing now.

Next Sunday, after returning from Mass and untackling her ass, Moll-the-Man realized she had a new and exciting secret — one she couldn't keep to herself a moment longer. She ran up the creamery road into Cheerful Nan's cowshed and then ran into Dowager's haggart and after that into Slipperslapper's welcoming room. She swore that the sad face of Jesus in her Sacred Heart picture had given her a little wink down off of the wall and for once in His life had even given her a wan little smile. She backed this up by spinning round and demonstrating the cute little wink she'd just received from Him. This was powerful evidence (she said) — the sign she'd been waiting for.

'Yes, mee noble Renardine, there's a heap of trouble in store for ye one of these days, the cartridges and double-barrel gun, the murdering footsteps of By-Jiggery and his cousins, Tommy's Tim and Bunnyfoot. They'll be coming to greet ye sooner than ye think and the blessing of God on all three of them.' Her eyes were full of fire. 'It won't be long now, mark mee word.' Then she ran back home, leaving her friends behind her, clapping their hands with joy.

Speckles continued to be a brave little hen and the Little Red Hen along with her. Moll's cockerel (Red Rascal) had the strength of a real live lion too. Every night, the henhouse door was clasped tightly shut with Moll's new hasp and the big stone wedged against the bottom of the door. The two creamery tanks were planted firmly against the big stone so that those other bloodthirsty villains, Mister Weasel and Mister Rat, couldn't find their way through. Moll's fowl were safe in their hiding-place, listening to the overhead branches tinkling on the galvanised roof.

2

Meanwhile, Renardine was standing at the gap in the Rishy Field. He shook showers of snow-spray off of himself and looked across at the dung heap in Moll-the-Man's haggart. It was time to put on his thinking-cap. He knew how women could be quick as lightning on their feet and make noble use of their ashplant across the broad of his back, should he ever cross their path. He recalled how the previous Sunday he came spying on Red Rascal from the depths of the monkey-puzzle tree. The cocky chap was crowing all over the top of the dung heap. What a pure picture-of-a-cockerel! He would have made a quick grab for him there-and-then if Moll-the-Man hadn't come storming down the yard, her ashplant to the fore. He shook himself and banished the picture of her fiery eyes and filled his mind with more cheerful thoughts about the contents of Moll's hen house. And now he was on the march.

Nearer and nearer he drew to her hen house wall, but there seemed no way in for him. The villain continued to think. Suddenly, he began to laugh. He had seen all these good-wife strategies the previous year, the new hasp, the big heavy stone and the creamery tanks lent in against the door in their efforts to protect their hen house from the likes of him. He had a new plan, and in spite of the dangers he must face, he was beside himself with joy.

'What a fine specimen of mouth-watering hennery ye are, oh, beautiful Red Rascal! Can't ye feel the romance of the midnight breeze? I have come to court ye, mee old friend, come to entertain ye. I have brought ye the gift of mee perfectly-sharpened teeth.' He could picture this beautiful shimmering cockerel filling the black expanses of the hen house with his raucous song — for the very last time, poor thing — and he licked his lips in anticipation. He jumped the stick. He found himself inside the haggart. He climbed up onto the dung heap. He squinted his eyes and peered in through the tiny gap between the four-foot sidewall of the henhouse and its sloping galvanized roof.

'What's this I see?' he thought to himself, licking his lips. 'A roost of magnificent hens dreaming away on their nightly perches with sweet thoughts of the farmyard, the ditch, and the haggart journeys that they think they'll be making tomorrow.' He couldn't stop the flow of his thoughts. There was an air of festivity in him. 'Ah-ha, mee fine young damsels, I am bringing ye a present of meeself this blessed night, the grandest fox in the whole of creation! Yes, ye poor ignorant hens, all asleep in yeer dreamland, soundly resting on yeer safe perches.' Meanwhile, the twiggy branches of the hawthorn tree continued to shake like tin against the roof of the hen house, and the wind continued to whoosh amidst the little leaves of the alder tree. A dappled shadow crossed the hen house wall where moonlight and shade were at play, but the hens (poor eejits!) continued to sleep, unaware of the sinister killer that would now bring evil on them.

And then it was too late. With the elasticity of a wildcat, Renardine wriggled his way in underneath the galvanized roof, working his way sinuously in through what seemed an impossible angle.

'I'm here! I'm here! I'm in mee heaven, in Moll-the-Man's hen house!' The excitement was killing him. 'Where will I turn to first, so spoilt for choice am I?' Flashing like a viper from his hiding-place on top of the wall, he pounced amid the sheer perplexity of the hens and ducks as they fumbled around looking for safety. He left terror in the hearts of every one of them as he savagely got to work before the sleepy load of old drakes could give the alarm. It was chop-chop-chop here and chop-chop-chop there — again and again. He brought down three or four snow-flaking young pullets and sunk his teeth into their necks, looking for their windpipe — oh, the surgeon that he was! Good God-in-heaven! Battlin' Sal's dear favourite, Speckles, was squawking for help in her final hour of need. Where on earth was Red Rascal, that great big oh-so-brave cockerel, that noble master of the farmyard? He was making his piss and hiding behind the two tea-chests, careful not to attend to poor Speckles' dying screams. With the last cackle-cackle he'd ever hear from her, she lay low in submission as Renardine continued to snap viciously at her neck.

And now was heard the bawling and singing (too late! too late!) of Red Rascal as a holy ruction filled the hen house. But Renardine had done what he came for and climbed out the way he came in. He marched to the cowshed where Moll-the-Man had hasped in her geese in readiness for tomorrow's inspection when she'd be selecting one or two of them for her sharp black-handled knife to feed her children.

Good geese! Ever-watchful geese! Not like those silly little hens. The geese sensed the coming of Renardine, and now they sang a song fit for the Cork opera-house. But in spite of their uproar, once again (a projectile of total fearlessness) it was chop-chop-chop here and chop-chop-chop there as Renardine spent a happy time of it, attacking several miserable geese simultaneously. Time and again his fangs covered the shed with the blood from their necks as he laid each of them low. This villain-of-a-fox was no clean killer like Mister Weasel who came to the hen house with the purpose of killing just one chosen hen for himself. Oh, you wicked monster! Was this the way to chastise Moll-the-Man's fine farmyard, Renardine?

Moll-the-Man and By-Jiggery ran out with their bicycle flash-lamps. They unbolted the door of their henhouse. Misery! Misery!

'Oh, mee fine hens - mee fine hens!' bawled poor Moll-the-Man. By-Jiggery's heart jumped in his chest on seeing his wife's terrible heartache over the state of her hens. He hated to see her looking so sad. Several hens were lying speechless, spread-eagled on the ground, their doleful legs giving the last lame kicking's of life. From her flock of fifty hens, Moll counted a meagre thirty-five left in what she'd call egg-laying health. She brandished her ashplant in her fist and uttered an unprintable curse against 'that whoor-of-a-fox — I'll tear the flesh off of his shitty arse!'

By-Jiggery owned a fine sheepdog, Shark, who loved to lie beside the fire at night. Not for him, the midnight prowl and killing of lambs like some of our other mad dogs. It was as if he knew what had happened to some of his predecessors — the bullet to the temple, the drowning, and the hanging-rope.

In desperation, By-Jiggery whistled: 'Shark! Shark! Shark!' His faithful dog came lolloping down the snowy yard. There wasn't a trace to be seen anywhere of our cunning Renardine. He had skipped his legs out across the haggart.

But suddenly and with a great leap out of his powerful body, Shark almost knocked down Moll-the-Man and By-Jiggery. The hen house was filled with his roars and snarls as he leapt to the top of the wall. And just as Renardine had brought down the hens from their perch, so now did Shark haul down this devil-of-a-fox and give him the most unmerciful chopping and mauling.

'Well done, Shark,' said By-Jiggery. 'Ye'll have an extra bowl of bones and goose-broth this very Sunday.'

'Ah-ha, mee clever Mister Foxy-Loxy,' screeched Moll-the-Man, 'ye tried to fool us by this unexpected bit of trickery — staying behind at the scene of yeer crime. Who'd have thought of looking for ye up inside the hen house roof?' With her heavy boots, she gave Renardine the fiercest of kickings, and with her ashplant, she gave him the grandest of beatings round his head and tail just in case Shark hadn't already killed him outright.

'Yes, Renardine (ye bleddy ould fool), ye're dead and killed alright,' she cried. There wasn't a kick out of him. Not a breath out of him.

In spite of her grief and her rage, Moll-the-Man was feeling a good bit better in herself. Before milking her cows tomorrow, she'd run and tell all the neighbours. She could see the smiles of Galloping Gret, and she was pleased for her. She could see the smiles of her good friend, Dowager, and she was pleased for her too — for Cheerful Nan, Slipperslapper and all the women that had feared this crafty old fox.

By-Jiggery picked up Renardine's carcass by the hind legs. It was true — not a move out of him. He was dead alright. He threw him out onto the dung heap as a bloodstained warning to any other fox that might come this way.

'Ah-ha, mee brave Renardine!' he said. 'What a fine pair of eyes ye have! And they're dead. What a fine pair of ears ye have! And they're dead too. What a fine set of teeth ye have, and they also are dead,' he crowed triumphantly and spat his venom into the yard. Then, with Shark and Moll-the-Man, he went back into the welcoming room and poured himself a mug of tea to celebrate a job well done.

But if a cat has nine lives, a fox — even Renardine and the blood-stained state of him, and he almost dead from Moll-the-Man's murderous kicking and the fierce beating he took from Shark — surely has even more lives to his name.

'Ah-ha, ye bleddy load of eejits!' winked the old fox - and in spite of his pains and his soreness, he couldn't help chuckling to himself. 'What a fine pair of eyes this old fox has! What a fine pair of ears this old fox has! What a fine pair of legs this old fox has!'

No longer attended by Moll-the-Man's boots and her ashplant, he now showed the world his most supreme cunning. He snapped up two fine young hens for himself. It was Little Ruby and along with her, Speckles. He threw them across his back and away he crawled, his body slouched down near the ground with the sheer weight of them. Out over the haggart stick he struggled, crouching under the bar-gate and into the Rishy Field. Back to his den and Prowler, his wary wife, and to his young cubs he hobbled. If ever he had a bit of cheerful news to tell them, it'd be this — how he had fooled the hens, how he had fooled the ducks, how he had fooled the geese and (best of all) how he had fooled By-Jiggery and Moll-the-Man and Shark, that impudent puppy-of-a-dog. Wasn't he the very devil out of hell! In spite of his pain, he had to laugh again.

Before you could blink, Prowler and her cubs were licking the blood-stains clean off of his noble battle wounds. Silence and happiness prevailed in their den, followed by plenty of high feasting as the happy pair and their merry young cubs made themselves a memorable banquet. The sun had not yet risen before they spat out the last of the chicken bones.

3

Sheltered and snug in a red ball of warm innocence, the little fox-cubs wrapped their tails round the muzzle of Prowler. Their screen was a wall of ferns and sheltering boughs as they huddled underground, silent and absorbed. They were safe — for now at any rate.

Hidden from Man, yet ever vigilant, the tip of their father's nose was all that peeped up. The sharp smell of pine resin was in the air, and the wind sang softly in the trees overhead him where the crows swayed whisperingly. The drowsy peaceful-ness of a winter's late afternoon filled the old fox's soul as he stared out at the starkness and the shiny ribbon of the river passing by. Memories, huge and beautiful, throbbed in his head, memories of farmyards and delightful geese and hens and drakes that he had once killed and devoured. There'd be more to come.

He sniffed once more. Suddenly, he felt unsettled for there was something new on the wind — he was sure of it. He thought he heard whispering, men cursing the briars that struck them across the face — thought he heard the scuffle of feet on broken twigs.

He was now fully alert, his fur standing on end. He couldn't believe it. His keen scent told him that his worst enemy was coming this way. Yes, it was Man — it was Man the hunter. Ah, the dirty heathens! Men and their wicked guns! He felt the blood buzzing in his ears and a feverish pain stabbing him through his eyelids. Suddenly, he felt old — so very old.

Here in this wood (he thought), Prowler and himself and their young family had lived a happy life — especially of late. Fate had been kind to them — too kind perhaps, nibbling on the sumptuous bones of chickens, of ducks, of fine fat geese from all over the countryside. Night after night they had feasted like lords decked out in their finery. Like men that had tasted well-seasoned wine, they had sat in the lap of luxury. Now panic filled the air around him.

Prowler stared up at him, and her eyes seemed to weep as she felt the trembling of fear coming out in him. They looked back at their young ones, nestling together in that cuddlesome baby-warmth of a sound evening's sleep. She felt old age catch hold of her as her mind cast frantically about for an answer, and she wondered whether she'd escape the terrible moment of death and get the chance to make old bones of her life. She went up to Renardine and rubbed her nose against his. They turned around and looked at the sad remains of Speckles and Little Ruby strewn around the corners of their den. And they waited. They waited.

There was only the sound of the crowbars and shovels and no bird sang its evening song. Dig! Dig! Dig again! There were three of them in it — By-Jiggery, and his cousins, Tommy's Tim and Bunnyfoot. Even the snow-blasted trees seemed to be sadly shaking round the den as they got to work with their tools . . . until finally, the home — the tomb — of Renardine was unveiled. Cunning in his last hour on earth, the wily old fox crawled out of his den as though he were some sort of sick serpent. With squinty eyes, he looked up at these ghostly monsters and their long-tailed shadows in the light. With his limping legs, he tried to supplicate them and draw pity from their hard hearts. Darker grew the fear in him.

'Indeed, ye are most welcome to mee home. I know it isn't much to offer ye. But, sad-looking though it be, it's all I have to offer ye. I-I-I-I have been somewhat unwell in meeself for the last few days, laid low with the wintertime bug' — that's what he seemed to be saying. In this grey time between life and death, he put on a performance fit for the Dublin stage. Look at the lustreless eyes of him (not a glint in them) as he takes the last look he'll ever get at the snow and the sun. His mournful song, his apology for living, and the sadness in him would sting the heartstrings of the Devil himself. You'd have to admire his bravery as he faced up to his death — in this, his final efforts to distract these killers from Prowler and her cubs. He slithered towards the boots of By-Jiggery so as to make of himself the ultimate sacrifice for their anger and hatred.

'Ye killed mee wife's hens. Ye killed her geese and ducks,' said the hateful eyes of By-Jiggery. His heart was as cold as the ice in the river. Not a flicker of kindliness from this gunman's eyes.

Renardine grew desperate. 'I am old. I am achingly old. Mee limbs fail me,' he seemed to say as he curled his forepaws up to his chest and gave a few hacking coughs. But for once in his life, his trickery failed him. Hunters and hunted stood motionless across from each other. Even the quivering waters nearby and the fairy folk of grotto and woodland held their breath at the sight.

Prowler, not to be seen slow-footed, came crawling out from the den and wrapped her body round that of Renardine in an effort to save her cubs. Behind her, in the depths of the den, she had covered them in the feathers of countless chickens till she was convinced they'd remain undiscovered in their afternoon sleep. Tomorrow (she prayed), they would follow their noses and discover once more the hills from where they had recently come. She would now join her noble fox in a brave death just as she had joined him in the joys of their life.

The three killers looked down at the two old foxes and their giddy legs shaking jerkily as death drew up before their eyes. CRACK! CRACK! CRACKITY-CRACK! The gunshots blared out across the frozen snowfields as By-Jiggery let loose the cartridges. With their sickening crowbars and pitchforks, Bunnyfoot and Tommy's Tim relieved their rage rapidly on the cubs below. There was scarcely a yelp out of them, and the crows tilted backwards (nothing to do with us) and floated away like black cinders towards Corcoran's well.

In a short few seconds, By-Jiggery and the men had drowned themselves in the foxes' deaths. All the cunning and speed of Renardine and Prowler had come to an end — to be made mere carrion for future woodland crows. Their furry muscles gleamed in the snow — their ruby blood, the sign of their sacrifice to save their cubs. And out across the river, the weeping ghosts of Renardine and Prowler echoed on their last unearthly journey away from the light of the Earth.

The men strode out onto the road. They had a mighty need to slake their thirst, and they quickly headed for Curl 'n' Stripes' drinking-shop. With the blood of the foxes still wet on their britches, they entered the shop and ran over to the fire. They pounced on the drink in an awful hurry to get their throats wet. Then they sipped the drink more slowly, and they shivered from the taste of it, and their lips became covered in froth. Turning their backs to the blazing fire, they reddened their pipes of tobacco, puffing loudly and sending wisps of smoke up to the rafters. The tobacco, the drink, the men themselves — all in perfect harmony after this evening's killings. They seemed as bright as a daisy field and raised their glasses to drink a health to the dead Renardine.

'Blasht it! — why weren't our glasses twice as big!' They drank to Prowler too.

Later on — and far more melancholic — they departed from the shop, their voices fading away behind them. Behind at the den all was quiet except for the little noises of grasshoppers and other night creatures, as if nothing had happened. Then the angry river began to murmur, and the treetops stirred into life, waving in the squally wind above the corpses of the foxes. The echo of the men's boots tramped up the road. The storm of anger had gone from their hearts, now replaced by a little poignancy.

'Such lovely creatures!' said By-Jiggery.

'Too true — wintertime is a hungry time for man and beast alike,' reflected Bunnyfoot.

The moon shone faintly, and the roadway was blue in front of them. By-Jiggery said goodbye to the men and entered his yard. The wind blew a little snow slantwise up into his face. With the scrub-brush, he brushed the snow from his boots. His face was wet and leaky, and there was blood down the front of his shirt.

Moll-the-Man heard the hobnail boots of her killer-of-a-husband as he stepped towards the door. He lifted the latch and smiled across the floor and came and sat down with her at the table. Soon, he was leathering into a huge plate of meat and spuds and washing it down with mugs of milk. He went and sat by the fire and took off his wet socks and hung them on the crane under the hob.

'Tell me this and tell me no more, did ye kill them all?' said Moll-the-Man.

'Aye faith, we did,' said By-Jiggery in between mouthfuls of spuds, and he wiped the milk from the corner of his lips.

'Power to the double-barrel gun! And even the young cubs — ye killed them too, did ye?'

'We did, begor,' said By-Jiggery. But there was a bit of weary sadness in his voice. His wife pretended not to notice it. She was tingled with pride in this lovely man of hers and in her relief for the rest of her fowl. She thanked God for the success of the killings. Galloping Gret would never again be reduced to the indignity of painting her geese red so as to deceive the fox.

Long afterwards, By-Jiggery went abroad to check the hasp and staple of the henhouse door.

'Never fear, mee brave little hens!' He counted all of the hens that had been left alive by Renardine. He counted the ducks and the geese too. Some of them were still awake, cocking an ear for the possible coming of their other enemies, Mister Weasel and Mister Rat. He carefully secured the hasp. He would sleep well tonight. He stopped in front of the Rishy Field to smell the pine trees around the haggart. He could hear the wind brushing the tops of the trees and the soft rain and the water of the stream chuckling on the stones. Then he returned and eased his poolie into the ashpit at the back carway. He gave a long look down the trail to where Renardine's den had been. It was back there inside the fence in the wood — where the foxes' lair was — now full of their ghostly spirits, young and old alike (he kept thinking). They were lying ignominiously among the chicken-bones, and the snow was coloured with their yellow piss. The lovely stars studded the black sky above their corpses, and the sad river rolled achingly onwards to tell the sea what had happened. Thinking of his wife's recent sadness, this had been a blessed day (he thought) and a delicious chill crept into his bones as he buttoned up his trousers. The killing had been something he simply had had to do (he kept telling himself). 'Twould be the same next year all over again.

1

On the day she arrived, none of us knew how a woman like White Snow could have such white hair — and at such an early age. It was something of a miracle. It was not until Red Scissors found himself down south in Tipperary Town buying a new mare that the news came back to us — the way in which White Snow had gotten the white hair. He had met up with a distant cousin of his (Napper-the-Lamb) who was also down there on a quest for a plough-horse. Napper lived out beyond Keeper Hill and was able to give Red Scissors a vivid account of the whole story so that he could bring back the unfortunate tale of the disappearance of the lovely auburn colour and the arrival of the whiteness in our newcomer's hair. He had met up with a distant cousin of his (Napper-the-Lamb) who was also down there on a quest for a plough-horse. Napper lived out beyond Keeper Hill and was able to give Red Scissors a vivid account of the whole story so that he could bring back the unfortunate tale of the disappearance of the lovely auburn colour and the arrival of the whiteness in our newcomer's hair.

It had been a bright shiny afternoon with the sun's fingers pointing everywhere and gilding the entire world when White-Snow (then a child of thirteen-years-of-age) went off travelling with her father, Dinjo. They were always together and as close as two sides of a dinner-plate, for her mother had died of her wounds during childbirth. Dinjo (amongst other things) was a woodcutter. He and his daughter took themselves and their horse-and-cart to cut the annual tree for their wintertime fuel — just like they had done the year before and the year before that. Their local gentry-man (a distant cousin of Lady Posh-Frock) allowed them the gift of this once-a-year access to his broad estates. He knew what he was doing — it was a handy way to get some of his diseased trees cleared away as well as those branches knocked down in the storms and to thin out any other unneeded bits of his timber crop.

The hearts of father and daughter were as light as a feather as they headed across the fields, the sun warming them by the minute. But all that was soon about to change. Dinjo had grown accustomed to the angle and direction of his axe-cuts over many years and the way in which the tree would be leaning. This time, however, when the axe-cutting was completed to his satisfaction, and he was sawing into the trunk like fair hell and not keeping an eye on the top branches, the tree seemed to have a mind of its own. You'd have to ask yourself — was some strange evil spirit lurking in this tree? For without warning it came crashing down on top of Dinjo, falling straight across his chest and almost burying his body into the ground with the dent it made. Oh, the sight of poor Dinjo, thus bespattered with his own life-blood!

'Father-father-father!' The young girl's heart leapt into her throat, and she threw herself across her father and buried her tears in his blood. Apart from the rambling spirits of the woodland, there was no-one else close by, and in the cruel unearthly silence, she gazed at the poor misfortunate Dinjo, the father she adored next to Jesus Himself. His glazed eyes were rolling round in his head as he tried to utter a few dying words to her whilst she (this heathen-of-a-tree!) tried helplessly to lift the fatal tree.

Would she ever forget his sad eyes — eyes showing that he was still aware of her presence, still able to recognise her? But the poor man could no longer call out her name. Oh, that he could for a second get back the gift of speech!

There was so much he wanted to say to her. 'I'm dying, child — go get me the priest! Go tell him come quick and hear my confession so that I can enter the gates of Heaven.' He couldn't even give her his fatherly blessing. He couldn't tell her of his everlasting love for her, and it was breaking the heart in both of their chests.

In the days following Dinjo's grisly death and after all the solemn obsequies of his funeral and burial had been accomplished, the child found herself in a bewildered state of loneliness — as though a sort of twilight had come over her. There were times when she felt dizzy and couldn't catch her breath, and she was constantly looking up at the clouds as though searching for a sign, as if wishing to fly away over Hurricane Hill and join her father and mother in the Beyond. For, with neither of them left to cheer her, the sunlight was utterly gone from her life. There was only the odd neighbour to come in and light the fire for her or help her look after the house and make sure she had a bit of dinner inside her. There was no-one to sit opposite her by the fire and while away the evening and burn the candle down in the long lonely night.

In the next few weeks, the young Clare curate (Father Simply) came up the mountain trail repeatedly, approaching the bereft young girl's half-door as gingerly as you'd expect. The sight of her tear-stained face troubled him greatly. Would she ever get back the soft smile he had known? Along with him, he brought the sweet music of his squeeze-box and gently began playing his haunting airs into her ears in the hope that his melodies would bring gladness back to her heart. But on these first visits (and for many more to come), the sad-faced child was unable to utter so much as a word back to him. The sight of that tree (the sight of her dead father underneath its trunk) would haunt her till the day she died. It was a miracle (the neighbours said) that the poor girl hadn't given up the ghost alongside her father from the shock and dismay at the sight of him, a sight no thirteen-year-old child was ever meant to look upon.

That was when the neighbours hit their chests in sorrow — such a change did they see in her before the year ended. Not one of the older men and women could recall an instance like it having ever happened before. Like a slow-moving cloud on the mountainside, the misfortunate child's hair started to turn by some strange magic from its lustrous auburn colour to a mixture of its future grey-and-whiteness, and they made the sign-of-the-cross and prayed that it wouldn't stay that way for the rest of her life. It was too much to bear. Hadn't they always stopped in their tracks to admire and marvel at the unusual colour of it — rarer (they felt) than the autumn leaves and outmatching even the beautiful colour of Lady Posh-Frock's ponies? Their eyes filled with tears when they recalled the deep love between a father and his daughter — how Dinjo had always been so proud of her lovely auburn hair. They remembered the way he used to sit her on the chair in the yard, the way he used to gently comb out her tresses in long sweeps through his fingers, the way he would patiently plait them into a single twisty rope right down to her waist. Then they shut their eyes and tried to forget.

2

Back here at home, a change was happening too — happening to our good friend, Taedspaddy. It had been his mother's dying wish for him to go and find a wife to take her place hereafter and to look after him. For a while, he didn't know what on earth he was supposed to do.

But then — in a blinding flash of light — the knowledge came to him and with the reins and the bridle he went off looking for his mare (Slippaway). Mindful of his mother's wishes, he washed and shaved and dressed himself in his one and only good suit, the blue suit with the faint red lines running through it. He put on his Sunday boots and combed his black curls with his dead mother's brilliantine. Then with a wing and a prayer, he leapt into the saddle and headed straight up through the pine trees and out passed Treacy's sandpit.

By now the sun was burning away the mists of the early day, and his heart began to feel as light as a bladder. He travelled out across the heather on the far reaches of the bog, determined to attack the high road round Keeper Hill and the rocky ford at Clashing River, the river known to the children as the River Sticks (the one in their storybooks). Soon, he could hear its waves brawling angrily where it came zigzagging its way across the remote valleys that surround our world before discoursing itself into Growl River and then into the mighty Shannon River near Limerick.

To the day he died, he would never forget that wild region of the bog and the sunlit day ten years earlier, long before White Snow had gotten her name or given him her hand and come to join him in the marriage-bed. It was the day when a lovely young girl (her own good self) had come on the scene and saved him from drowning in one of those deep and treacherous bog-holes, the day when he'd been planking turf alongside his father's brother (the Gog).

They'd been working like blazes, airing and dressing the final stages of their turf, and had finally planked up the last bit of it, leaving it in neat tidy rows. It was a grand and glorious sight to be looking at, and they now had time to soak in the tranquillity of the day. They'd an awful thirst and a hunger in their bellies. The Gog sent Taedspaddy to the spring-well below in the gully to fill the kettle for their afternoon tea.

A few minutes passed by, and he started thinking that his nephew (blasht him!) was an awfully long time gone. Was he ever coming back with the spring-water so that they could unwrap the sandwiches and boil the mug of tea over the bit of kindled heather?

It was then that this noble-looking girl came riding by like Jesus on her ass (Scallywags). It was a year before the tragic death of Dinjo when she was still only 12. She was out searching for her father's stray cattle. Down through the gully she came, carefully sidling Scallywags round the danger-spots of the bog. And then — in front of her — she saw the bog hole waters churning themselves and sobbing with an unusual sort of sound. A gusty wind seemed to hurry behind her, as though an unknown force was driving her and her ass towards the edge of the bog hole.

Saints-above-us! — she was in the nick of time to prevent a terrible disaster. For there in the treacle-dark waters, she found what seemed the remains of poor Taedspaddy floating aimlessly about. All she could see were the two bits of his struggling arms and head sticking up out of the mire where he'd slipped and tumbled in. A lump came up in her throat.

Such a thing had happened to others, and she realised the poor man was about to sink down to his final resting-place amongst the fairies of that place, unseen and disregarded by the rest of mankind. It was as if she'd been given a kick in the ribs, and she jumped down from Scallywags and tied him to a nearby bush.

It must have been some sort of miracle (she thought), some plan in the mind of God or in one of the heavenly angels, that had guided her to this very spot and at this precise moment to try and save this poor man's life. The ass wasn't slow either in acknowledging what had happened and could see that his help would be required the very next minute.

She led Scallywags to the edge of the bog hole and directed his eyes to the legs of the man and (you're the best little ass in all Ireland) whispered those well-known ass-whispers into his ear.

Leaning out over the bank, she tied the reins round Taedspaddy, all the time crying out desperately: 'You're far too young to die, poor man — far too young!' She and Scallywags fiercely toiled and struggled, pulling and dragging as never before at the frantic reins and all the time letting out a string of silent curses against the bogland fairies (those filthy basthards) and their fiendish cruelty in trying to drag away a young man from his place on God's earth. She thought her lungs were going to burst from all her efforts. No untamed lion, however, could have applied itself more energetically than she did and with the last gasps of her strength, she and her ass hauled Taedspaddy, bit by agonising bit, out from the mire until he was safely landed on the bank.

The sight of him lying there, stiff with the cold — with no more than a kick left in his body and at the very doors of death — sickened her stomach. She hadn't a second to lose. She opened his mouth and began breathing the life back into him with mouthful after mouthful of her own breath, all the time pummelling his chest till she finally saw him shudder and open his eyes.

Hearing her cries, the demented Gog came running through the heather, his heart in his mouth when he saw what was happening. They stripped the shivering Taedspaddy to his skin and laid him flat on his back. They hung his wet clothes on the furze bushes to dry in the wind. To see him there, so frightened and whimpering like a lost child — ah me! They brought the kettle of freezing spring-water and time and time again pelted it into his face to revive him. They washed away the mud from his body. By this time, the Gog had uttered to the skies every childhood prayer he'd learnt at his mother's knee, and all the time, he kept looking at this strange unknown girl and asking himself whether she was a real child at all or was she a ghostly fairy child or whether she had come down from the skies like the angel Gabriel. It was indeed a miracle: how else had she appeared on the scene so suddenly when there wasn't a single soul around them anywhere?

The strangeness of that memorable day, the almost-drowned Taedspaddy and the lovely young girl appearing just in time, was like a scene from a fairy-tale. Once the poor man came back to his senses, the tea and the sandwiches were long forgotten, and the kettle was lying at the bottom of the bog hole where he himself might have ended his days. Instead, he saw the face of the smiling young girl kneeling over him and rubbing the warmth back into his legs, his chest, and hands. A feeling of intense warmth and gratitude swelled up inside him. The silent tears rolled down his jaw and joy swam up to the surface and into his helpless eyes. It passed into the girl's eyes and then came back again into him.

3

That was ten years ago, and now it was the month of April with the air soft and the sky clear. He puffed out his cheeks and drank in the cool breezes that were up around Clashing River. He looked a noble sight, seated high on Slippaway, as he plunged onwards passed the ford and out of the river.

All the time, he kept mumbling to himself, 'I have coom for ye, I have coom for ye.' He didn't know what else his shy tongue-tied mouth would say once he reached the young woman's yard, and (again thinking of his mother's pleading words), he tried to summon up all the courage that his heart could muster.

His guardian angel, however, was with him and steadfastly led him on, the smoke dribbling aimlessly from his pipe, up through the shaggy woods behind the mountain and out passed the bog. He was tired and weary but steered his mare determinedly on till he came to the narrow path that skirted the pine plantations on the slopes of Hurricane Hill. At last, he was there.

He drove Slippaway down the yellow lane and into the yard. He entered the half-door, the shafts of sunlight streaming in behind him. He felt as excited as a springtime calf and took off his cap with the usual polite *God save all here* on his lips. He bowed towards the young woman in front of him, unaware that both her father and mother were dead. His eyes had room for nought but herself — the same child, now a woman, who had once had a head of hair more colourful than the woodland chestnuts, a head of hair, however, that was now as white as snow. He was struck dumb at the sight of this former child that had once smiled down on him at the side of the bog hole. She had blossomed into a tall and stately woman.

'I have coom for ye, I have coom for ye,' was all that the poor wooden man could stutter in the silence of her welcoming room. Renowned as the rest of us were for our inability to keep our tongues quiet for a single minute, this was one day in Taedspaddy's life when long speeches and finely-chosen words had sailed away with the wind, and his aching heart could say no more.

And then the fates that rule the clouds smiled warmly down. 'You are welcome, kind sir,' she said. She always knew he would come for her. Time and again her dreams had shown her this man's sad face on that sunlit day in her childhood when she drove her ass to the edge of the bog hole — the way the hand of God had directed her through the gully, the fierce struggle and rescue, the bewildered face of the drowning man, his grateful eyes looking up at her, the joy she felt in saving his life.

She took Taedspaddy's hands in hers and shook them warmly. It was all so like a dream: one minute she'd been busy with the cabbages and spuds in the skillet pots at the side of the fire, the next minute she was packing a few bits of her best clothing into her father's old suitcase, leaving the remnants of her old grey life forever behind her — the new life mapped out in front of her.

She closed her front door for the last time and with a happy heart, scrambled up behind Taedspaddy onto Slippaway's back. The two of them went sailing merrily (if not quite at a gallop) across the wild lands that would lead them the long trek to Clashing River and eventually down to the forge and Sheep's Cross. In that precious moment, there was no mansion of any lord or lady that Taedspaddy would have wished to call his own, so high, so happy were his undaunted spirits — hers too, the woman we'd forevermore know as White Snow.

4

Following the whirlwind of their meeting, the life of the happy twosome was seen to change with gathering speed. With White Snow beside him, Taedspaddy developed a new lease to his life. Not since his mother's death had he appreciated the goodly smell of the brown earth and green grass. Now he could hear once more the morning song of the blackbirds and larks.

We all saw the change in him. He had a jaunty spring to his everyday step, and his limbs itched to be out working. It was as if a rosebud had burst open in his chest — all those untapped energies lying asleep in him, once more pouring out of him as though the smiling spirit of his mother had come rushing down and back into him. And he raised his eyes to the skies to thank her in her new home beyond the clouds.

Like her husband, White Snow was up before the cockerel had even blinked an eye. She went about her tasks with a will and a driving force. Armed with her bucket and distemper-brush, she helped Taedspaddy whitewash the inside and outside walls of their little thatched nest — the pig house and hen house too. She went back across the bog and brought home a dozen of her hens across Clashing River and added to her store a number of ducks and geese. Round the edge of the yard, she planted several flowers and loved the smell of them, and she swept and cleaned the yard each day. Before the year ended, she sold her bit of land back home without a moment of regret along with the cottage and its red-tiled roof. Everything was a pleasure to her.

5

It was many years later. Bunches of dark clouds came rolling lugubriously down the hillsides from behind Corcoran's well. White Snow never saw the threatening nature of those clouds, so busy was she at her work. She was beyond in the seventh field, hoping to bring in the thirty-six trams of hay like the previous year and all the other years that she and Taedspaddy had lived together. But this time, she was working on her own, Taedspaddy being away tending the forestry these last few weeks.

She threw the metal chains over the base of each tram — time and again — her back and shoulders soaked in sweat and the insects clinging to her. This was the way with her — the chains round the base of the tram rather than spending half the day firing the hay into the horse-and-cart. She yoked the tram's chains onto the tackling. With her whip, she drove the hard-pulling horse and the chained tram downhill and into the hayshed rather than wait for the horse to lumber down the field with his heavy cartload of hay forever slowing him down. It was a new way of working that none of us had ever heard tell of.

It was getting on for dusk and those mysterious cold dews were falling fast, replacing the earlier breezes. Working at wind-speed, she had drawn twenty-five of the thirty-six trams into the haggart. No man (let alone a woman) had ever matched this staggering amount of work. In the following days, when news of it reached us, our brains were so addled that we were left wondering where on earth this woman from the other side of the mountains had gotten so much strength. Some of the more imaginative among us (the wicked old gossips) said that as soon as they were born, women up there were put under the cow that was chained to the half-door for this very purpose and that such a sound nurturing at birth was the source of their Samson-like strength. Be that as it may, the twenty-fifth tram was the last tram that White Snow would ever throw her chains round. She had (even for her) over-worked every muscle in her body.

'After all,' (said a tearful and heartbroken My-son-Jack a day or two later), 'she hadn't the mechanics of an alarm clock inside her, had she?' He had always admired her greatly.

White Snow was standing in the yard, her work done for the day. She took off her working wellingtons and put her head in the bucket of cold water to cool her head and wipe away the sweat and midges from her face. All of a sudden, she felt something like a sledgehammer hitting her a blow in the chest. She must have known it was her heart. She staggered across the yard where she fell at the half-door, never to rise again. There she lay — like a small bird with a broken wing that had fallen out of its nest, helplessly awaiting its fate, its heart still pumping furiously. She couldn't move a muscle and, knowing that her hour of death was close at hand, she lost consciousness.

Meanwhile, Taedspaddy was returning with their children from the other side of the wood. They were as happy as a field of thrushes, singing their summertime songs as the horse carried them behind him in the cart. As soon as they entered the yard, they saw the sad state of their mother at the half-door and set up such an almighty roar that the birds in the trees round the haggart almost died of fright and fled. Between them, they carried White Snow into the welcoming room and lifted her onto the bed — the children all the time (mother, mother, dearest mother!) dancing round their dying mother and bawling at her to get up out of that godforsaken bed and come back and join them.

Taedspaddy, though he knew his dear wife hadn't a sin on her soul, sent for Father Honesty to come and give her his blessing and final absolution. And though Doctor Glasses hurried in along with the priest, there was nothing he was able to do for her in spite of all his ministering. White Snow had had an almighty stroke and was dead inside a week, her soul soaring off beyond the clouds on its final journey to meet her maker.

It was impossible to feel the depths of Taedspaddy's grief and the fierce heaviness of the pain in his chest. His previous joy — listening to the little birds singing in the laurels and the howling winds knocking at his windows during a stormy night when he was safely locked in the warm arms of White Snow — was all gone from him in a quick flash.

A day or two later, he dressed himself in his wedding-suit and placed White Snow's coffin on his horse-and-cart. He would take her with Slippaway and the cart on the sad journey back across the mountains to be buried in a final resting-place alongside her mother and father. With the children in tow, he crossed Clashing River. It was a long and painful journey, the tension in them almost unbearable. Not a word was said between any of them till they reached the graveyard. Taedspaddy asked his children to hand him down the pick and shovel and with the tears hopping from his eyes, he opened up the grave. The family knelt down silently and prayed the rosary over her coffin. Little did the good man know — it wouldn't be long before his own soul would be sucked up into the skies to come and join his dear wife.

6

A year to the day, he was coming home from town with a few bags of messages and six cream buns for his children. The children heard Slippaway clip-clopping her way along the creamery road towards the yard, and they ran out excitedly to meet their father. He had been spoiling them more and more since the death of their mother, and they knew he'd be bringing home a gramophone record or two (he loved the music at night around the blazing turf-fire) and a few big bags of their favourite peggy's-leg sweets. They raced one another up the lane towards the lace of the horse-and-cart. They looked up at their father. He was as still as a church statue — stone cold dead. He had (we all agreed) died of a broken heart. Doctor Glasses said he had been dead all the way home from town. The faithful mare had delivered her last rites for him.

The following evening, the praises of White Snow and Taedspaddy reached a new dimension in our little church in Copperstone Hollow. The words love and romance were foreign words in our part of the world — although we had our own words for being warm-hearted and loving to one another. But, led by Father Honesty, everyone agreed that this was the end of a beautiful love story, a match made in heaven between Taedspaddy and White Snow from the day they met at the bog hole. And (said Father Honesty, growing to his theme) if the angels have wings in Heaven, there never had been two happier souls than the two of them — than Taedspaddy and White Snow, the woman from beyond the mountains, who had once dragged him away from the arms of death.

The following day was the day of Taedspaddy's funeral. There wasn't an echo of man, woman or child left behind on our lanes and fields as we all found our way up the long winding road towards the bog. We crawled out passed Keeper Hill and on towards Clashing River and Hurricane Hill where our men made use of the few pick-axes and shovels they'd brought with them. They reopened White Snow's grave and with bell, book and candle, lowered Taedspaddy down next to his beloved wife — peaceful with her at last under the soft sod. His uncle (the Gog) came down and started a new life at the ripe old age of seventy, he and the heart-broken children all pulling together and in harmony, working the land — a sight to be seen.

SCALLYWAGS

1

Whenever they were home from Dang-the-skin-of-it's school, Moll-the-Man's children scampered all over the hills as though they had a need to cast off the dark days of wintertime. They were often up to untold mischief in their efforts to annoy the older generation, and that's when their mother would threaten to brain them with the leg of the stool or throw the yard-brush good-naturedly after them.

'To hell with the lot of ye! Don't be tormenting the rest of us with yeer antics, ye young scallywags!' It was her usual half-hearted way of chastising them, and then they'd laugh and go dancing down the creamery road as though the scallywag label was a well-earned rosette handed out to them at the town's show fair.

There were times last autumn when the hillside seemed too small a place to contain them, times when they made raids into the orchards of Old Stroller and Galloping Gret, times when they trotted off gathering blackberries but preferred instead to destroy their faces with red juicy stains as though they were on their way home from a pig-killing or were a wild bunch of red Indians newly-arrived among us. By the time they got home, they'd have eaten far more than they'd have put in the jam-jars their mother had given them for collecting the berries, and their bellies would be belching with the gripe from all the fine feasting. It would make a stone laugh.

On some days, their wildness seemed akin to vandalism and only a step short of cruelty. They raced across the Valley-of-the-Pig and made sure that most of the old ladies who lived there — even Old Gentility and she ninety — never got a wink of afternoon sleep. They stole the eggs and nests of small birds like the robin, which they brought home to show off to their father so he could make a study of them. They ran after their ass (Short-Arse), swinging off of her tail and trying to get up on her back and ride her through the dock-leaves in the Rishy Field. They pelted stones at Galloping Gret's sow and ran amok amongst her revered flock of guinea hens. They caught the screeching ginger-barred cat of Simple Simon and swung it round and round by the tail before firing it out over the ditch.

After such sturdy work, the older ones (Lippy and Philly) galloped off with the younger ones to the foot of the tree in Red Scissors' lane. From the top branches, they lifted their trouser-legs and let flow a stream of their hot poolie down on top of the heads of Young Jim and Leppity who were struggling to climb up after them. That's when you'd hear the most inventive foul language (friggin' basthards) from the screaming mouths of the younger ones — even from Battlin' Sal.

As if that wasn't enough, the next week they ran down past Echo Bridge and let loose the two fat sows of Ducks-and-Drakes in through Red Buckles' gate to stumble their way through the alarmed calves and send them maddeningly round and round the thistles. The list was endless. The young scally-wags indeed! Moll-the-Man might well have thought of a somewhat different name for her children than that.

Of course, there were other more sedate moments when the gentler urges of nature took hold of them. That's when you'd find them making bangles and necklaces for one another from the field-flowers — especially the younger children (Young Jim, Leppity, and Battlin' Sal). These three were unlike the older boys and were harmless as of yet, spending a good deal of the day dreaming their lives away on the flagstones that ran across the yard stream — playing with the brown and ginger caterpillars who lived at the foot of the oak-tree and allowing them to weave their way across their legs. They'd collect handfuls of horse-dung from the road and mix it up with the mud after the rains to make their toy-farm ditches and then make their berry farm-animals with haw berries (cows) and fir-cones (horses) and with the white berries (sheep) from the bushes, before Lippy and Philly (the rascals) came up behind Battlin' Sal and squashed the juices from these berry sheep into the little girl's ears - just to hear her (go 'way, ye pair of basthards!) curse and swear at them before the two of them ran off laughing.

Later in the day, the whole pack of them would traipse across the Rishy Field on a sort of pilgrimage to pay a polite visit to Battlin' Sal's cubby-house, which was situated in the depths of Old Stroller's dyke. Once there, they took their pretend tea like lords and ladies from the broken bits of crockery and the rusty tin cans on her wooden shelf-boards. Then they raced off and paddled in the river where they collected the pink and lavender stones to bring home and draw their mother's face on the white flagstones in the yard. But when evening came — tired and worn to a thread and after all the day's jobs were finished to their mother's satisfaction — they would climb the ladder and lie on top of the hay in Old Stroller's hayshed and sing their many school songs.

2

However, after their most recent outbursts, Moll-the-Man was determined she'd establish some sort of fresh rhythm in their lives. She took a good look at Leppity, who was eating a roast crab-apple on the ditch. Since he was the fastest runner amongst her children, she called him in and gave him his orders for the day. She handed him the two sweet-gallons and the small green bottles that he could stow in his pockets.

Then she said, 'Take yeerself over to the church and fetch back as much holy water as ye can carry from the church barrels.'

He knew the distance — his three big brothers had travelled the same three-mile stretch a year back when they brought home the little puppy, Lightning, to comfort their good friend, Clever Jack. So much holy water would be a heavy load for young Leppity to carry all that way. But Moll-the-Man knew her son and that, though still only nine, he was well suited for the task. She and Sweet Birdsong would need enough of it to bless all their farm animals — especially the two plough-horses, who'd get a special dash of it before the day was out. The rest of it she'd splash on the others (a long list), especially the seeds for the new crops that would sprout much better after their blessing — and not forgetting the ass.

Leppity was a cute little fellow and hadn't gone to school for nothing. Once he was out of sight and had passed Old Sam's stile, he hopped in over the rusty gate at the side of the river. He lay down on the riverbank for a blissful hour or two, listlessly sunning his cheeks and arms. Ah, the life for a man like meeself (he thought) and was as happy as the nearby bees and butterflies, having escaped from the work and drudgery above in the farmyard. The holy water in the church barrels could go to blazes for all he cared, and he began filling his gallons and bottles with the pure river water, careful to avoid any of the froth from the river's floating cattle-piss.

When he thought he'd been sunning himself long enough and saw that the sky was turning more of a pink than a blue, he wobbled his way home with his heavy load of holy water (the heathen little actor that he was) with a look of sweaty fatigue on his innocent face.

Neither Moll-the-Man nor Sweet Birdsong ever got to know it, but his big brother (Philly) had also played this devilish prank the previous year and, would you believe it, the ass and the mare, the sows and the poultry, the spuds and the cabbages, the mangles and the oats, the barley and the hay — they were never seen in better shape! God-in-His-Heaven must have been scratching his head and frowning inwardly. It seemed that the waters of the river were more than a match for the priest's sacred barrels when it came to the blessing of our animals, seeds, and implements. Enough said.

SLIPPERSLAPPER

1

Matty-the-Lamb was Slipperslapper's nephew and a pure Trojan when it came to the working of her sixty acres. Each morning while we were still on the broad of our backs in our dreamy little beds — before we had wiped the sleep from our eyes or had stirred the salt and butter into our eggs — Matty would have milked his cows and exchanged the milk for skimmed milk and butter, and he'd be back home with his ass-and-car from the creamery. He'd be whaling the cattle-feed into his four calves and getting the two pigs ready their dinner-feed. He'd be filling the two potato-sacks (one sack with the Kerrs Pinks spuds for the house-table and the white Arran Banners for the animals). He'd be filling another sack with the cabbages, cutting out the hearts and most of the outer cabbage leaves to give to the pigs, keeping only the juiciest leaves for their own dinner of fat meat, spuds and milk. Yes, the list of Matty's jobs was as long as a church litany. And all that work took place even before he'd given himself time to say a prayer or swallow a bit of breakfast!

This left the rest of us scratching our heads and at a loss for words. His method of working was his own peculiar way of looking at life. The birds of the air (he used to say) were put on this earth to spend every hour of daylight as wisely as they could, and God had given a similar task to all other creatures, man included. It meant that during the cold months of winter, he behaved with the same nondescript efforts as the birds in the bushes and spent each miserable morning fast asleep. But now it was springtime, and we could see that he was working himself to the bone. He couldn't go on working like an animal, day in and day out, could he? He wasn't a man-made machine with a set of gears on him to be oiled here and there, was he?

And to confirm this very point, a cry was soon heard on everybody's lips, 'Poor Matty! Oh, poor Matty! Will ye look at the state of him!' It was true — his arduous work had turned him into a gaunt ghost of himself.

At the best of times, he had never been a giant-of-a-man and soon he was as skinny as a bed-rail. What with all the ploughing, the tending of the turf abroad in the bog, the harvesting of the hay and the thrashing of the corn, all done at an extreme pace that Matty — and Matty alone — had always set himself, the farming had turned out to be far too much for his poor frail frame.

And then it happened — and all too quickly. The poor man was found dead whilst sitting on the lace of his ass-and-car bringing back a load of ferns from the wood for the bedding of his cows. His gentle ass (Lazybones) wheeled him into the yard and put her head in over Slipperslapper's half-door to bring her the sad news — a scene fit for a painter in oils if ever there was one.

The news of Matty's death was hurried down to us by the women from the hills as they drove their little ass-and-cars down our way on a Saturday visit to Father Honesty's confession-box. Red Scissors had always said that hard work never killed a living soul, but he was wrong this time. Seemingly, it had killed poor Matty and, after waking his corpse in the grandest style possible, the entire parish went to his graveside to do him the solemnities of a noble burial. They could do nothing less, could they?

2

Now that poor Matty was no more, Slipperslapper was beginning to work herself up into an ever-increasing turmoil and to lose some of her mind. She knew in her heart-of-hearts that, unless she got herself another working man to take Matty's place, she'd end up inside in the corpse-house like him from all the slavery she'd have to do on her farm and become another of Lazybones' passengers on the lace of the ass-and-car.

The poachers brought down the news (they being the only ones ever seen wandering through the fields after midnight) how one starry night when they were cycling their bikes and lamps into the moonlit hills, they had come across Slipperslapper wandering aimlessly through the fields beside Growl River. On another night, they saw her strolling around through the woods. What on earth was she up to? What was she trying to tell the rest of us? Was she hoping some ancient nymph from fairyland would come flying down from the tree-tops or up out of Growl River and carry her off in his powerful arms to the land of romance?

Father Honesty wasn't much use. All he succeeded in doing for her when next she found him coming in through the half-door was to bring with him a hairy and toothless old farmer (Ugly-Face). He took off his hat and leeringly introduced himself. He had the nerve to say he'd just turned fifty. Slipperslapper could have died laughing for the bleddy liar looked at least a day or two over seventy. Of course, the old bugger had come to cast his eyes on her sixty acres of land and to walk across her fields to see if they were any good in the hope of extending his own bit of land.

When he saw Slipperslapper (or rather when he saw her sixty acres), old Ugly-Face didn't waste a single second. With a step and a jump, he went as far as pushing her into town and in through the church gates and up onto the altar-steps. But, in spite of Father Honesty's smiling urgency for her to get a move on and marry old Ugly-Face, she became as fidgety as a hen about to lay her first egg.

At the last minute — and just as the old slyboot's hands were about to make an eager grab for her finger and put a ring on it — a small thought suddenly worked its way into her head. It was a fruitful and wise little thought, inspired not by the holy priest but by her very own guardian angel. All of a sudden, she saw in her mind's eye the picture of her future cold bedroom. She saw the icy arse of old Ugly-Face rubbing up next to her in the long and lonely nights. Shiver the thought! In a fit of panic, she turned on her dainty heel and flew like a bat out the church door, Father Honesty and his startled vestments tearing along the yard behind her for he could see he hadn't yet earned the bottle of whiskey that old Ugly-Face had given him. Slipperslapper went sailing down Jinnet Street, frightening the life out of several innocent schoolchildren as well as the bemused jackdaws round the market cross.

3

The antics of Slipperslapper (even the children began to see it) outmatched all of the day-to-day antics of the rest of us. She couldn't stop thinking of Matty and a restlessness (almost feverish) increased its daily hold on her. She was letting the little farm go to blazes. We heard she'd gone into town to replenish her store of clothing as she thought the dusty old clothes inherited from her mother (Mad Norrie) were far too dowdy for her. From Fanny Farthingale's Dress-Shop, she came home one evening with an ass-and-car-load of coloured ribbons. These were to replace the ones she'd tied in her hair for the previous proposed marriage to old Ugly-Face — the marriage that had never taken place.

Men, chasing after their cows to milk them, found that, in her effort to greet the new spring season, she had beaten them to it, having risen up earlier than the corncrake. From inside the lid of her flour-box, she selected the finest of these coloured ribbons and, mindful of the honeysuckle below Shy Dennis's shack, fished out her mother's dress with the pink and yellow flounces on it so as to celebrate the rising year the way that lady used to do. She couldn't help herself, or perhaps she wanted to give the idle-jacks something to talk about. With no sock to spare, she put on Matty's brown pair of boots.

Her days started the same way — up at dawn, sniffing into her nostrils the air's pure freshness. She cut her yards of ribbon into long bands and made streamers of them, which hoisted onto the tresses of her hair, tying them with safety pins and with little red bows at the end of each braid. She put on her mother's sunbonnet and adorned her wrists with daisy chain bangles. She put on her father's cocked hat and his peacock-blue jersey and his buckled belt for a sash. She was almost ready. She stood outside the half-door, admiring her hairy shins and making awkward attempts to squash her ample breasts together, which seemed to be fighting with each other like two wildcats in a bag. Then she went down to the yard stream and took a look at her reflection in the stream. What she saw was the look of a rakish pirate from one of her mother's storybooks, and she let out such a war-whoop of pleasure that all the crows flew out over the ditch. Dressed in her head-rags and ribbons, she could now sing the song of nature, and she paraded out the yard past the dung heap, a sweet-gallon tucked under her elbow and it full of pebbles for her to shake. With her stick, she whaled onto the gallon-lid and made as much of a racket as she could. She then hurled her boots down the lane, scattering the flies that were dancing in the horse dung. Moll-the-Man's terrified rooster started crowing at the sight and speed of her.

When My-son-Jack saw the finery of her as she came tearing down the road, he yelled, 'Mother! Mother! Come quick, will ye? Look at Slipperslapper, the world's latest thunderbolt and the lightning coming out of her arse!'

'All she needs is a pair of buttercups in her ears,' said Dowager and they both split their sides laughing.

The breezes impelled Slipperslapper on. She burst out over Free 'n' Easy's stile and passed the lazy-eyed cows of Simple Simon, her eyes scanning the field as she stooped to pick up a pheasant-feather and stick it in her hair. She took herself on over Old Stroller's stile and leapt across Cackles' spring-well before scaling Moll-the-Man's top field where Moll's children were chastising the ass. She galloped on towards the blue gates, blessing several bushes on her way and greeting several young trees. With the colourful fashions she was wearing and her sweet-gallon and stick and pebbles, she far surpassed the dizzy juggler in the Daffy-Duck circus, and the sun shone down on her in utter disbelief for it had never before witnessed a woman so outlandish as this.

4

However, the days of her alarming behaviour were about to come to an end. Her downfall would result neither from the fine embroidery of her dresses (although the rest of the women envied her this daring) nor from her gallon-drum. Instead, it was a slow but steady rumour that no one really knew how old she was. Without the war-paint on her face, she looked to be old enough (said the old gossips) — she could be as old as a hundred-and-one. As always, they overdid it. But she was certainly well past the age of childbearing, in spite of the previous courtship given to her by old Ugly-Face. Father Honesty was sent for a second time. He prepared himself for what would be a singular visit for he wasn't quite sure how he was going to handle it.

A few of the gossipy old women had gathered at the flagstones outside Slipperslapper's yard, their ears cocked back so as to hear the conversation — the way they were used to doing when some poor soul was reciting her few miserable sins inside in the confession-box. No, said Slipperslapper, she didn't know how old she was. No, she had never thought of her age until now. After much prompting and winking from the women (they were now peering in at the half-door), Father Honesty guessed her age to be around the fifty mark. He had been well primed by those nearest and dearest to him and realised that Slipperslapper was the sort of woman who'd be more than loathe to stand up against a man-of-the-cloth and would bow to whatever wisdom he would be able to drag up.

Gently and fatherly, he reminded her (almost patting her on the knee) that it was a small scandal for a woman of her wise years to be seen abroad in such colourful clothing as Fanny

Farthingale's dresses, that it was doing untold damage to her soul, that it was high time for her to go back to the shop and buy a more suitable set of garments for a decent woman of her age. Before he left her welcoming room, he gave her his solemn blessing out of his holy water bottle and ordered her to dress herself in the customary black clothing from now on.

'Good man, yeerself,' said the women as he returned to the yard and headed out to his motorcar, and they smothered themselves in delight, knowing that they were no longer going to be outshone by this common old outsider who had come down from Ambush Wood to buy her farm only a few years back.

A day or two later, a very sad face appeared among us. It was a most disconsolate Slipperslapper. She was no longer wearing the brown boots, and she was wearing a new black dress that reached down to her toes. She had equipped herself with a white wimple underneath a black bonnet. From that day forth, in obedience to Holy Mother Church, she would never again greet the new spring season with her colourful antics but would wear no other raiment other than the aging and decent black. There'd be no trace of her lipstick and powder. She threw the green tam, the sunbonnet, the cocked hat, and her mother's flowery dress into the flames of her turf-fire.

'Amen to it all!' she sighed, and she wiped the tears from her tired old eyes. She felt deeply alone, more so than ever before in her life. Nobody wanted to look at her, dressed as she was in her black widow's weeds. Why would they?

5

Spring had turned into summer and the tinkers had left for Kerry's Puck Fair, leaving a flea-ridden puppy behind them. Slipperslapper came down the lane, a sack on her back. Moll-the-Man's children ran up to meet her and crowded round her. 'How d'ye do, Slipperslapper — where are ye off to?' they wanted to know.

'I'm going to the river,' said she.

'And what have ye in the potato-sack?' said Leppity.

'I've a tinker's pup, and it's covered with a thousand fleas.'

The children gathered closer and heard the faint and suppressed whimpering from inside the potato-sack. 'And what are ye going to do with the puppy?' scoffed Lippy. 'Are ye going to teach him to swim?' The other children laughed uncertainly.

'I'm going to drown it,' said Slipperslapper without the blink of an eye.

They couldn't believe their ears. For though Lippy and Philly had once tied a tin can to a stray dog's tail to see the performance it would make, here was an entirely different story: the old mad-woman was about to kill an innocent puppy.

'Surely not?' they shouted.

'The very thing,' said she defiantly.

They felt helpless and could see that Slipperslapper was more excited than usual. Did they but know it, her heart was pounding the blood right up into the roof of her head. She led them across to the ditch.

'Don't be shy, little children. Go and fetch some rocks, big ones so we can weigh down the sack.'

Suddenly they were frightened, but of late they had become dutiful and obedient as a result of their mother's renewed efforts to guide them into good behaviour. Without thinking, they ran along the side of the ditch, gathering in big stones. Not a word did they say to one another.

Slipperslapper walked steadily on, the children following behind her, carrying their stones. To her it was like the killing of a pig. When she got to the bridge, she tied the reins firmly onto the railings and then raked out some even bigger stones. She threw them into the river, testing the depths of the water to find out where the deepest holes were.

The dazed children crowded round the railings, craning their necks forward so as to gaze through the bars of the bridge and listen to the cheerful sound of the rippling river. How often had they banded together at this bridge and looked in over the railings to see the river rushing merrily by? How often had they shouted and cursed underneath the bridge to hear the echo of their voice? How often had they counted the sleeping brown trout in the haze of a quiet day when they could see the black fish-shadows on the floor of the river? And now, not a sound other than the despairing whimpers of a tinker's puppy in a potato-sack. It was all strange to them — a mixture of excitement and sorrow for what they knew would be certain death. They couldn't tell one another how they felt — that they needed to cry out to their mother to come and help them. Yet here they were — each one alone in themselves — with their inexplicable fear, their guilt, and their shame all rolled into one.

This bridge and this river, the saddest place on earth. And if ever there was a time to say their prayers, it was this minute — prayers for the hapless puppy and for God to forgive them. They couldn't take their eyes off of the potato-sack. What would their mother say when they got home? What would they tell her? All the poetry of fairy fields and woods that had always been inside in their hearts had vanished.

'Stand back, lads!' shouted Slipperslapper, her voice echoing off of the metal of the bridge. She held the frightened little parcel of the sack out over the glittering railings. Just as the lonely pig that, knowing its fate, had once cried out agonisingly for mercy, the miserable puppy now howled as if to ask for mercy (take pity on my innocence!) and struggled to get out of the sack.

The mad woman lowered the sack out over the railings. She dangled it for a second and then slowly lowered it into the river. To the eternal shame of Young Jim, Leppity, and Battlin' Sal, not one of them begged mercy for the puppy. It was as though they were entranced, so anxious were they to see the drowning since they had never seen a drowning before.

The reins and the sack swayed back and forth. Down, down and ever down into the bottomless waters, that seemed to be welcoming the unwanted little bundle into the realms of oblivion, the sack fell into the deep hole with an echoing splash.

And then there was silence. Nothing but silence. And the silence was followed by an even deeper quietness — a quietness which none of the children had felt before. It was the beginning of wickedness worming its devilish way into their young souls and sunlight stopped its sunning and clouds stopped their clouding. In that single moment, the children realized the horror of what they were looking at — at what they were agreeing to — the act of drowning a small creature! They saw the heart-rending puppy kicking at the sack under the surface. They saw its hopeless struggle with inevitable death. They heard the last low whimpers.

After a supreme effort, the puppy loosened the bonds at the mouth of the sack. He was free. He was in the river. The children had never before seen such a sorrowful expression as the look he gave them from his forlorn eyes. Their pain and compassion would last them a lifetime. Tears seemed to be streaming down its face. Not even the pig, when man is about to stick the knife in his throat, had ever looked so pitiful. The killing of this puppy was their very first great sin, and they thought to themselves: could they ever be forgiven? No —never!

It took less than a minute for the puppy to die. Even the flies stopped buzzing, and the crows stopped their awkward melodies. God seemed to be looking down and pointing his accusing finger at them, and they felt like hiding their naked souls in the waters of the river alongside the drowning puppy.

Supremely brave little puppy! A minute before this, his nose had been twitching for air as he kicked out at the river. Now he was gasping for a final breath, and his eyes were glazed like the dead pig's. He swam a few feeble strokes towards the bank, but his little body was too weak and at the same time his lungs were filling with water and still the children hadn't raised a finger to try and stop this cruel death. They knew if their mother ever found out what they were up to, she'd have belted their legs with her ashplant the length of the yard. What harm had the poor innocent puppy ever done them (she'd say)?

The puppy gave a final shudder and floated for a second on the surface, his body circling around and round, twisting his hairy whiskers. So small and so shrivelled, like a wet dish-clout folding in on itself. Then he stopped kicking and sank down limply into the river's black hole. No soft death was a drowning. A slow kicking death was a drowning. A dirty teasing death was a drowning. The children had time to ponder on what had been done and they felt the sickness over the death of a fellow-creature. Even the river seemed to have forgotten its movement and seemed still. A large piece of the carefree innocence in each child had died this day. They looked for the sun, but it wasn't there. They looked for the birds, and they weren't there, though a horrible serpent had taken over the sky.

CHERISH AND
GALLANTRY

1

A few years previously, Lippy and Philly had already started school but their younger brother (Gallantry) was still at home for one more year. His daily life was as peaceful as a monk's, almost unworldly. He was the sort of child that never felt lonely when he was on his own. With his deep and intense eyes (like his father's), he always found time for childish reflections as he sat on the lace of the empty ass-and-car, listening to the faint breezes of the early morning whispering their soft voice into his ear. He had time to gaze at the ditch across from him, crowded with wildflowers, and watch a nearby spider at her web. He listened to By-Jiggery cutting up the logs with the bowsaw and liked the harmonious sound it made and the luxuriant smell of the wood.

A little while later, he walked down to the stream near the road where he'd hidden his father's disused old bicycle lamp and began smashing it on the flagstones to disintegrate the insides of it. Like his big brothers, he was intent on breaking anything that came in sight so as to see what was inside it and what made it work. Ah, the budding scientist that he was! Of course, there were one or two unexpected lessons to be learnt, and he was surprised to discover that anything smashed — be it the clockwork car from the lady in the big house the previous Christmas or the wax doll from his aunts in far-off Baltimore — was not going to be easily mended!

Meanwhile, Cherish (his one true friend apart from his two big brothers), was also up and about and as carefree as the birds in the bushes — at least until next year's dreaded school-imprisonment should come her way. Like Gallantry, there was nothing to upset her peace of mind except for the odd ass-and-car ride with her father (Handless Rody), jogging off to the creamery or out to the bog for a load-of-turf. To please her mother (Goodness Mary), she took herself down the haggart among the nettles in search of a few fresh eggs. When this small task was done, she bent her footsteps down the slope to meet up with Gallantry and give him a bit of a respite from the intensity of his daily daydreaming.

She found him on the flagstones — he and his old flash-lamp. He looked up at the dark shadow crossing above his head, the gleaming sunlight almost blurring his vision of Cherish. Like himself, she wore no shoes except for Sunday Mass. She was wearing her green dress, the one with some pink roses on it. A happy light passed between the two little souls and from that moment onwards, it was going to be eyeball-to-eyeball as they got ready to play and pass their morning together.

Cherish peered down at the smashed lamp and the blue graphite inside it. She saw the sad look in Gallantry's eye. It seems she had arrived in the nick of time. As usual, she had the power to distract him from the torn insides of his lamp and transport him elsewhere.

They took out their hidden store of coloured stones, which By-Jiggery had brought home from the river and stored in the base of the hawthorn tree next to the tar-barrels. Pink ones, rusty ones, mauve and lavender ones. With an armful of these, they attacked the empty flagstones and drew four big circles with uncomplicated upturned mouths — the faces of their parents. They put the finishing touches to their artistic handi-work by drawing seven cattle and a field of sheep — unusual sheep in that their wool was a torrid red! The flagstones soon became a messy entanglement, a blaze of bright colours, which only one or two happy woodland fairies, lurking in the nearby dyke, could have looked upon with a proud smile.

The little adventurers sprang to their feet and took themselves off to the upturned pony-and-trap in By-Jiggery's stable. In its darkness, the years of bedding had softened the floor, and their bare feet could simply purr in across the doorway. Their eyes gradually adjusted to the shadows of the dark. They crept into the well of the trap and lay down snugly inside on the soft warm blankets, looking up at the empty nests of the wagtails who had long gone off to feast on insects. They lay there, resting, pretending they were asleep, and they purred with pleasure. The lazy day was humming with languor, and the buzz of the day's flies was everywhere. They could hear the geese and hens strolling round the wheels of the pony-and-trap. Like themselves, they had picked their way in from the glassy sunlight of this summer's day, which had been piercing them in the eye.

Moll-the-Man came out into the yard. With her shovel, she was about to fire the dung and slurry away from the cowshed door. In her apron, she brought out a dozen crab-apples that she had been baking in the fire. She came in through the stable door. She reached into the pony-and-trap and handed the crab-apples to Cherish, the lady of the imaginary house inside in the trap. Like a prince and princess, the two children then dined heartily on the roasted feast as though it were a castle banquet, and the slanting light of the sun cast its rays directly in the door on them in this secret hidey-hole of theirs.

Shortly afterwards, they hopped down from the trap. It was time to be on the move and catch the warm sun elsewhere. They headed along the creamery road, swinging their hands and scuffing their feet — Gallantry as always following behind the heels of Cherish. They'd soon be at the little girl's house where he had often ventured with the prospect of a slice of bread and jam from Goodness Mary. They raced each other as far as Shy Dennis's shack across from Fort Dangerous, home of the mischief-making leprechauns, and were soon at the house.

As always, Gallantry was pretending to be the little brother. Today was another day when Cherish would offer to bring him into her make-believe dreamland, all the time looking back at him and beckoning him on. She led him to her father's shed and helped him up onto the piles of turf stacked against the back wall. On top of the turf was a wooden box and in it snuggled her tiger-barred cat (Whiskers) on a sop of hay. Around her were her newly-born kittens, their eyes gazing up at them.

One or two were brave enough to begin crawling out from the box and onto the turf. With one eye on the cat, Gallantry timidly stroked the fur of the boldest kitten, the cat looking on disinterestedly. Through the air-slits, knifed high in the walls over their heads, the wagtails brought food into their screeching young at the speed of light. In and out they flew, cheekily whipping the cat's fur as they feathered their way out over her head — daring new wagtail adventures, which might have been their last ones, if the tired cat hadn't had other matters on her mind and been quite so peaceful.

From there, Cherish led the shy little boy to her cubby-shop — a place where none of the grown-ups ever showed their faces — where she and Gallantry would get themselves a few more hours of this day's charming blandishments. Its shelves were three old lat boards and some heavy cornerstones holding them level and in place. Handless Rody had brought the lat boards and stones down here, taking them from the rickety old barn, which had had its door shattered in the heavy snows the previous year. On these lat boards, Cherish had her glass jars and tin mugs and accumulated bits of broken glass, willow-patterned crockery, beads, rocks and discarded utensils — all hunted out along every ditch and dyke. On one of the nearby pine-trees nearby dangled a rusty old kettle, her prize possession, like some Christmas decoration.

Before they sat down to tea, they had one long-drawn-out task to do. Mindful of their previous joys of making necklaces with field-flowers, they gathered fistfuls of purple wildflowers and, provoking once more the concentrated furrowed lines on Gallantry's brow, laid them out on the shelves of the cubby-house. As a finishing touch, they made themselves two bangles with the flowers and their task was complete. Gallantry placed his bangle around the wrist of Cherish and Cherish placed hers around Gallantry's.

'Let's have tea,' said Cherish. 'I'll fetch down the mugs.'

Gallantry needed no encouragement and got down the rusty kettle and filled it with water from the stream. Cherish took down the tin mugs and poured out the water. From her store of wealth (the coloured trimmings and broken bits of glass and crockery), she gave Gallantry a slice of her best pretend bread and jam. Such tea-making and delicacies you never did see! Such eating of sweets wrapped in wads of newspaper, as the two of them continued to sip their tea and bowed their heads to each other and pretended to be important people having high tea below in the big house. A warmth seeped from one set of eyes into another set of eyes and the field fairies smiled triumphantly on such innocent friendship.

It was time to bake the cakes for next day's teatime, though this sort of work wasn't quite appropriate for a prince and his princess bedecked in their bangled jewels. There was plenty of dry mud nearby (grey and a little on the hard side). With a stick, Gallantry dug out a little pile of it and, through a battered old strainer, he sifted out the smaller stones, the earth having to be clean and fine like his mother's flour. He filled their two mugs with the last of the water from the kettle, and with it, Cherish tried to soften the clay with her hands but found it unworkable. She crouched over the rusty kettle and, turning her back on Gallantry, bent her knees and filled the kettle coyly with her own hot poolie. She poured the poolie over the mud-heap and it worked well, giving her a well-textured cake, which she separated into four smaller cakes. Gallantry marvelled at the cleverness of her. She placed the cakes in neat rows on the shelves. Gallantry marked each of them with a cross, just like he'd seen his mother doing. They'd bake nicely in the sunshine. They ended their cubby-house play by pouring for themselves a plateful of soup from the pee-water, which they pretended to drink. Delicious!

It was time to clear away the implements and the refinements of their fine living. They turned over two of the lat boards and made them into beds for themselves to lie down on. For a while they pretended to be asleep, but they were too excited. The afternoon air was deliciously cool on their outstretched legs, and they lay dreamily looking up at the sunlight and the afternoon's fluffy clouds that had raced in from faraway Galway.

Cherish then got busy, humming happily to herself as she cleaned each article in the stream. She washed down the lat boards and neatly stacked the jam-jars and tin mugs. The many small coloured stone sweets she stored on the lower shelves, saving them for some other time. Looking back at the finished tidiness of the cubby-house, Gallantry again marvelled at the skilful housewife that was his little friend, Cherish.

By now, the setting sun had begun to give up the ghost, and the hills around Handless Rody's little farm were turning purple and charcoal. Mysterious shadows came towards the two small children and put an end to their play. Daylight would soon be passing altogether, and the little playmakers grew afraid, feeling the penetrating eyes of the Boodeeman peeping out at them from the bushes. They ran back into Goodness Mary's haggart where they felt safe and secure. It had been another gift-of-a-day, and they were as hungry as a pair of tigers.

The mountains had finally lost all the red smokiness of the sunset, and Gallantry took leave of his little friend. He ran down the creamery road and into the apron of Moll-the-Man, his mind full of his day's teatime labours — full of bangles, kittens and wagtails.

2

One sunlit Saturday, Cherish and Gallantry strolled up as far as Shy Denis's shack and went down the lane to My-son-Mick's cowshed. They were on a mission and wanted to take a peek at his newly-born calf, who had been confined till now inside the four dark walls of the cowshed. Mick (they knew) was about to let the little fellow loose and out onto the wide expanse of space. It would give them the chance of a precious and memorable day.

The big man lifted the calf in his arms and staggered out with him into the Goldfinch Field. He placed him gingerly down midst the startled cows and his ass (Grease Lightning). The children were wide-eyed in anticipation and held their breath as the startled calf wobbled onto his feet. The little creature gazed at the great big universe, a huge space previously unknown to him and beyond his wildest imagination.

A moment later (and to the delightful screams of Cherish and Gallantry), the little fellow stabbed his back legs up at the clouds as though he were about to challenge them. Then he raced around the demented field like some runaway train. His fierce enthusiasm frightened the life out of Mick's old ass and drove his cattle head-over-heels towards the only hiding-places they could find — the dyke. They tumbled in and there they would remain (the simpletons), peering out at the strange sight of a tearaway calf that had become the brave new owner of their field. The children clapped and clapped. They then had to laugh outright when they saw My-son-Mick lying on his back and kicking his legs into the air. He was doubled up in an uncontrollable fit of joyful laughter, the big silly child that he always was.

3

During their schoolyears, which passed somewhat uneventfully, Cherish and Gallantry were still young enough to run races with each other and play hide-and-seek amidst the ferns round the river. They counted the apples, as yet unripe, in Curl 'n' Stripes' orchard and planned future raids there. In Red Scissors' hayshed, they fought happily with one another and at times boxed the ears off of one another. They took the rusty bowlee-wheel rim of the milk-churn and marched up the hill with it. They belted it down the hillslope, scattering any stray cat or dog that might have the temerity to be in their path. And then they marched all the way back up and started all over again.

In the late afternoon, watched only by the rooks, they sat alongside Lippy and Philly (now home from school) on the fallen pine-tree in Old Sam's grove where the older boys handed out fags from their collection of stolen fag-butts. They attempted to smoke them like Lippy and Philly till their stomachs were sickened to death. Then they crossed over the singletree and watched that big child-of-a-man, Red Scissors, towering over them and hanging down by his boots from the outstretched limb of the beech tree on Simple Simon's ditch. Oh, how Red Scissors missed his own childhood! These were leisurely days of magical music that neither of them would want to forget.

However, during these days of uncertain adolescent growth, Gallantry preferred the silence of his own private world. You'd catch him listening from afar to his brothers as they gloated over the spoiling of some new orchard or the theft of half-a-dozen spuds from their mother's burner. Each morning when he looked out the window, he saw the world in a different light from them — as though it was looking back in through the glass and staring him straight in the eye. In the evenings, he sat by the fire like a motionless heron, his finely-tuned ears filled with the tales of the visiting card-players — tales of wealth and glory that could be earned in far-distant lands. At these times, a restlessness crept over him. He was like a cat caught in the briars or a rabbit before the glare of the ferret, and he couldn't understand what all this change in him meant.

Whenever he had the chance, he strolled off to one or two secret places that only he knew — places where he could content himself in admiring the growing life of the springtime lambs, chicks and goslings. He spent hours down by the river and was never as happy as when he was walking undisturbed in the hills or found himself in the depths of the woods. Nor did he steal the eggs from the birds' nests like his older brothers did but spent hours watching these same birds wheeling round in the sky and listening to the cheerful songs of blackbirds and thrushes.

Some days, he wandered across Free 'n' Easy's nine acres and over as far as the forbidden Fort Dangerous, hoping to hear the faint whispers of the bygone Danes, whose ghosts (he knew) still lurked there. He tiptoed into the middle of the forbidden fort and sat there for a while, listening — listening — forever listening — to see if he could hear the laughter of the little leprechauns. And at dusk, after his daily tasks were done, he crept down as far as the waterfall beyond Echo Bridge to keep step with Gret's two noble sows. These were the times when Moll-the-Man saw (as only a mother could) the changes in her young son as he struggled with his new growth, and she was afraid that she was losing sight of him and he of her.

Cherish too was beginning to feel she had lost the little boy that once she played with, and to please him, she stole Fatty-Matty's ass from the Ragwort Field and offered it to him to ride round in her father's haggart. Below in the river, the children living at the waterfall caught a small trout in their canister and made a gift of it to him. His brothers stole the hurley-stick and slither ball from behind Old Stroller's bedroom door and promised him the next pig's bladder when they'd be going up to Jack-the-Herd's pig-killing in the Valley-of-the-Pig.

For a time, all these ruses succeeded in bringing Gallantry back to his childhood playfulness amongst them. But being at one and the same time a child as well as trying to act like a man was now a difficult problem for him. He was too young — too fragile — to compete with stronger men. And yet he was too old to let spontaneous laughter get loose in him and join in the younger children's games as in those happier days of his recent childhood.

Cherish found herself in the same predicament and had to admit to herself that there were days when she had entered a new and secret place. Whenever she looked in the looking-glass, she (the little girl of previous daylight merriment) found herself coming face to face at times with a brooding darkness that was trying to transfigure and re-shape her into the world of adulthood. A strange tenderness began to consume her spirits. There were dreamy occasions when she felt she was fading away from the earth altogether — when her eyes and ears grew cloudy as though she were being dragged along by some magician or one of the heavenly angels. But (like Gallantry) she was doing what was natural — discarding her childhood feathers and taking on the comeliness of early adulthood. There was a sadness to it all for no longer could she throw herself into childhood's laughter, no longer could she climb the rotten tree and look across at the pink clouds marbling the sunset over in Clare, no longer could she paddle along the riverbed with Gallantry. These days had gone for good. She and Gallantry were two-of-a-kind, approaching a new world.

4

A week after visiting My-son-Mick and his calf, Gallantry was hurrying along towards Miss Friendly's glen. He had a bunch of his mother's flowers and some loaves and cakes and was heading for Sally, his aged grandmother. She was sick on the bed after falling off of her ass-and-car down in the wood while loading her cart with bedding ferns. The nurse (Black Bess) who usually tended to the needs of Sally, was laid low with the flu-bug and couldn't get herself back in harness for a while. Gallantry would spend a day getting the messages for her down at the shop, and, with her directions, he'd be able to get her the bit of dinner and put back a little health into her. He'd put a broom to her welcoming room floor as well as the yard.

The day was hot and dusty. Wishing to avoid the long journey round by the road, he strolled on across the fields towards the Hooshian's meadow above the river. He saw the youngest of the Hooshian brothers loitering at the gap, a lad three years older than himself. It was as though he'd been expecting Gallantry to come this way for he certainly wasn't out catching butterflies or eating redcurrants for himself. He was a big strong lad and went by the quaint name of Give-him-the-left for he had a reputation for rowdy brawling.

When Gallantry found himself at the gap, Give-him-the-left stepped out in front of him and put his hand out to stop him passing through the gap.

'Ye're trespassing on mee father's lands,' said he with a smirk on his face. This was unusual, for no-one among our God-fearing people had ever heard tell of the word trespassing.

A second later, the row rose up between the two of them. Gallantry (and here we must tell the truth) was feeling manly from all the hard work he'd been doing of late — like helping his father sort out the hay-reek — and he clenched his fists and got ready to put up a bit of a fight. Admittedly, it was he who struck the first blow. But he was no match for Give-him-the-left, and the bigger lad struck the second blow straight into Gallantry's stomach, knocking the breath clean out of him. He then struck the third and fourth blows and countless others until Gallantry's poor nose was a river of blood.

The poor boy now knew that he was still a child and not a man, and he burst into an uncontrollable fit of tears. Such savagery was completely new to him for he had been treated with the utmost kindness since the day he was born.

And at each blow from Give-him-the-left there seemed to be a number of unheard-of oaths: 'I'll dismantle yeer jaw and put a few more wrinkles on yeer forehead for ye — I'll make a crow's dinner out of ye!'

Gallantry finally curled up and lay in a heap at the gap. Give-him-the-left wiped the blood from his knuckles and went away unruffled, whistling his merry way across the field. Poor Gallantry! There was no one present to comfort him. How he longed for Lippy and Philly to be here with him! How he longed for the comforting touch of his mother's stout arms that would soften the hurt on his face and heal his breaking heart!

He wiped away the tears from his blotched eyes and staggered onto his feet. He realised that Give-him-the-left had disappeared from view, and he continued his journey through the gap. He couldn't come to his grandmother's door (she being the biggest gossip in the entire world) with his face in such a state of disrepair. The old fairy-woman would be sure to broadcast it the length and breadth of Tipperary, thereby ensuring that everyone would know that he (soft in spirit, soft in heart) was not yet a man when it came to the use of his knuckles. He headed down towards the river, intent on wiping the bloodstains from his face.

What he now needed was the strength that lay in Cherish these days. If only his childhood friend had been here with him, what an energetic beating with her fists she'd have given Give-him-the-left! He remembered the day the previous year when Batty, the youngest of Red Buckles' children, was going to the well to fetch home a bucket of water. Cherish was returning with her own overflowing bucket and her mother's ashplant across her shoulder. In the middle of the road stood Old Stroller's angry terrier (Whalloper). He had turned himself into a vicious thug-of-a-dog ever since Lippy and Philly gave him the kicking of his life after Old Stroller had fired his double-barrel gun out over their terrified heads when they'd robbed his orchard.

The terrier came face to face with little Batty and then ran straight at him, ready to make a raid on the seat of his britches. You should have heard the squeals out of the misfortunate Batty. You'd think he was about to be killed.

In the blink of an eye, this little scene drew a sturdy reply from Cherish. Until then nobody had known the power in her elbow or the strength of her anger. To save the little arse of Batty from being eaten raw, she ran at the terrier and downed the entire contents of her bucket of water on top of his head. When the enraged terrier recovered from the shock, he decided to attack her own rear-quarters. That's when her strength turned into a complete tornado. She took her ash-plant to Whalloper's skull and beat him to within an inch of his life until he was left whinging at her feet, begging for mercy. On that day, she had turned herself into quite the young heroine amongst us. She had shown us a passion which any man would be proud to share in when the years rolled by. Dowager ran out and held poor Batty in her comforting apron, and he told her of the saving graces of Cherish. She cocked her crooked finger (the one the ferret had disfigured years back) to her lips.

'Tell me this and tell me no more,' said she to My-son-Jack, 'did ye ever see such a wonder-of-a-child as our Cherish — and the beautiful rose that's in her cheeks when she's hot and vexed? I ask you, aren't a child's looks deceiving? She might be a pure pearl and the prettiest flower in the garden (again those big words of Dowager), but she's a born savage when it comes to beating the life out of a wild dog like Whalloper. Fair play to her!'

5

On the day of his chastisement by Give-him-the-left, Gallantry was to realize that he had at last become a proper man. He dragged his dazed body across the field to where the crossing-stones would lead him to his grandmother's house. Suddenly, he heard the shrieks of girlish laughter destroying the day's calmness. It was coming from the depths of the sally-hole, screened off beneath the bank of oak-trees. And then he heard the playful splashing of the water being pelted about in the river by a crowd of girls — like a herd of wild horses let loose.

He crept down through the oak-trees and peeped down into the sally-hole. And there in its depths was a pile of young women and they full to the brim with flushed-cheeked happiness. There was Leggie Lizzie, Fiery Fluff and their older sister (Brazen) along with half-a-dozen other innocent young girls, none of whom had yet experienced a man's pleasure. In the middle of the pool, they shone like silver mermaids and the branches of the trees reached down like hands to fan them. They had slipped out of their dresses, vests and knickers, leaving themselves liberated and free from their mothers' daily dominance and the forceful aggression of their older brothers.

If a whole lorry-load of Lady Pock-Frock's Christmas chocolate gifts was to be put in front of his face, Gallantry would not be tempted to compare them with the unblemished vision of these bare-arsed angels, now ripening from girlhood into womanhood themselves and the happy laughing innocence of their voices, themselves and the flush of their pink cheeks and their soft bellies and wobbly breasts swaying with every movement as they cavorted and churned up the water in a shower of rainbow drops with their weather-worn feet. Each of them seemed conscious of wanting to be little children all over again, and they ran mad-cap round and round the pool, their hearts wishing to shout out, 'Look at me! Look at me! I am alive!' And that fairy creature (Fancy Free) and her sister (Happy-Go-Lucky), both of whom lived amidst the nearby trees, sang their fairy-songs in the girls' eyes, in their ears and hair and tickled them deliciously.

Quicker than a blink, our beleaguered hero forgot the wince from Give-him-the-left's fists, forgot about the aching cramp in his jaw, forgot the blood running out of his swollen nose, forgot his torn knuckles. With the illicit and furtive sight of these nature-nymphs he even forgot his torn heart and his abandoned pride — all gone from him like a field of goldfinch after a handclap. A strange feeling of longing and lustfulness stirred inside in him at the sight of these beautiful water-nymphs — a sight which no other man had ever seen before.

Then suddenly (were his eyes deceiving him?), he spotted the majestic limbs of Cherish and she fairer than all the jewels of India. For a moment, he was struck dumb. This very night (he felt) he would wear away his praying knees, thanking the Blessed Virgin a thousand times over for the gift of his two eyes and for the lovely charms of his Cherish and seeing her in all her natural finery.

The little girl, who had once been his childhood friend, was now a beautiful woman and all his previous lifetime of childish happiness in that silly little cubby-house, in that ramshackle pony-and-trap, in that topsy-turvy turf shed, now disappeared from him in a single thunderbolt. If only he had the hold of a pen, he'd have written much: she had a beauty beyond any previous song, poem or music he'd ever listened to, she had the alluring freshness of new poppies, she had hair the crispness of polished ferns, and the sunlight made a halo round her. And the cream of her was like the new milk, and the pink of her was like the new apples. There and then she tore his heart into smithereens, and he realized he had completely fallen in love and that Cherish would keep him in her thrall forevermore. His heart had always been as soft as butter, and if ever those river fairies felt like dancing a jig-step, it was at this precise moment in time — the moment when our boy-man fell on his bended knees in pagan worship of Cherish.

Long after the young ladies had dressed and departed, Gallantry sat by the water's edge. He bathed the wounds to his face but not the mortal wounds in his heart: these he'd keep open. With his head in the clouds and his feet floating above the earth and not knowing how he got there, he reached his grandmother's house. For the rest of that day and the next day, he stayed with her. In his efforts to drive to the back of his mind one or two sinful thoughts that kept rushing to the forefront of his head, he worked himself into a solid frenzy.

He scratched his head and he thought to himself, 'I have just walked the high banks of the river. I have spied on the bare-arsed beauties, and, for a moment or two, I have experienced a life that I never knew existed. The rest of the world can go to blazes. What are the likes of my previous companions when compared to these fine women!' To his surprise, he found no stain of shame or sin attached to what he had just witnessed — only beauty in the pearly laughter of young women's naked madness. He saw above all the beauty of Cherish, and he would keep it a secret in his heart till the day when old age would come and catch a hold of him and carry him off to the Beyond.

The following day, he scurried home at breakneck speed to his mother, drinking in the new breezes of his manhood. A happiness like never before was bursting up inside in him, up through his chest and out through his body like the hot milk rapturously pouring out from a young cow.

Later that evening, he tumbled into the settle-bed and lay silently alongside Lippy and Philly. In secret, he folded his pillow protectively in his arms and planted kiss after kiss on the back of his hand, kisses which he'd go on practising with that big mouth of his, kisses which one day soon he'd be planting on the raspberry lips and laurel-berry eyes of his charmer.

6

A few days later, Cherish was sitting uncomfortably on top of the sharp-edged load of turf and because of this, her ass (Quaintways) was having twice as heavy a load to pull. The turf began to cut into her backside and to redden her legs, and she was as cross as a briar.

There's a small river (just a stream) that crosses the Road-to-the-Hollows where, having skilfully negotiated the rocks in Growl River and the winding path out of the bog, she had the misfortune to see the cart's axle sinking into the mud of the stream and jolting to a halt. She was angry with herself, especially as she was so close to home, and she gave Quaintways a few tidy smacks of the ashplant across his back. Try as he might, the stubborn old ass couldn't get the wheels dislodged from the mud, though Cherish kept pulling and dragging at his bit. He felt he'd had enough of her nonsense, and he knelt down in the middle of the stream in what seemed to be an act of prayerful supplication to some strange ass-god. The cart-load of turf then keeled over and spilt around the road, and Cherish's anger completely exploded. She was like a rat caught in a henhouse.

The wilderness fairies (the trickeries) were nearby and searching for their angel-friend, True Love. Though they had hitherto been treacherous enough to drown one or two young girls in the bog's dark holes, on this occasion they were in a far friendlier mood and had plans to ambush Cherish and Gallantry.

Gallantry was on his way up towards Sweet Birdsong's hen house to bring home a clucking hen. He had reached the Road-to-the-Hollows when he came across the plight of

Cherish and her load of turf. True to the name he'd been given at birth, he gallantly reached out his hands to rescue her. With his father's penknife, he cut a few bushes from the ditches and placed them round the wheels of the cart. He gave Quaintways a long look from his eyes (no ashplant for you, my dear little ass!) and whispered those traditional words of kindness into the ass's ears and nose, 'Aren't you the best little ass in the whole of Tipperary!'

As a result, the wheels were set free, and Quaintways was led over to a patch of rich grass that promised to assuage the pain on his back from Cherish's angry ashplant. The two of them began pelting the sods of turf into the ass-and-car until the load was bulging again. Gallantry led the nervous Quaintways along the road to Sheep's Cross — Cherish, walking beside him rather than sitting back on top of the turf. In silence, they listened to the hum of the cartwheels and the metal of the ass's hooves. A dovelike glance of thanks sped from Cherish's eyes and landed in the heart of Gallantry, and then it sped back from his eyes and landed in the heart of Cherish. This, however, didn't last long for like any other youth with a thorn in his backside, Gallantry (in spite of their merriment) was beginning to feel the discomfort of his new love. No amount of coaxing from those same wilderness fairies was able to put a stop to it, and his cheeks were soon as red as his mother's jam, and his tongue was a river full of rocks.

Then he remembered the four apples that his mother had given him to present to Sweet Birdsong as a gift for getting the use of her clucking hen. He stopped the ass and decided he'd not be going up there now. To distract his amorous thoughts, he took them from his pocket and gave them to Cherish. It seemed as though she could read his mind for with his small gift her heart melted away like last winter's snow, and she felt a sudden light-hearted giddiness that comes to all young lovers at moments like this.

They sat in abstract idleness on the ditch, as carefree as tinkers on a summer's day — with the hills all round them and the sun overhead them. Cherish handed one of the apples back to Gallant and the two of them munched and munched, and the silence bound them ever closer together. Were you there beside them on the ditch, you'd see in them the indolent grandeur of the nearby foxgloves and honeysuckles and the warmth of the summertime bees and the singing of summertime birds in the bushes. It seemed as though their dreaminess would last a lifetime. The ass looked bemusedly across at the two of them as if to ask were all humans as distorted and daft as these two soft-hearts?

7

They couldn't stay there all day, and they went on past the forge till they came to Handless Rody's yard where they unloaded the cart. Cherish took Gallantry by the hand and led him across to last year's pile of faded turf-remains on which the horse's tackling had been thrown. They climbed over the tackling and peered down into the little bay reserved for the next newly-born calf. And there (as of old) was the cat (Whiskers) and around her was stretched a warm load of kittens. She reached down and took one of the kittens from the cat and, as she stroked it, her sparkling eyes met those of Gallantry. Like a dog with a rusty kettle tied to its tail, he could have cried aloud with the pain from the tender looks she was giving him. Then she let the kitten crawl back across the turf to its mother. Freedom once more for the kitten but if only Cherish would let Gallantry have back his freedom so that he could run off and hide in the depths of the wood. He couldn't tell her (he was far too shy) how the magic of love had taken hold of him. He would be sixteen the following Saturday, a young age for a man's thoughts to be getting so confused. Take Sweet Birdsong's eldest daughter (Bridie). She was seventeen and still classed as a child. Never in her life had she worn a stocking, and she was still wearing her ankle-socks for Sunday Mass. Not a shred of paint or powder had she ever worn on her face nor had she ever heard tell of such nonsense as love. So, what the devil had caused Gallantry to get so soft in the head and fall headlong in love?

Seeing the serious and hurt look in his eyes, Cherish jumped down from the turf and led him out behind the shed, balancing on top of the stone-wall, and disturbing the afternoon nap of the hens and geese. Gallantry (how easily the young can forget past pain) caught her joyfulness and was soon as happy as a field of thrushes.

They tiptoed out the orchard gate where the early apple-trees were full of flowers. The damsons were nearby. They climbed onto the ditch, and Gallantry reached up his hand because the branches had always been too high for Cherish to get at them. He took down a damson or two and gave them to her. There in the shadow of the branches, her pretty face was close to his, and he gave her these fruits of his love. Wishing to emulate love and destroy the threads of shyness that had always gripped him to his mother, he jumped down casually from the ditch. Cherish jumped down after him, and he caught her in his arms in case she should fall awkwardly and twist her ankle. Between their two eyes everything began to move with a speed that blinded them. As though suddenly aroused from their childish dreams, their young hearts beat fast and there was no thought of the past or the future and the clocks of all the world stopped ticking. In his unexpected arms, a boy had become a man and a girl had become a woman — far away from their childhood world. The sun's rays swam through their hair, washing them in its light, and their hearts danced like a kettle on the crane. Cherish offered Gallantry her delicately-angled jaw, and he gave her blushing cheek a shy little kiss. Fair play to him! — he was like a jaybird that had stolen the grapes from the barrel, and he knew he would always give her the moon and the stars thereafter. Though plain-featured compared to the loveliness of Cherish, he had brought her a true friendship with his apples and his damsons and a pile of restored turf and (after much dithering) this shy act of a boy-man's kiss.

There was still a little daylight left for Cherish to walk the dusty road with him and show him her secret blackbird's nest. His shredded heart had no time for even a multitude of blackbird's nests for he'd be forever looking at the rosy cheek that he'd just kissed. He took the last of his fag-butts from his pocket. He took out the matches and cupped his hands around the flames as he'd seen his father doing. He put fag-smoke to the heavens, and he laughed and laughed, no longer mesmerised by the pearly smile on Cherish's lips. She turned away from him and with a little chuckle of childish ecstasy, suddenly sped across the orchard and back to her frowning mother.

Gallantry looked after her retreating heels. He couldn't explain the intangible sensations he was feeling — this new feeling of love. This day of the upturned ass-and-car and its turf, this day of the apples, this day of the damsons was the greatest awakening influence in his life. He had reached down deeply into a secret place inside in him and wanted to stand on his head and waggle his legs in the air.

He made his dreamy way home. The tenderness of the kiss had transfigured him, and his head was full of Cherish's merry eyes after he'd planted the shy kiss on her jaw. Her shiny laughter was still echoing in his heart.

1

Whereas our women went to confession every month, the mission was the one time in the year for our men to examine their conscience and prepare themselves for the coming of Canon Eloquence, the esteemed holy man from Kerry. He'd be coming to give our souls a good overhaul (what Dowager called the treatment) and put our men back into shape. For the mission was the time when everyone needed to cleanse both body and soul and put their best side forward. Our older girls would spend the night in their hair-curlpapers getting ready for such a momentous occasion. Mothers would be busy spitting on the iron, and there'd be the smell of mothballs and fresh linen round the fireplace. There'd be the smell of boot-polish wafting to the rafters when By-Jiggery took from the bottom of the press (his glory-hole) the polish-tins to attack the shoes and boots. Like the rest of the men, he'd have to shave his cheeks till they were as shiny as a saucepan. He'd pull out his best dark blue suit (the wedding suit and not the usual check one that he wore for Sunday Mass), and he'd air it the night before in front of the fire. He'd have ready his stiff collar and his striped tie and his new pancake cap.

Before setting out for the mission, both he and the older children would be given a bit of Moll-the-Man's brilliantine to put on their hair rather than the soapy water. Moll would dig out her wedding-brooch that had been locked away behind the bedroom altar, and she'd spend a while polishing it and giving it the little dab of butter. Such detailed preparations as these had always been the way as far back as we could remember. We knew that the time of the mission was an event which came only once every second year and then went away again like the wind and the rain. It could not be missed.

In the men's eyes, it was something of a nuisance — a sheer necessity that they had to put up with. It had been drummed into their heads ever since childhood that they were only the sheep of the flock (the poor scholars) and that the holy missioner had something like the power of sheep-dip to root out any maggoty irritations that might be on their souls.

The women were a good bit different and were gladness itself to see the holy man coming into their church. His fervent arms would embrace them and make their fidgety souls perfect for the onward journey towards the Beyond when their time came to die. That's what he told them the previous visit — that he was the fence round their burgeoning grasslands (such sweet words) and with something like relief they had not forgotten what he'd said to them then. They trusted him completely.

Back to the men — they shuddered in their boots and made the sign-of-the-cross. They'd now have to take the shy little trip inside the confession-box where they'd be asked to unveil their souls.

'Blasht it! Do we have to go through that old rigmarole again?' they groaned. Stripping their souls naked was no laughing matter, and to confess their sins to another man (albeit a priest) was something they usually reserved for Eastertide — something that had to be done annually under pain of mortal sin. They'd have to pause from their work and think long and hard about the business of the sins they'd supposedly committed against the commandments laid down by God. This was a difficult task that left them scratching their heads. They had very few sins they could think of. Unlike the old gossips (ah, it was those old crones who certainly had a lot to answer for), the men hadn't had time to go bad-mouthing one another, what with the plough and the hayfork forever calling on them. No man (except a passing tinker) had ever stolen an ass or a cow or had beaten their wives for fear an army of her brothers would arrive at their half-door and beat the shite out of them, if not kill them outright. Nor had they molested another man's wife as the same rule applied there too.

And now it was mission-night and the congregation were all inside the church, locked in like cattle in a pen. The women trotted into the belly of the church and up into the two galleries to get a proper look at the holy man when he came out to perform on the altar. There was a vapour of fresh polish and candles percolating the air at the front of the church. There was the odd little feather in one or two ladies' hats, the gloves slimly on their wrists, and a jewelled brooch or two on a few jacket-lapels.

The men quenched their fags and trudged sheepishly into the back of the church, their inherent shyness preventing them from entering too far up towards the altar. They placed a knee on their caps, their broad shoulders crouched over the rosary-beads that were dangling from their fists. One or two of the older men stayed next to the door as though ready to make a bolt for it should the missioner point a finger of scorn in their direction, and they lifted their anguished eyes up to the statue of Our Lady. On some of them there was a smell of farmyard manure that'd knock a bull down kicking, and one or two of these poor souls occasionally dug their black-nailed fingers into the seat of their britches to itch themselves.

The first few pews were reserved for the rich farmers who had given handsomely to the coffers of the priest from the compulsory annual church taxes. Every Easter these tithes were read out from the pulpit. Many a poor man (like Dinny Buggerman and Larry Woebegone) had lobster-red ears on him when he was forced to hear the humiliating words read out about the few brass coppers he'd been able to give — unlike Captain Scratch-mee-back's offering of fifty noble pounds. There'd be a deadly hush, the odd little smirk and titter out of the rest of the congregation. The only thing missing was the applause for the rich man, as though the God to whom we said our prayers was a greedy one, as though poverty was as much a sin as avarice.

Rambling Jack looked round him at the wizened faces nearby. He didn't know what to expect. This evening they might be told (it had happened before) that they were good-for-nothing rogues, one and all, and he pitied his own skin as well as everyone else's. He was never frightened at the rage of a mad pig being killed, but he was as frightened as hell of the missioner and the power of his tongue. If matters turned out like last time, Canon Eloquence would be quick to lay out the parish's sins in front of them. It wouldn't have entered the holy man's head (said Rambling Jack to himself) to think he had one or two little foibles of his own to account for when it was his turn to reach the pearly gates of Saint Peter. He reached into his pocket and pulled out his rosary beads. They had been hanging on the bedpost since the previous Sunday, and he used them only when he came to Mass. Like the rest of us, he absentmindedly let the beads drip-drip-drip through his fingers.

Around him was the sound of a church-load of rosary beads and the sibilant voices of the congregation like a Cork orchestra filled the place with whispery uplifted holiness. 'Look at us poor scholars,' he said to himself. 'How odd it seems — grown men and women and we all waiting to be chastised as though we were back inside the school-house door.' He tried not to feel the anger that was boiling up inside his shirt. He gazed out through the stained-glass windows at the dignified haze of the emerald pine trees that rose sky-high on the backbone of the mountains.

In the missioner's earliest childhood, when he was no bigger than a cabbage-leaf, the church and he had been like two sides of a sheet. He remembered the day he entered the church-door in the gloved hand of his devoted mother. That's when he fell in love with the smell of the church, with the polish, the gleam, the incense, the starched white altar-cloth, which capped the circular rails like fuchsia bushes in the snow. He had been as quick as lightning in learning the heavily-printed Latin responses at his father's knee — quick too to grasp the various sequences and times of the movements round the altar. He had carried the huge book from the epistle-side to the gospel-side of the altar without once tripping over his shoelaces - even though he was a mere young starling seven years old. And all the while, his mother would be there in the front pew and smiling up at him. He'd an uncle who was a bishop (she said), and a day might come (she said) when he too might get to wear the tall mitre like Bishop High-Hat beyond in Clare.

He tried to forget the Easter evening when he was forced to wet his britches during the night-time ceremony of Tenebrae. Candle after candle, the church had been gradually darkened by the man with the tall quencher until the entire place was as black as pitch. This was in sorrow for the terrified Jesus whilst he was waiting for Judas and the other assassins to waylay him in the Garden of Gethsemane the evening before his cruel death on Calvary's cross. He had always been scared of the dark and during Tenebrae's gloomy service it wasn't just the darkness of the church but what followed after that. Several bursts of repeatedly rapping wooden boards blasted their racket across the church's macabre emptiness, mourning the infamy of what had happened to poor Jesus and the way he'd been manhandled. After what seemed an eternity of this living nightmare, the lights of the church were all switched back on. To his mortal shame, he saw the warm stream of his poolie making a slow and sinuous river out onto the centre of the blessed sanctuary. The other altar-boys (a nudge here and a wink there) saw it too. The likes of this had never happened before. To taint the altar space like this was (they said) the same as hitting poor Jesus a slap on the jaw, and they cruelly taunted him thereafter. How could he or his mother ever forget it?

But that was long ago, and things were different now. Though he was a man of small height (no bigger than a wren's quill, as Dowager would later say), he was meticulously neat, and no tailor could have turned him out better in his colourful vestments. He was a man (thought My-son-Jack) that had eaten well, with a great pair of jaws on him and was a little on the paunchy side round the middle. He hadn't a wrinkle on him, and his scented face was as shiny as a sweet-gallon, and you could tell that he didn't smell like the rest of us. He was wearing immaculately-polished shoes, pointy and like the ones in Fanny Farthingale's Dress-Shop window. My-son-Jack took it all in.

As the holy man stood facing us on the altar steps, he fidgeted with the ring on his plump finger and examined his closely-clipped nails. And then he gave us a perplexed little smile. But Dowager was no fool, and a little thought was already creeping into her head: it was his small ferrety eyes - they had the glint in them, which one often sees in a man of intelligence like Doctor Glasses, but she wasn't sure if there wasn't a little bit of the pitiless hawk in him this time round.

He called on Our Blessed Lord to bless us. We echoed him with a thunderous Amen. You'd have to admire him — a man who had prayed so fervently for us even before he'd set foot in Tipperary (so Father Honesty told us). Then he put his shush-finger to his lips, and we all sat down in a subsided hush and with an air of expectancy prepared ourselves to hear what he had to say.

But after the opening bouts of our honest hymning — after all the polite little bows and smiles from our holy guest — the weather was about to change, and the soft tenor of his voice to fade away into history. He paused as though cogitating a little wise thought in his head. He leaned down from the pulpit, frowning and scowling rather than letting us have a few more of his lovely smiles and dimples. He told us that he'd come to save us from the fiery furnaces of Hell. We knew this to be true as we'd often been told it during our schooldays, and some of the men had long believed that they were already halfway towards these very furnaces, and others (their wives said) were too far gone to be saved (although a few might yet be shep-herded back into the fold this evening). The women, on the other hand, felt they were safe enough.

Bit by bit Canon Eloquence intensified his frown, and his pauses grew that little bit longer and more unsettling for us. He was a well-practised man in this art of holding a congregation in suspense. This caused the odd little nervous cough, which was hushed away by a wave of the holy man's imperious hand.

'Ah, my little clover-field!' he whispered, and his sermon now took on full steam. You could see his white teeth — none of the rest of us had a tooth in our heads. The cheeks of the women were soon on fire as if they'd been drinking a little too much hot punch. They knew he was going to give them a fine old time of it — as good as a deathbed sermon. They could almost read his lips. Of course, his words would be wrathful at first. What else did we expect from him? But there'd be forgiveness for us before he came to the end of his sermon. His wrath and God's forgiveness (which would surely follow) had always been put into the same mixing-bowl. That was the way of things — surely, we all knew that?

It wasn't long, however, before we sensed that something was wrong. He started painting a far coarser picture than any of us had ever expected. He introduced us to a foreign God, one that was far removed from Jesus and His cross, a dark-shadowed God that we could not recognize, a cruel and pitiless God and a vengeful and fierce God — not a merciful or good-natured God in the form of Jesus who had comforted Mary Magdalene or had spoken gentle words to the adulteress or to the woman-at-the-well or to countless other lost souls. He droned on and on, his wrathful voice startling us and hitting us full in the face. The eloquence had clean gone from him.

'Blasht his hide!' whispered Rambling Jack to By-Jiggery. 'Look at the triumphant eye of the little bantam-cock — here again and chewing the same old cud. The bishop should have put a padlock on his gob.'

By-Jiggery had to agree. 'He's like a scratched and broken gramophone-record that keeps on repeating and repeating itself,' he mumbled. 'Ye think he'd change the needle and give us a new kind of song, wouldn't ye?'

Within five minutes, the missioner had turned himself into a lather of sweat from demonizing the sinners in our midst. Some of us closed our eyes, and we all sank down like little field-mice, fidgeting and folding our knuckles and sniffing our noses. Lucky were the men who had taken up their station at the back of the church. They'd be the first out the door when the sermon was over, for they'd sooner meet a hedgerow of sparrows than stay listening all evening to the likes of him.

Dowager was one of those who decided to close her ears to him. It didn't matter a ha'porth (she thought) that he'd got himself the learning of things or had the lofty rhetoric of the spoken word. His high-handedness was not going to put the fear-of-God into her or the fear of the brimstone, which he supposed was waiting for many of us.

'Repent! Repent! That's what I say,' he cried. The wrath of God would come down on some of us (especially the men, said he) if we didn't atone for our wrongdoings. And at these words, it seemed as though John-the-Baptist had been reborn this very evening. But where was the sackcloth? Where were the rags and the bare feet? Where was the dry sandy desert that Our Saviour's cousin had patrolled? Where were the locusts for the missioner's breakfast next day?

Moll-the-man looked at her watch. Her face was as long as a tinker's fiddle. Could the missioner really have been ranting on at us for the last twenty minutes? Like Dowager, who was sitting alongside her, she was finding it hard to listen to him. What was the use of his thundering against sin and the devil that he supposed lay inside most of us? There wasn't a word of truth in it. This evening, unlike any other evening, had turned out all wrong, and there was to be no happy-ending to his words. The holy man had spoken to us as though we were a pack of heathens, but we knew we weren't wicked sinners. This was no place to listen to a man like him, who considered everyone a sinner to be led back onto a supposedly straight path.

He concluded his sermon with, 'Let there be an amen to it all,' and this time we did not echo his amen. Throwing his eyes to Heaven, he offered us his final benediction and gave his fist a resounding pound on the pulpit, which woke Dowager up from her peaceful slumbers.

2

It was the second evening of the mission. We were all shep-
herded into the church again by Father Honesty. We waited
for the missioner outside the confession-box — waited for the
scourging, as My-son-Jack called it. By telling him all our sins,
we'd ensure the success of the mission with the cleansing of
our souls.

In a short while, there formed a queue out as far as the
front door, consisting mainly of the men, who hadn't been
inside the confession-box throughout the entire year. Since it
was a day later, we had all been given time to think of the
missioner's lofty words, and we had calmed down a good bit
and recovered from our initial anger. We were eager to wipe
away the malady in our souls as reported to us by the well-
minded man the previous evening. What shocking tales we
would have to compose and put into his sensitive ears! It's a
wonder that he wouldn't die of the sick when he heard it all, as
each of us would try desperately to embellish one little sin
after another in such a way as would be appropriate for a holy
man like him to hear.

The confessions soon began. It would take the whole evening
and maybe half of the night before we had let all our so-called
foibles escape from our lips. A good few of the men were more
than fretful, for they had those secret sins-of-the-flesh that no
honest priest would like to befoul his ears with. And when at
first the holy man didn't hear these commonplace sins
mentioned, he was greatly puzzled, for he knew that such sins
belonged to most men. So, he began to prod each of us in turn.

'Have you any more secret little sin to tell me? Come on
now, don't be shy.' He was as nosy as an old crow behind a

thrashing-machine. Armed with the varieties of our many sins, he'd be well-prepared for the wind-up sermon that would conclude the mission the following Saturday when he'd be sure to whale into us like fair hell all over again.

But the missioner didn't get it all his own way. For (bless the bit!) whom did we see standing at the door of the confession-box? Why, it was none other than the hitherto intractable Red Scissors himself — the only man never seen inside the church all these years, back now in the enveloping folds of Mother Church. His guardian angel must have caught him by the two ears (said Rambling Jack) and dragged him in through the church doors.

There is always laughter (thank God) even in a rainstorm. May God have mercy on the soul of Red Scissors. He went into the confession-box, feeling that he was safe behind the screen. Inside his head, he had invented an outrageous range of wicked sins with which to fill the missioner's holy ears.

He started to confess his weaknesses, one by one, 'Father, please forgive me, I am an awful rogue, and I have sinned some terrible sins in my lifetime — enough to frighten any saint in heaven.'

'Go on, my child! Go on!'

'I have been injecting mee seed into the tinker-women these last four months. They can't keep away from me, and they're the ruin of mee poor soul. Three of them (forgive me) are now with child!' The rest of the men, queuing up outside the doors of the confession-box, were as quiet as a church mouse and desperately trying to hear what the rascal was saying to the holy man. Would the missioner be able to do the magic-trick that no other earthly priest had ever been able to do before? Would he be able to reconvert the heathen that was Red Scissors? From his unholy gob he kept pouring out lie after lie after lie — it'd surely land him in the bowels of Hell. There had never been such a long list of sins. Fifteen minutes came and went by. You would hear a pin drop, and we were all left wondering how Red Scissors had remembered so many sins, and would he ever get himself out of the confession-box? He would have the missioner know that he had broken almost every commandment in sight. Indeed, so inventive and creative was our hero, that he should have been writing a manuscript for the rest of us.

Canon Eloquence (fair play to him) was no fool, and at last he began to realize that what he was hearing was nothing less than a pack of filthy lies, nothing less than a criminal act against Holy Mother Church and the blessed sacrament. White-faced with rage, he came bursting out from his side of the confession-box. But Red Scissors was no fool either, and he had beaten him to it, making good his escape as far as the church-door. The startled onlookers saw the holy man in hot pursuit, his white soutan fluttering behind him.

'Put that Satan out! Put that Satan out from the House-of-God!' — hoping that one or two of us would take a flying leap and bring Red Scissors down like an escaped calf. But (blessed be the spirit of Red Scissors!) the humourist was long gone out the church-gates, and Merrymouth's drinking-shop (an arch man, he's a credit to us all) was full of the tale of it that same evening. And for many evenings to come, the antics of Red Scissors were greeted more cheerfully than a Christmas dinner at many a shop-counter and even down in the town itself. However (as he himself said), it was to be his last song and testament inside in the church, and after that, he went back to his horses and cattle and became his own self once more and never darkened the church door again.

3

It was the day after the mission, and Old Stroller had brought out with him his billhook to cut back the briars and the long nettles. In his pocket, he had his usual penknife and the ball of twine. He asked the older children if they had enjoyed the missioner's new tonic-water. Then Lippy stepped out from the crowd of children and said that he himself would be able to do just as fine a job as the missioner if given half the chance. Oh, the impudent puppy — the same rascal who had thrashed Mick-the-Walking-Hayshed and brought him to his knees in a recent brawl.

Old Stroller cut down two long saplings with his penknife, and he paired them and fashioned them into a cross. He fixed them securely with the twine.

'Ye have yeer mission now,' said he, and he went and sat himself down near the well and watched the proceedings unfold. Lippy made the rest of the children line up behind him and when all of them were ready, he paraded them round the outskirts of the Rishy Field. They all followed his lead, repeating the words after him as he started his psalming:

'Blessed be the stars at night!'

'Blessed be their sister, the white moon!'

'Blessed be our mothers and fathers!'

A long list was following from the high-and-mighty lips of Saint Lippy. The Rishy Field hummed to the tune of it as the rest of the children processed round the ditch behind him. Reaching each of the four corners of the field, he made them bow towards the ditch in a friendly salutation like the missioner had done when he first entered the altar. From his mouth, he let out a loud volley or two of his own Bog-Latin, frightening the little birds from their nests. The other children tried in vain to repeat his mighty words.

The procession at length got back to Old Stroller and he reminded Lippy, 'Blessed be the missioner, Canon Eloquence.' And with one voice they all blessed the holy man. For they had to agree — he had spoken what was only the truth: there was need for much improvement in them all, men, women, and children.

Old Stroller scratched his head, 'Which of ye is going to say the missioner's finish-up Mass?'

'I am,' said Lippy since he was the only one old enough to have ever set foot on the altar the time he'd been asked to serve the school-leaver's Mass on his last day at school.

Old Stroller galloped off home and brought back a long scaffold-board and two half-barrels and a tin can or two. The missioner had had his moment of triumph, and this was now to be Lippy's moment. Philly ran off home and fetched out By-Jiggery's best Sunday shirt, which was hanging on a nail near the dresser and ironed and starched for next week's visit to the church. Old Stroller placed the scaffold-board across the two upturned half-barrels to make a makeshift altar. It was agreed that the children were going to honour Our Blessed Lady. Battlin' Sal brought back two jam-jars from her cubby-shop in the dyke and filled them with wildflowers from the Rishy Field. Young Jim remembered to retrieve the Infant-of-Prague statue from Moll-the-Man's altar in the bedroom, and Old Stroller added a finishing touch with his penknife and fashioned a smaller crucifix with the twine, which he placed in a jam-jar.

Dressed in his father's long white shirt, Lippy gave a supreme performance, assuming the missioner's angry voice and gestures. The holy man would have been proud to witness it. He mumbled and droned his own version of Bog-Latin again, occasionally raising his papery whispers into a very loud and snappy shout, which shook the three smaller children half to death. It was like the mission all over again, and a new sense of holiness filled each one of them. It was a glorious moment, and Lippy vowed he'd bring a gift to Mick-the-Walking-Hayshed and put a smile back on his sad face. Then he bobbed down into a fast genuflection, kicking the tin can with the skill of his big toe and using it as an altar-bell. The older ones smiled at one another: their big brother had the makings of a fine priest, a fine missioner, in the years to come.

From time to time Leppity and Battlin' Sal hit their rusty mug with a stone — the mug stolen from Gus Gilton, which Cherish had once used for wetting with her poolie the mud-pies for herself and Gallantry in those faraway toddler-days. Now it became a second altar bell, and it gave an added solemnity to the entire performance. Were it not so serious and solemn a ritual, this Mass in the Rishy Field would have been a grand addition to the Daffy-Duck Circus.

'And what of the missioner's wind-up sermon?' inquired Old Stroller.

'Yes, give us the sermon!' the little ones roared. 'We want a sermon, blasht ye!' They were beginning to get uppity. Lippy now proved himself a winged angel and delivered the finest sermon they were ever likely to hear. His energy was inexorable, and they were all entranced. He spent the next half-hour filling their ears with the most unrecognizable gibberish, a load of strange God-inspired words that not one of them could understand. Old Stroller had to smile and chuckle to himself. This latest recruit to the priesthood had deluged the field in his unique Bog-Latin, and all the children clapped and clapped. With merry tears in his eyes, Old Stroller (isn't that lad the devil's own at the missioning!) clapped his hands too. For a finish they begged their big brother ('Please, Lippy, please!) to give them just one last little procession round the Rishy Field before the sun left them and the dark cloud-shadows of Galway came and annoyed them all.

It had been a great afternoon, a fine version of an innocent childhood mission and free from any sacrilege. And if the pope himself had hopped out over the ditch that very minute, he would have shaken them each warmly by the hand. For there was in them an unreal aura of peace and harmony, most unlike the strange feelings that had come into them at the death of the tinker's pup and the pulverizing of Mick-the-Walking-Hayshed and the death of the foxes in wintertime. And this new feeling was gentleness — the softness of a baby. Indeed, it could be said that for this singular moment in time, they felt themselves to be pure holiness for they had turned themselves into little angels and could have flown away out over the bog and Keeper Hill before the day ended. They knew now that it was better to be good little saints rather than devilish sinners. But being children and still a-growing, how could they be expected to maintain this religious fervour for the rest of their natural lives? In their books at school, they had learnt that even a few of the Jews had once fallen by the wayside when they were seen shouting their vociferous praises of Jesus (Hosanna to the King-of-kings!) on one day and demanding his death on the very next Friday.

Old Stroller then wound up the proceedings and said a little prayer of his own — that the children would hold tough and stay on the winning side against the Devil. The mission (for all its drawbacks) had given them a head start. He knew it and even the children knew it. It was time to go home. The sun, the sky and the pink and lavender colours all fled away from them. Grey misty clouds took their place in the Rishy Field and inky shadows appeared over Corcoran's well. With sad hearts, they retired in a troop from their little bit of paradise and the darkness drove them back into their yard where the hens and ducks were already fast asleep on their roosts in the henhouse.

DAISY

1

In the middle of Dowager's bedroom was a totally out-of-place obstacle — Harpy, the grand piano. For modesty and decency's sake, it acted as a stop-gap between the parents' bed and the bed of Mary-Anne and Little Nell during their childhood. For some unknown reason, Miss Friendly, on her deathbed, had left it to Dowager as a reward for her ten years' service at the big house. Still a child, she had gone down there on the day she left school (aged 11) and had stayed there till the day she married Warbling Will ten years later.

When news of the piano's whereabouts spread abroad, everyone was left scratching their heads, for it was a very curious thing for a posh lady like Miss Friendly to have done, since neither Dowager nor her brothers and sisters had ever played a note of music, and no music was ever heard played in their little house till years later when Warbling Will played a few old polkas on his battered concertina. But even then, he did so only on a few special occasions like a child's baptismal day or (better still) the birth of a child.

You'd imagine that a showpiece such as Miss Friendly's grand piano would have been the talk and envy of the open road — that it would have been displayed at every opportunity in front of the jealous neighbours. But no, not one of the children knew what to do with the wretched thing or even if it was a musical instrument at all for it was always covered in a thick film of dust, an act that some foreign grandees might have regarded as the next worse thing to blasphemy. Worst of all, inside its lid was kept some of Dowager's most precious items: the icing sugar, the nutmeg, the raisins. Family law forbade the children to touch any of these items for she had eyes on her like a hawk, and she assured them that they'd take the short road to Hell if they ever stole from Harpy, the grand piano.

From their hidey-hole under their blankets, Mary-Anne and Little Nell were forever eavesdropping, listening to the talk of the cardplayers at the other side of the hob when these happy chaps came in out of the cold for the copper-counting and the serious games of card-playing. By this time, Dowager had hurried all her children off to bed early. It was for the good of their souls (she said) since the cardplayers' language, depending on their excitement after winning a game, was somewhat coarser than usual — though it was rarely, if ever, over-polite on these good-humoured occasions.

There were other times (these were seldom) when the older children were allowed to stay up and sit on the cardplayers' knees in front of the cheerful fire. There were one or two lucky occasions when even the little ones were allowed to stay up a bit later than usual whilst the table and cards were being set out. This was by way of celebration; maybe their father had sold a beast or two at the fair. For the next half-hour, they got themselves thoroughly spoilt before ending up kneeling down to say their prayers in front of the fire. After that, the girls shyly put on their chemises. The boys, like the men, did not have to undress as they always slept in the shirts that they wore during the day.

The general rule, however, was for Mary-Anne and Little Nell to kneel on the damp potato-sacking in their bedroom and busy themselves with their long list of prayers — thanking God for His goodness and asking Him to bless their animals and crops — praying for the dead and for all the sick souls before ending up with the God-bless-me prayer. Heaven help them if they made the mistake of creeping into bed before saying this almighty list of prayers, for Dowager would have her hawk-eye ready again and, as with any attempt to steal from the piano, would once more threaten to beat them half to death with the broken leg-of-the-chair if they didn't offer up their nightly prayers to God before hopping into bed.

After all the excitement of the card-games was finished and the cardplayers had stepped out the front door after taking the holy water from the font, Dowager and Warbling Will were able to get a bit of peace for themselves. This was a special time for them with no children or cardplayers left in the house to annoy them or interfere with their thoughts. That's the time when Mary-Anne and Little Nell had their ears cocked closer than ever to the chimney wall, listening to the lofty stream of conversation that always seemed to pour out of their parents' mouths. They'd stay glued that way till their eyes grew heavy with sleep and even at that hour of the night, it was the devil's own job to get a wink of sleep, for Dowager could talk the legs off of an ass and would stay talking across the firelight to Warbling Will for half the blessed night. In these nightly conversations, the subject of cousin Daisy would often be to the forefront when they could hear their mother sighing over something she called Daisy's unusual bouts of sanctity.

By now, they knew that Daisy was one of their closest relations and that she lived a mile from their own door at a spot where the road dipped down at Red Scissors' well and came to a sharp elbow-point leading up the lane to the Little Bald Plain. Running across the lane was a small stream, barely a trickle in summertime. If you turned the ass-and-car sharply left and followed the next lane further up the hill, you'd come to a nook among the pine trees. In that sheltered spot lay the little thatched house of Dowager's older sister, Nancy. She'd married late in life to Dan-the-Cooper, a hill farmer with oceans of black cattle to his name. Miracles do happen, and in spite of their advanced years in life, God had been good to them and had given them the gift of four children: Jack (the eldest) and the twins (Ned and Nan) and Daisy, the youngest child.

When this little girl was five, the year prior to attending school with her big brothers and older sister, she would spend the morning helping her mother keep the place ship-shape while her father was abroad in the fields, working away like blazes at the hoeing and weeding of his early crops before going on to trim the briars on the ditches. Dan was a man who never seemed to stop working. It was the same with Daisy's mother, Nancy. With a face as red as a turkey's gobble, she could be seen enveloped in the washtub's steam and soap-suds of a Monday morning, rinsing the bedsheets before laying them out on the bushes where they quickly dried. After that, she had a hundred-and-one other jobs to do — far too many to mention — and there was never a time for her to stand still gossiping.

Daisy was being brought up in the same vein, and her workload was always a tall order for a child as young as five. She had to dodge the snapping jaws of the two fierce sows blocking her way to the haggart in her search for eggs hidden in the nettles. She had to tiptoe round the ducks who were drinking up the pissy swill at the sinky pool outside the pig-house door before she could collect the thorny bushes for her mother to light the fire. She had to sweep the dung from the yard with the long-handled brush (not too roughly lest ye loosen the cobbles). She had to help her mother clean out the flies and the milk-scour from inside the two creamery-tanks.

It was something of a miracle that Daisy was still alive, seeing the narrow escape she'd had from death that very same year. What had happened to her was all-so-predictable — everybody said so at the time. After finishing her jobs, she wiped the sweat from her brow and went in the door to get herself a mug of water from the bucket. She was tired beyond belief and sat down on her stool by the fire whereupon she slipped into a doze and fell with a crash into the hot ashes. The folds of her dress got caught on a burning log, and the flames tore into her flesh.

Her father was coming across the yard to get his billhook and return to the field for the briar-cutting when he heard the roars of Daisy. He rushed in the door and quickly wrapped his greatcoat round her. Her mother rushed in a second later and ripped the dress off of her back to see for herself the damage to her child's body. The blisters were already forming round the child's waist.

A month previously, a certain poor woman had scalded herself by tripping over her skillet-pot whilst straining the boiling water from her spuds. The parish priest had mentioned a young widow who lived at the back of the bog. He said she had the cure for almost everything — especially the burnt limbs (even Doctor Glasses had said so) and that she had healed the burns and blisters on the poor woman's arms. The same young widow now came sailing down the hill on her piebald horse (Black Jack). From her hip-pocket, she produced her mother's own hand-me-down ointment that had been made from the heated paste of dried-out laurel-leaves, mixed up with a good dose of unsalted butter. A month later, there wasn't a single mark left on Daisy's body — just like the arms of the woman who'd been straining her spuds. It was nothing less than a miracle, and it was talked about for months. Father Honesty and Doctor Glasses never stopped singing the healer's praises. Praise-be-to-God for the life-saving powers of the young widow from beyond the bog.

2

Daisy's school-years sped by quicker than a wink and were now gone. Then, came the next May — the first real month of the year when everybody had finally shoved to the back of their minds the harsh days of snow and winter and when April's showers and all the dark clouds had finally drifted out over Galway, and the sun had drunk up all the puddles. Listen to the whispering oak trees on the ditch with their new leaves, shiny and clean as the holly. Behold the many hawthorn trees showing off their snow-white flowers and the wild violets smouldering everywhere with vivid colour and spreading themselves round Daisy's bare feet. This was the loveliest time of the year with all those flowers and blooms to celebrate Our Blessed Lady and all those church processions and nasally hymn-chanting round the church grounds and Our Lady's lofty statue being carried on the shoulders of the red-and-white-robed altar-boys.

Father Honesty took a long look at Daisy. She was at an age when she was growing big and strong (he thought) like the crops in over the ditch, and he had no hesitation in picking her out to crown the statue. She reminded him of Our Lady's own good self, what with her clear angelic face and her fingers forever laced round her rosary beads every Sunday during Mass.

Her mother too was taking a long look at her these days and wondering about her, days when she saw her go off behind the cowshed in her search (though she didn't know it yet) for a surprise gift to bring back to her — maybe cutting an unexpected bunch of wild roses for the house-altar with her mother's scissor, maybe discovering a rare duck-egg or two.

Nancy would steal a peep out the back window and see her little daughter in the middle of the ducks and the way they'd slowly rise up from their nests in the dock-leaves to greet her, almost tripping over her feet, the sunlight shining on their feathers — the way Daisy's nimble feet moved towards the haggart-gap, dancing round a proud young hen as she paraded her chirping chicks out the field-gate, guarding them with her motherly cluck-clucking.

These were Daisy's most joyful days — a far cry from the day of her burnt body. Like the flowers and the trees, the child felt the fullness of life tingling inside in her. She was happy in other ways too, for it was no great loss to be free from the imprisoning drudgery of her schooldays and all on her own whilst her brothers and older sister were abroad in the bog, slaving away at the turf.

The happiness that was walking hand in hand with Daisy had been noticed even before the day Father Honesty had picked her out to crown Our Lady's statue — on the day of her first holy Communion when she was only nine. Her Communion robes had an outstandingly silky sheen to them that reminded the congregation of how close to an angel this child had grown. Her face that day took on a new complexion like an innocent saint from the pages of her prayer-book. Up until then, she'd been reluctant (though few knew it) to kneel down in her bedroom during the long-drawn-out imposition of nightly prayers. But now — like an ugly duckling turning into a swan — as soon as the blessed host passed her lips, she found she'd become a new child and had cast off her old self once and for all.

The year after she had left school, she was ready to take the sacrament of confirmation along with the other boys and girls her own age. She was 15. Once more, it was the month of May and the holy bishop himself arrived in his posh motorcar from Clare. During the ceremony, he was to give each child the traditional slap on the jaw to remind them they were now strong and perfect Christians — that they were nothing less than soldiers of Jesus Christ. Daisy was dreading this slap to the jaw as her mother had told her that one side of her face would be blood-red for the rest of the week. Shame on you, Nancy, for frightening a guileless child this way, for the kindly old bishop merely gave her cheek a gentle stroke with his fingers.

Slap or no slap, after this new meeting with her Blessed Saviour, Daisy was seen to increase even more (if that were at all possible) in sanctity. She was going to show the world she'd become a soldier of Christ, and she promised she'd stand beside Jesus till the day she died. Wasn't that what the bishop had meant when he bent down and whispered those words into her ear?

Before the summer ended, people were starting to worry about her, seeing the extravagant differences between herself and other girls. Before attacking the main tasks of the day, she dressed and then washed her face in the icy waters of the yard-stream. After that, she took her father's bike from the shed and cycled into town to attend Mass and receive the blessed host in holy Communion. It was a miracle she didn't break her neck and kill herself on that ramshackle old thing as she raced across the hills in order to get there in time — five miles in and five miles back.

As she pedalled home, no bird ever flew with such a light spirit as she did. Her cheeks were aglow with pinkiness. Her heart was full of a new burst of holiness. By accepting the host so regularly on her tongue, she had increased her love of Jesus more than ever, and she imagined the tall trees winking down at her as if they knew how she felt — almost whispering their softness into her soul. She hummed a little tune to her crock-of-a-bike, knowing that Jesus was deep inside her heart and soul and would never leave her.

Winter came along. The kindly old priest in the town (it was Father Bountiful at the time) began to worry like everyone else. He could see that the farm at home had begun to take second place to Daisy's desire to come to Mass each day. He had expressed his priestly anxieties to her mother. Daisy was becoming far too engrossed in her own saintliness. Might she be losing her mind altogether (he asked himself)?

Nancy spoke to him the following Sunday. For as soon as her daughter came home from the altar-rails, she'd see the way she was: sitting on the upturned ass-and-car and dreaming her life away, brought back to earth only by the anguished cry of an adventurous drake caught in the bushes round Nancy's private bit of garden.

As the old priest listened to Nancy's sad worries, he was left scratching his head. He'd have to do something — surely, he would. By now there was something else: Daisy was as slender as a blade of grass for she had begun fasting from food on Fridays in order to chastise her body, something she had read about in a book of the saints. This was a new one — starkly in contrast to the ways of her parents and Jack, as well as the twins, Ned and Nan.

One morning as she was leaving the church, Father Bountiful decided he must act. He caught hold of Daisy's arm. It was a day that had started off bitterly cold when the snow was almost a foot deep, capping the neighbouring fields and making the laneway behind Daisy's house far too treacherous on which to have been seen cycling her father's old bike to town. He was bent on forbidding her from cycling all that way to Mass during these cruel days, and he advised her (even begged her) to give the altar-rails a miss now and then — at least on these fierce wintry days (he said).

'Even Jesus would not be expected to do what you're doing, Daisy. You're a pure saint if ever there was one — with one foot already inside the gates of Heaven.'

Daisy was quick to answer him. 'Yes, Father,' said she (and he saw the worry-lines on her forehead), 'but if one of my feet is already inside in Heaven, tell me this — where is the other foot?' She already knew the answer — where the road to Hell lay — and Father Bountiful went off into his presbytery smiling reluctantly. He had lost his battle with Daisy.

3

Daisy and her sister, Nan, were now fast approaching the first stages of womanhood. Nan was 17, and she was 16. Their mother smiled and smiled. How proud she was of her two pink-cheeked beauties!

'As pretty as two beautiful wildflowers in a field of thistles,' said she. She felt she could almost write a song about them — their coral blue eyes sparkling like a sweet-gallon full of shiny water, like dewdrops on a new flower in the dawn, their teeth (unlike the rest of the young women) as white as a bone in the sun, their hair as wavy as the sea. These were her thoughts — if only she had Dowager's words to back them up. But something was missing. Though they crossed the fields to get water from the well, they had never been known to mix with the rest of the growing boys and girls or spend happy childhood days carousing along the riverbanks or seen at the top of the high trees, shouting and cursing like Dowager's children (those young galoots as their mother disdainfully called them). To give them their due, Daisy and Nan lived a fair bit away from the rest of the children — too far to be seen traipsing down the road from their home beyond the forge.

On mornings when Mary-Anne and Little Nell were sitting on the logs in Old Sam's grove, they'd think of their two cousins and wonder whether they were a bit on the lonely side. From their home across the fields, surely the two of them must have been tired of hearing them roaring and bawling from morning till night and thrashing the life out of the countryside.

Their big brothers, Lofty and Bill, had other thoughts about Daisy and Nan — that, as lovely as their looks were, their two little noses were pointed a bit too high in the air.

'Let them go and bury themselves,' snapped Lofty indifferently. 'They are far too good for the likes of us with the smell of cow dung on us — them and their skimpy dresses and they always shining like a pair of dolls,' said Bill. There was no love lost between the two lads and their cousins — or so thought Mary-Anne and Little Nell.

Yet, in spite of their strong denials, the temptation fairies (led on by the Devil and his wicked band of fallen angels) had already come stamping in the doorway and were enthroning themselves blissfully in the hearts of these two doomed boys — especially Lofty. He was 18 and had already been feeling those unmentionable hidden tremors in the blood of his lower body that had caused Dowager to drench him with a bucket of water the previous year. He was just a year older than Nan. Bill was the same age as Daisy. Had Dowager known the thoughts that were creeping into her sons' heads, she'd have either put a hairclip in their hair (Why, don't tell me it's turning into little girls that the two-of-ye are — with yeer sheep's eyes gawping at Nan and Daisy?), or she'd have given them a wallop of her yard-brush in case their thoughts were brazenly given to lifting up the young girls' skirts to see the colour of their knickers.

Do you know the spring-well below at Old Stroller's stile? It sometimes went dry during the summer months, and Dowager's children had to take their buckets up to Red Scissors' well. It was at this well that these two fair damsels — their shiny eyes and their smiling fat lips — came each day for their buckets of water. Without looking up at the sun, Lofty and Bill seemed to know to the minute the time when Nan and Daisy would be arriving with their buckets. You'd see the two fidgety simpletons — and their faces for once washed clean as a new copper — dawdling in embarrassed shyness not far from the well, as though they were in search of a new species of wild rosebush, so intently did they gaze at one bush or another. They were utterly unaware (it seemed) of the presence of the two fair damsels stepping down across the fields with their buckets.

Bill began cutting off the heads of the nettles around the well hole to protect the soft limbs of the girls when they arrived. Lofty was expertly pulling up the roots of the thistles with the aid of his switch for a similar reason. Our two young knights were making sure that the visiting girls would not get stung by the nettles or torn amongst the thistles and that their ladylike route to the well would be unimpeded. They left no holds barred so that these fair creatures could get into the side of the well and fill their buckets.

The two stately girls arrived, dressed in their summery dresses. With them they brought their angelic smiles and their shiny eyes and teeth. They brought their polite laughter as well. Lofty and Bill had no words in their stuttery mouths to offer them. Why on earth were these boys so blasted shy? What on earth was wrong with the pair of them? They were like fluttering birds inside a winter's cage at the sight of the girls' soft beauty. As Daisy and Nan got down to the task of filling their buckets, the two odd fellows could be seen running away towards the metal bridge and disappearing in over John's Gate and out across the Bluebutton Field.

That night as they lay in their settlebed, Lofty swore that Nan's eyes were as blue as a robin's egg. Bill swore that Daisy had hair as yellow as flax. Lofty vowed that he'd give Nan the moon if only he could get the price of it. Bill swore he'd go one better and give Daisy the whole of the sun. Ah, such poets were they! And for the rest of the summer, these two poor lovelorn scholars sang like the larks in the morning, and the hearts in their chests went tra-la-la and tra-la-la time and time again.

FANDANGO

1

With the old horse (Fuldoon) now dead, My-son-Jack and Fatty-Matty were on their way to Galway to buy a new plough-horse to take his place. By the time they reached Prodigal Hill, the moon was already drifting over the ditches, and an hour later, the first few stars had made an appearance when they were passing Twin-Rivers before riding into Borrisogandery.

Once they were there, they hopped down and tied their mares inside a haggart-gate so as not to lose sight of them. They crept across the haggart and climbed into the top of the farmer's hayshed where they shook out a few sops of hay to make a tidy little nest and shelter themselves from the wind. And there they slept soundly for the rest of the night, as snug and contented as any two bugs.

Next day was Sunday, and they woke up to the tune of church bells — woke up also with the hunger of a poor widow in Lent. However, they were not heathen enough to go dirtying their copybook like Pon-mee-oath did by stooping as low as that rascal had done a few years back. It was here on this very spot — enough to destroy his immortal soul — the time he traipsed in the back door of the chapel belonging to those he called the black Protestants.

He sneaked into the sacristy and drank a whole bottle of their Communion-wine while the service was at its height abroad in the church. After that little sin, he made a raid on a sackful of unblessed hosts. To this day, men crossed themselves at such an unheard-of act of blasphemy and the glori-fied way in which Pon-mee-oath told the drinkers in Curl 'n' Stripes' drinking-shop his merry tale of adventures when he got home.

'Why, 'twas only the house of the black Protestants,' said he, 'and a few sops of stale bread and a drop of their pagan wine that I was swallying.'

The devil that was in him — he couldn't leave his tale alone and went a step too far when he added how he'd gone out into the church and traipsed up to their altar-rails a second and third time to get his lips at the wine and the wafers. His tale-of-events, however, was met not with buffoon-like laughter by the rest of us but with silence and a shaking of heads in our sheer disbelief at the insolence in him. If there was a shred of truth in his words, we were left wondering if a shocked Saint Peter would ever be kind enough to let a sacrilegious rogue such as him inside the gates of Heaven when he died.

No, that was not to be the unholy route our two new adventurers would take in their search for a sound plough-horse. There were other ways of staving off hunger rather than desecrating a poor Protestant chapel, and they now went and found a little farm on the outskirts of the village where they were sure to get enough food to keep the wolf from the door. Of course, the two of them hadn't turned into canonised saints overnight and believed that a bit of innocent thievery wouldn't damn their souls entirely. So, they stole half a dozen mangles and turnips from the field of a very good farmer and began eating them raw. They stole four duck-eggs from a good woman's hen-house that would nourish them on their way. With the hatpins from their coat-collars, they'd prick the ends of the eggs and suck out the fine medicine inside. They were also well-armed with a package of biscuits from Curl 'n Stripes' shop — but these they had paid for with sound money (or so they said).

What with the fine night's lodging in the hayshed and the feed of vegetables and the package of biscuits, they felt like two young princes as they strolled round the deserted streets of Borrisogandery, waiting for next day's horse fair to beckon them on towards Galway.

They knew when they got to the Shannon Bridge that buying a suitable stallion for the plough would be a job requiring a scrupulous knowledge of horse-flesh, backed up by a bit of foxy cunning in the give and take of bargaining. The Galway jobbers were the devil's own when it came to buying and selling horses (we all knew that), but our friends were as determined as hell to get the right horse and, fearful of the threats of Dowager to brain them with the tongs if they came home empty-handed, they both felt confident of success.

Two years previously, the jovial Hammer-the-Smith, like many a Tipperary man before him, had made this self-same journey. However, the poor soul had come back empty-handed. For when the Galway Horse Fair was almost over, and the horse traders were fading off into the dusk, he found himself getting desperately fidgety and began rushing up and down the streets in a last-minute effort to get himself a horse.

My-son-Jack and Fatty-Matty had listened to his sad tale a number of times, and they were now about to benefit from it. Before they set out, he had given them a dose of fatherly advice, describing in detail the dismal day that had let him down so badly — how he spent the whole afternoon investigating every blessed horse along the town's main street, then up and down the backyards and alleys, testing their hooves and fetlocks, their teeth and temperament — to such an extent that, in the end, he couldn't make up his mind which horse was best to his liking. They were all such fine-looking animals.

There had been an added factor to all this that had troubled him a good bit. Like the rest of us, he had always heeded his mother's warnings — this time to be more than careful before foolishly handing over his few hard-earned banknotes to a few Galway unknowns. As a result, and before he knew it, the daylight had crept away on him. Would he ever forget the sorrow he felt when he finally got home after his fruitless search for a horse?

For the rest of that week, he had kept to his bed and was as sick as an old corncrake. He lay there cursing the two sides of his mother for her over-anxious warnings. He was a holy show (said he) opposite the neighbours: no fine plough-horse to bring him joy after his forty-mile trip, nothing to boast about to the friends who had waited in the yard to greet him on his return. And (worse still) a week later, he was forced to head off — this time to Tipperary Town and make do with what proved to be a second-rate animal. Poor old Hammer-the-Smith! It was easy to see how the likes of him could get sore and heavy-hearted — especially as he'd been as good as gold the livelong day amongst those strange Galway men and hadn't treated himself to a single glass of stout or a drop of whiskey. He made a vow he'd never set foot in Galway again and said that the homeward trek had made him feel as miserable as an old woman driving home her bad-tempered ass in the rain. And neither My-son-Jack or Fatty-Matty felt like laughing.

2

Around that time, there was a dance in fashion in the town institute and at the Platform Dances-in-the-Fields. It was known as the tango and came from Argentina. It required more than a drop of twists and turns in it, and it was far better than any of the lazy slow waltzes. Dancing its mazy steps gave the hairy old men a chance to lace on their Sunday boots and come out of hiding and attack the dance-floor. For once in their ancient lives, these old rascals could catch a grip of a comely young woman and press their bellies up against her. One or two of the merry souls got more than one firm uppercut to the jaw for placing his hands firmly on an innocent damsel's arse rather than round her waist — as though the wily old devil was ignorant of the proper dance graces and procedures of the new dance. Would life ever change?

'What sort of a fandango-of-a-dance is this new tango?' said some of the older women, who had no interest whatsoever in going off with their men to try out a few foreign dance-steps. These old beldames had to laugh when their weary men came home after their dance and showed them what they'd been missing and did a few fancy currywhibble steps for them round the floor, their heads full of the twists and turns of the new crazy dancing.

My-son-Jack and Fatty-Matty, having purchased their fine Galway stallion, and at no great cost, now carted their lovely beast all the way from Portumna towards their own purple hills, having given him the name Fandango rather than Tango. The young stallion soon got used to this name, and the road passed by as quick as a jig-step. They made a grand procession — the two cautious mares and the reins that tied them to the back of the cart they'd bought in case Fandango got a bit too amorous. They ran the cart along the grassy verges of the road so as to keep the sharp stones out of their stallion's hooves and, wherever they could, they took the shortcut across the velvet fields. Buying this fine beast had been a glorious adventure from start to finish, and the two heroes were more than satisfied with themselves and their stallion and with all the fine drinking they had done, still rattling around inside in their bellies.

Next day, they got as far as our own Abbey Cross and glided up past Gret's Kill, by which time the cocks were crowing, and the cows were well and truly milked, and the sun was a faint blur aching in the sky. To see them — they were as proud as two young turkey-cocks. The children skipped out expectantly and lined the roadway to greet the mighty adventurers. How astonished was the look in their eyes as they beheld the high-stepping Fandango and welcomed him into their midst, none the worse for wear after his long journey. You would think he'd come down to us from the moon.

At Hammer-the-Smith's forge, the two men got busy, examining Fandango's hooves and his hocks and especially his shoes, to make sure that no damage had been done to him. With his delicate pen-knife, the smith removed one or two tiny pebbles from his front hooves. And then they took their prize down to the river with the inquisitive children following along behind them. They led Fandango into the river and soaked him in the waters of the sally-hole to cool any ache that might still be in him. They knew he'd be finding himself in a very strange place, and they continued to whisper those bits of encouragement and endearment into his ears that any stallion would love to hear.

An hour later, their new prize was reluctant to leave the coolness of the river. They made use of the Cindy-powder mixture and gave his legs a good rub of it. After that, they gave him a feed of oats and water — just a light feed and not too much in case he got the wind and cholic trapped in his stomach. With the back of his coat, My-son-Jack wiped away the surplus water from his back.

Warbling Will came down to watch and placed a warm blanket on Fandango before taking him up the road and crossing the yard where he proudly presented him to Dowager. She took out a bottle of holy water and shivered her new stallion all over with its contents, making the sign of the cross on his eyes, his ears and nose. And though the two men had returned tired and weary and with a full growth of beard on them and their coats a bit dirtier and shabbier than before, the smile on her face now told it all: she was as happy as a queen on a throne. It was clear she was not going to be stopped from expressing her happiness, and she invited all the well-wishers to come in and see the razzle-dazzle of her fine new beast. They were chockful of joy. She cut them several thick slices from the ham that she'd prepared in celebration of this great day. Everyone whaled into the meat as well as the fat onions that she'd thrown in to make up a juice and soon they were all scraping their plates clean — even the ailing Warbling Will.

That evening, My-son-Jack and Fatty-Matty sent for Rohan, the bonesetter, whose knowledge of asses, ponies, mules or horses was renowned the length of Tipperary. He came at once and gave Fandango a right good scrutiny before passing his judgement.

Said he, 'Believe me, I sin meeself, if this isn't the finest horse to ever grace the fields of Tipp'rary,' and from his back-pocket, he took out a bottle of his mother's holy water, and Fandango was blessed (if not canonized) all over again — even his belly and privacies, so that he might sire a fine foal the following spring when coupled with Red Scissors' giddy young mare (Hot-Lips).

There was still a deal of money left in the two horsemen's pockets after their victorious exchange in Galway. Along with Rohan and Hammer-the-Smith, they decided to celebrate with a proper carousel. Down at Curl 'n' Stripes' drinking-shop, they bought an indescribable amount of whiskey and coupled it with what they labelled the medicine (the raw-gut potheen), which had been hidden in the base of Warbling Will's press cupboard. It still had the corn-seed in it. In the twilight, the four of them sat on the singletree across in Old Sam's grove where they proceeded with great reluctance to throw the whiskey down their throats and smack their lips — a toast (they vowed) in praise of recent times and the acquirement of their noble Fandango. It proved to be a long and powerful drink and the rooks in the rookery did not get a wink of sleep from all the fine singing they were forced to endure this blessed night. Eventually, all four of them staggered home and collapsed in their beds where they slept far into the next day, dreaming no doubt of Galway and the successful horse fair and what everyone hereafter remembered as a rale full booze.

3

It was the beginning of springtime — a time fresh and green — and the blackbirds were at their finest. Herald-the-Post came storming into the yard with the news that Dowager's older brother (the Little Yellowhammer — he could whistle as good as any yellowhammer bird) had been taken to his bed with a dose of double-pneumonia. The whole world knew what a killer this was and that it might put a finishing touch to both his lungs, poor man.

When she heard this very sad news, Dowager was agitated beyond belief and pushed Warbling Will out the door to go down and fetch the ass (the Lightning Whoor) so that she might tackle him to the ass-and-car. For a change, the sulky old ass was in the best of possible humours and was already at the field gate, his heart rustling inside in him. He was glad to escape from the confines of the bull-paddock and get himself out onto the road. After all, this was springtime — and springtime can bring out the best in all of us, even in sulky asses like him.

Warbling Will led him back up the road and into the yard where, much to the children's surprise, he took to the tackling and chains at once — to the carting in the shafts and Dowager's gentle encouragement. Then she set sail towards Old Sam's stile and, knowing the ass's regular forlorn spirits, she put the whip soft-and-easy to his back, and they tripped on their merry way to the Little Yellowhammer's sick-bed in the cottage he was renting near Sammy-in-the-fields. This prized lodging had long been the Little Yellowhammer's home in return for looking after this sporty old fellow's Cheltenham racehorses and keeping them in fine fettle.

The Lightning Whoor soon worked himself into a steady rhythm, prancing gaily past the pump outside Lackey's Bicycle Shop. See those swanky ladylike legs of his and the chains and tackling swinging and swaying in harmony with his hooves. All this, the swanky stepping and the shifting of his arse and tail would cause any lady-ass to fall helplessly in love with him.

Lo and behold, it was at this moment that Pat-the-Bear's snow-white ass (Sleeping Beauty), a fleshy young she-ass that had recently replaced the good man's own dead ass, escaped from the gate at Mick Murty's meadow and hurtled down the lane and out onto the creamery road where she finally entered the gateway of High-Hands farm at the Slippery Gap. That's when the two asses met up and began neighing heartily to each other from inside and outside the ditch and giving each other the winking eye with more than a passing interest. And just as a garden flower yearns for water, so had the Lightning Whoor reached an age where he yearned for a she-ass's companionship.

'Neigh-neigh-neigh,' went the two of them, melodiously braying in one and the same accord. There was so much ass-talking to be done. Pat-the-Bear's she-ass was a rare one indeed — a true beauty, equal in stature to Dowager's own rough-diamond-of-an-ass. There were none of the usual bloodstains round her eyes or her ears or on her privacies where the blood-thirsty flies had left her alone (thank God).

The two asses were at once completely captivated by each other and nothing could shake them from their joy. They stuck their hooves into the ground — one ass inside the ditch and the other outside on the road. Clearly the arch woodland fairy (True Love) had moved in on the scene and overpowered the pair of them. Ah, what merry sport they would have one fine day! Oh, what noble young asses they'd produce if given half a chance!

They continued to speak to each other in an ass-language that Dowager, for all her years' experience, didn't understand.

'Bless my soul, I haven't seen ye these past ages,' the Lightning Whoor seemed to say.

'And how has that master of yeers been treating ye this last while?' Pat-the-Bear's ass seemed to say.

On and on went the charming discourse of their ass-talk, as if they had the livelong day to converse with one another. Who knew when these two handsome creatures might set eyes on each other again. It had become an ass's love-tale — the tale of Sleeping Beauty and the Lightning Whoor. Ah, Love herself, the sweetest of all virtues!

'What on earth's to be done now?' cried Dowager, seeing her ass's hooves stuck so firmly into the ground. The minutes were ticking by, and she started working herself up into a fine old fit of stormy temper. At this rate, she'd never get to see the Little Yellowhammer. He might even be dead before the evening was out. No jab of her reins could do the trick. No swift snap of the bit. Not even the famed curses of Dowager (Coom on, blasht ye, ye ould shitty-arse!) could work the miracle on this wretched eejit-of-an-ass.

Pat-the-Bear came out across the road to size up the situation and give a helping hand with a few sound kicks of his boot into the Lightning Whoor's belly. The ass wouldn't budge. Dowager took out her infamous hatpin from the side of her blue-basket hat, and she fixed it into the heel of her ashplant. Shoving the hat-pin up into the ass's arse was always her last resort, but she may as well have tried counting a shower of moonbeams as move him.

Madge Roundabout, the Ballad-Boy's wife (he never seemed able to get out of his bed), had been watching this charming little spectacle whilst she was digging her spuds and pelting them into the bucket. And now, with that little light laugh of hers, she stopped and leant on her fork. She was a well-known lady of great intuition when it came to farm-animals, especially asses, and she wiped the clay from off of her hands and stepped tidily out the gate.

'God spare ye the health — I've the very thing ye've been looking for,' said she, just as poor hapless Dowager was about to untackle the ass and pull him the length of the road with her two good arms. This old fool-of-an-ass (she thought) would think nothing of kneeling down on the road as though he was saying his prayers and staying there till the Guards came along and carried him off on a stretcher to Nackers' Yard — or else shot him there and then on the spot.

A minute or two later, she saw Madge running back from the house with an old stocking and the steam rising up out of it. Inside it, she had a boiling beetroot. She now took over and waved everyone aside. She took up her stance — as close as she could to the Lightning Whoor's tail and the cart. She clutched the stocking in her gloved fist and gingerly tied it round the ass's unexpected tail — as far away from him as she could so that he wouldn't feel the heat coming out of the beetroot. Then delicately and ladylike (almost elegantly), she rammed the stocking-with-the-boiling-beetroot in under the ass's tail, as close to his arse as she could.

With eyes of the purest fire, the startled creature — and he on the verge of a memorable courtship with Pat-the-Bear's Sleeping Beauty — thrust his two fine legs out into space and took off with the speed of a bullet, dragging the mystified Dowager and the cart after him and, at the same time, kicking lumps out of the road and almost throwing the poor woman and her hat into the dyke.

Ah, fame at last. It was said in several drinking-shops during the course of the evening that this misfortunate beast shot out passed the red sports-car of the Bearded Vet, who was on his way home from Limerick. It was reported also that Dowager and the Lightning Whoor spent a day-and-a-half getting back their shattered senses. Fame too for Madge Roundabout and her boiled beetroot-in-a-stocking. It had done the trick that no one else could have done, and this became true in more senses than one. For when the Little Yellowhammer heard tell of her famous exploit with the beet-root, he damn near wet his bedsheets and fell out onto the floor from the fits of spluttery laughter he took. His whistling-skills came back to him in no time at all, and he entirely forgot about his double pneumonia. In future (thought Dowager), Doctor Glasses would have a handy way of treating anyone with the double pneumonia: mention Madge Roundabout and her stocking-with-the-boiled-beetroot that was shoved up the Lightning Whoor's arse. That'd be medicine enough for anyone.

4

Going to fetch Fandango and Fatty-Matty's horse (Shout) from their respective stables was never a hard job: no need for coaxing, no need for the whip or the foul curse, no need for administering the wellington boot or the shortness of temper or the brutish chastisement that some other horses endured and expected every day of their lives. Fandango and Shout were the most honest workers and were never reluctant to start a day — and now more than ever since it was the start of ploughing time. The kindliness and the whisperings into the horses' ears by Fatty-Matty and My-son-Jack inspired the pair of them to the very height of horsemanship and ploughing took on a new edge. There was no horse-fly or horse-bee out looking for the sweet smell of ammonia underneath a horse's tail that could stop them whaling their way across the early-morning ploughing-field. See the flashing blades of the ploughshare silvering its way above the dark clay, turning the grass from frosty green to brown clay time and time again, trimming it as neatly as a man's beard after making friends with the well-stropped razor of the town's barber (Tom Slappity).

Warbling Will came down to John's Gate to inspect the work. He could see the power in the horses' legs and the sweat hopping off of the two farmers' jaws as they took it in turn to steer the speedy plough. He laughed to himself seeing the men struggling like blazes to keep up for they hadn't time to light their pipe or give so much as a cough as the two gallant beasts opened up the straightest of furrows, the ploughshare cutting deep and regular drills. What a magnificent sight (he thought). Flawless the teamwork, one horse stepping on the soft grass, and the other one keeping pace on the hard-pulling sweaty clay, one horse always on the right side and the other on the left as they strove up towards the headland, the ditches answering them back when they drew themselves back-back-back in perfect harmony at the turnabout, one in the bigger circle and the other in the lesser circle, scarcely pausing to draw a breath.

There was no need for words of guidance (coom oop! careful now! steady! whoa!) as they stamped their hooves and pushed on firmly down the field towards the lower turnabout before Warbling Will could even blink his dreamy eye. He was tired these days, and it wasn't long before he had seen enough for himself. He shook his head and headed up the road a happy man, leaving behind him this precious bit of the day when the hearts of Fandango and Shout beat as one. He took with him their memory — the fire in their legs and the steam on their backs spiralling its way to the heavens, out over Simple Simon's ditch and into the blue sky beyond Corcoran's well.

My-son-Jack had almost forgotten to look at his pocket-watch to see if it was time for Dowager to bring out the tea and sandwiches. Suddenly, he saw his mother appearing at the gate as though she was a visiting angel with wings on her back. She stood for a moment with her hands on her hips, her sweet-gallon of tea at her feet, and the doorstep sandwiches wrapped in newspapers. She gazed in wonder and admiration at the two ploughing beauties. It was an even better sight to her wise old eyes than the little birds and the bellflowers all over the sunny ditches.

Later on, in the cooler and fading light of afternoon, when ploughing time came to a halt all over the fields, My-son-Jack and Fatty-Matty inspected the noble new ploughland. They stowed the plough away in the ferns by the ditch after scraping its share clean with their sharp flinty stones.

And now the legs of Fandango and Shout called out for their scrutiny — legs that were aching like the legs of our mighty Tipperary hurlers after the fray. The two men took them down to the river, scattering the cows that had been peacefully sheltering from the flies in under the metal bridge.

Now was the most important part of the day, the time for precious silence, the time for peace. And those woodland fairies (the springtime maidens) could only stare out from the wood and admire the two great horses and their stout-hearted masters. Slurp-slurp-slurp! Fandango and Shout mopped up the cool river water — for ten minutes and not a minute more, since too much water would damage the wind in their lungs. It was time at last for a bit of sport, and the horses rolled over in the sally-hole and kicked their restored legs into the air.

The men had to smile, and they sang the honest praises of their horses, 'Could any men in Ireland have a better pair of horses than ye?' said My-son-Jack.

"Where did ye get yeer legs from?' said Fatty-Matty.

They bathed and soothed their horses' burning hooves and hocks all over again, tending to any swelling that might have appeared on their limbs — up as far as the fetlocks. After all the playfulness, they took them out of the river and up onto the grass. It was time at last for them to tend to their own needs, and they took off their wellingtons and cooled their feet and the aching fire that was in their ankles. Underneath the bridge where no women could lay eyes on them, they took off their shirts and britches and swam bare-arsed around and around in the cool of the river. They were like little children all over again. Heaven (they thought) must surely be a moment like this.

5

Fatty-Matty led Shout back to his own stable. After the afternoon's cosseting by the two ploughmen, Fandango was for once in his life as free as the birds in the sky. For the next half-hour, he cantered round and round the bull-paddock, the last sunbeams of daylight caressing his shoulders.

See him — mad as a March hare and striking his hooves out defiantly towards the hillside plantations. His evening was bliss — like music to his ears. Could life ever get better than this?

Fandango! Oh, Fandango! Alone for the first time in your life and without the support of your good friend, Shout, what ringing devil was it that suddenly worked its way into your head? Why (blasht it) did you gallop over to the dark corner of the field where the orange ragwort grew most tall and strong? What was the great force that now distracted you? Was it the thought of the coming harvest days and the merriment amongst the hayfield farmers? Were you yearning for the nose-nudging of your noble friend, Shout? Were you listening to the echoes of the ploughshare clashing with the clay and the afternoon song of the river nymph fairies on the other side of the bridge? Why did you forget yourself and just this once eat of the deadly root that you'd steadfastly avoided from the day you left Galway?

Yes, Fandango, the noblest of beasts, ate the poisonous ragwort. Too late! Too late! He knew he'd done wrong and realized that something terrible was happening to him. His legs became frail, and he felt as weak as crumbled powder. He staggered to the lower gate and from there into Fatty-Matty's yard. By now, the sweat was rolling down his sides like rain splashing off of a reek. The faintest of whinnying arose from his gaping nostrils and a rasping sound from the depths of his belly. I ask you, was this what so fine an animal as himself deserved?

You'd have to be there in the yard to witness the grief written across Fatty-Matty's face — the appalling pain in him as though he'd fallen into a thousand thorn-bushes. And yet he had the presence of mind to send Lofty and Bill racing to the doors of the Bearded Vet to tell him that the life of the precious stallion was in ruins if he didn't get back quicker than a falling star.

The sad news had quickly spread across the fields and a crowd of men, women, and children came running towards the yard. A minute later, the Bearded Vet was seen leaping out of his car. He saw the exhausted Fandango lying on his side and the demented Fatty-Matty kneeling in front of him, gently stroking him. The poor man's tearful voice was no use to poor Fandango now. No amount of *coom on, mee beauty, ye're the best little horse in Ireland* would work the magic for him. Fandango's eyes were burning in his head, and his despairing whinnying came from far away, scarcer and scarcer by the second.

The crowd groaned — to see how Fandango's eyes never left Fatty-Matty. He couldn't even lick Fatty-Matty's trembling palm — the palm with a few grains of oats now held out on it, the palm from which he had so often eaten the icing sugar at the end of a hard day's labour. He strove to talk to Fatty-Matty in that horse-voice of his that only Shout could have ever recognised — a voice over which he was soon to lose control. Vainly he tried to rise but was too weak now to pull even a feather let alone a plough.

He rolled onto his back, his feet kicking feebly at empty air as though it were some sort of living thing. The Bearded Vet knelt down and shone his torch into his eyes. He lifted apart his dry lips and examined his gums. He shone the torch into his ears. Then he grabbed a sack and began violently rubbing his legs and chest. Fandango didn't even move a muscle.

There was one last resort. He told Lofty and Bill to hurry to the barrel in the barn and bring back as many buckets of water as they could. They scurried back with the buckets again and again and the vet unleashed their freezing contents all over Fandango's sides and onto his head in a last effort to restore him. Little good it did him.

Nothing so dreadful had ever before been seen in our midst. The yard was cloaked in silence — just the hollow sounds coming from Fandango's throat. The crowd saw his body shaking and constricting as he tried to convey to them his heartfelt sadness — saw his eyes half-closing, the lids thick and dry. There was a thin stream of fluid running from his nostrils. There wasn't a murmur from them. Then they heard the ghostly whistling sounds fighting their way against the nasal obstructions as poor Fandango snorted to clear a vent in his nose. The Bearded Vet had witnessed something like it before — but only in textbooks. Fandango's coat had started to turn unkempt and lustreless.

My-son-Jack had been searching in the hills for a hurley-stick-makings when he heard the heart-breaking news. He came galloping along the road, his younger brothers and sisters struggling to keep up with him. He entered the yard, fingering the rosary beads in his pocket. He pushed the crowd aside and ran towards his horse. From across the yard, Fandango raised his ears, hearing the well-known footfall of his master and feeling his presence. The big man knelt down alongside Fatty-Matty, the air stifled in his throat so that he could scarcely catch his breath. Fandango turned his head away and little sob-like sniffles quivered out of him as though he were ashamed to be seen dying, no longer serving his master.

My-son-Jack stroked the dying stallion's jaw. He put his arms round his neck and nuzzled him for the last time. Then he threw his body across him and let loose his tears. For a second, Fandango felt a delicate strength flowing back into his legs from the body-touch of his master. It was only for a second — just a second — and then it vanished.

Demented from crying, My-son-Jack left the yard and sat down on the house-step outside Fatty-Matty's half-door, knowing he'd hear Fandango's cheery notes no more. The after-world of olden-day horses would now be calling him: 'Come home, Fandango, come home! Come and join us in the green pastures that lie hidden from the eyes of men, beyond the clouds and the Mighty Mountain.'

There was one more labour for this great animal — one more determined effort before leaving us for the last time. He lifted his shivering head. He staggered to his feet. The crowd couldn't bear to look at this vision — this spectre — and the birds in the groaning trees were silent. Fandango stumbled and wobbled round the yard. Was it a dream? Was he trying to reach the field? They stood back to give him a space.

'Keep back, lads! Keep back!' they whispered.

But Fandango, hearing the sobs of his master, lurched drunkenly towards the house and the half-door where Fatty-Matty sat next to his good friend, his comforting arms around him, his own tears mingling silently with the ants on the doorstep.

Fandango reached the doorstep. Could it be possible? It was as if he was trying to say something to his master: 'Don't cry! Come now, Jack — dry your eyes!'

My-son-Jack raised his head. The look of astonishment on his face — would anyone ever forget it? The crowd saw Fandango standing beside his master there in front of the house. It was something he himself would never forget. In all his life, he had never owned a horse so loyal and true as the noble Fandango, who even at this moment of death was compelled to offer him this final act of devotion.

More was to come. Fandango took a step past My-son-Jack and leaned in over Fatty-Matty's half-door where the house-fire blazed lively. From deep in his belly he gave a last sad note to the house-fire, a whispering whinny of goodbye, a last secret voice between himself and the house before falling on his knees on the doorstep. He had paid his homage to

My-son-Jack and Fatty-Matty — to life itself. Sergeant Death drew near, and Fandango's head drooped low, his tongue hanging out dryly and traces of black blood oozing from his mouth. That's when he died. His spirit flew away over the hills, and the birds flapped their wings and sped off in terror as though now knowing the ghostly spirit of death.

My-son-Jack, Fatty-Matty, and the Bearded Vet took the tarpaulin from the barn and reverently covered Fandango's naked shame — his death — from the eyes of the crowd. An orchestra of flies began to surround his corpse. All that toil — all that service to Man — all gone. The snivelling crowd walked over to the half-door and said goodbye to the dead stallion — the stallion they knew had come among us only a few years earlier — and then they crept away. The two men wanted to be alone with their dead horse.

A short while later, My-son-Jack left Fatty-Matty and took the shortcut across the lord's estate. He fingered his rosary beads and knelt beside the grave of his grandfather, Dandy, to tell him of his sorrow over Fandango, the horse that (like Dandy himself) had come to Tipperary on that long journey from faraway Galway. The day was getting cold, and he rose to go home. The bats and owls slipped by him and the idle swans cruised their careless way along the surface of the big house lake as if nothing unusual had lately happened.

For days to come, it'd feel like the end of My-son-Jack's life. No more would Fandango have those visions of green pastures or of creamery roads, no more would the children see him rolling round, deliciously tickling his back on the grass below in the bull-paddock in the reddening sunset of evening, no more would they see him good-humouredly teasing the Lightning Whoor, the cantankerous ass, no more would they watch him ploughing the fields or cavorting with Shout as the two of them raced the length of the bull-paddock, no more would Fandango bawl out his heartache when the Lightning Whoor was tackled for his run to the creamery or the forge, leaving him sad and alone, no more would he run and look out over John's Gate to greet the children when they called out his name on their return from Dang-the-skin-of-it's schoolhouse.

Next morning, the men were up even before the cockerel had started his impudent crowing. They took their shovels and pickaxes across the haggart. My-son-Jack, along with Fatty-Matty and Red Scissors, buried Fandango in a big black hole in the depths of the Callow Field. He'd not be going to Nackers' Yard, and they drowned him in their tears afresh.

The following Monday, as the children headed off to the schoolhouse, they saw Fatty-Matty passing by with Shout. He was heading for Hammer-the-Smith's forge to get him his new set of horseshoes. A strange thing — stranger than all that they learnt in school each day — was happening before their eyes. For, as soon as Shout reached the gates of the Callow Field, he fixed his hooves steadfastly into the ground and set up a mighty din — a terrible din that they'd never heard before. His yellow teeth grimaced in an angry snarl, and he raised his front legs in the air in an effort to leap out over an imaginary ditch.

Fatty-Matty was no fool, and he opened the gate. He had sensed what was in the mind of his noble beast. Although Shout hadn't a notion where the men had buried his good friend, he raced across the Callow Field towards the spot where Fandango lay cold in the grave. It was as though from somewhere far away — beyond the skies — the dead Fandango was calling out to him. He could feel the ghost of him close at hand. One thing was clear: Hammer-the-Smith would have to wait a good while yet before putting on his new shoes for him.

Round and round the grave tramped the sorrowful Shout, like a priest that ceremoniously walks round a coffin with his incense and thurifer. Then he whinnied for all the world to hear. He whinnied, and he whinnied, and he went on whinnying. It seemed as though his own heart and the dead soul of Fandango were (and always would be) locked together as when once they ploughed the fields in springtime.

Instinctively, Fatty-Matty took off his cap, as if in reverence. Who would have believed it? The whinnying voice of Shout told him a tale that no human heart could ever supplant, could ever equal. For, there in the Callow Field — there, in front of the children — in something akin to majesty — Tipperary had witnessed the innermost heart of Shout, had witnessed his final toast to the very best of horses, our truly-beloved Fandango, the stallion that had come from Galway. Enough said.

MORNING GLORY

1

Benbow was a small farmer and with his wife, Sally, lived at the far end of High Straits. Even before the sun burnt away the mists, Benbow (in spite of owning his little farm) was out on the roads working in all sorts of weather alongside Gus Gilton, Nate Jimmy, and Red Buckles as a ditch-trimmer and filler of potholes. Benbow and his companions shared a bottle of milk, a few slices of bread-and-jam, and some currant cake. And whilst other small farmers cocked up their noses when asked to do small jobs such as this for the council ('what — the likes of meeee — and meeee a farmer!'), there was no shame in such honest work — at least not for Benbow and his friends. It was regular work. It was safe work too. The money was also heavy enough in the pocket and kept them laughing.

The minute he entered the welcoming room, Benbow would place his wages on the dresser behind the sour-milk jug. Only then did he hang up his hat on the nail with his usual greeting of God save all here! With his wages on display, he felt as proud as a cat. Sally counted out the heap of coins. She cut them in half. Then she cut them in half again. Finally, she cut them once more into yet smaller halves. It was like cutting the playing-cards before the big game. This last small share she gave to Benbow — an eighth of his working wages. Benbow now had enough money to warm his pipe with a squid of Curl 'n' Stripes' tobacco, enough too for his weekly supply of stout when he cycled his bike down to the drinking-shop to play cards in pairs alongside that king of cardplayers (Nate Jimmy) at the forty-five hand-wheel.

Morning Glory was the only child of him and Sally, and the bond between the three of them was as complete as the wheel and metal rim on their horse-and-cart. In the evening, in between tending to his rabbit-snares and shaping the wire and his whittle-sticks, Benbow would place his chair in the middle of the floor. With his hobnail boots, he'd beat out a fanfare and beckon the little girl to come and sit on his kneecaps.

With the tobacco-pipe forever stuck in the corner of his mouth, he threw his short, stubby legs out across the floor and lifted her onto his shins and then slowly up into the air: 'Blasht the bit,' he squinted, 'are ye telling me ye still can't see Dublin?' and he'd shake his head confoundedly as higher and higher (the rogue) he lifted her. The delighted squeals and the panicky excitement of her as she gazed down into his eyes (the laughter still echoes to this day) took her breath away, and she couldn't help wetting herself down the length of his britches. What the black beetles in the turf-box made of it, as they made a frantic run for the half-door, was never recorded.

If the weather was fine on those weekends when he wasn't working, Benbow would take his little daughter out to listen to the puffing winds and the small birds chirping and to breathe in the rich smell of the pig house dung. Together with Sally, they fed the hens and turkeys with so much mash from the skillet that the feathered flock could never complain.

Suddenly, he'd catch the child by an arm and a leg (a leg-and-a-duck he called it) and twirl her round and around (an inch from the ground) before laying her down gently in the yard.

'Again! Again!' she screamed. They were like two boisterous puppies playing, and it was as if the rest of the world wasn't there at all. And Sally and her bread-baking floury fists would be leaning out over the half-door, laughing flush-faced to see the complete love between her little daughter and her sound man. He was like a big child (she thought).

If he reached home early from work (the weather preventing the trimming of the ditches or the mending of the potholes), he gave Morning Glory the most unforgettable rides on the handlebars of his bike. The joy and beauty of it all: the breezes piping their soft serenade, the sky-high mountains, the long dark aisles of the perfumed pine-forests which seemed as if they were about to come walking down to greet them. The old schemer would stutter his rattling bike here and there across the road and threaten to pitch the two of them headlong into the dyke — all this accompanied by the child's playful screams, masking her utter delight and affection for her father as she snuggled into his body.

He always had a spade and a billhook and brush strapped onto the crossbar. As well as that, he carried a billycan for their tea and a few roasted crab-apples or raw tomatoes and a slice or two of soda-bread wrapped in a wad of newspapers so that he and Morning Glory could lie down stretch-legged amid the forest's greenery or at the edge of a murmuring river and have what he called a right royal tea for themselves.

2

The day came when Morning Glory was seen scurrying off down the road to Dang-the-skin-of-it's schoolhouse. In her pockets, she carried a few roast spuds and a hard-boiled egg.

When she got home, Sally made it her business to help the little girl write her homework into her copybook, ensuring that the copperplate curves were the right way slanted and sloped, that the sums were accurately totalled, that *The Lady of Shalott* was rote-learnt little by little each night throughout the year.

Later in the evening when the candles and the lamp were lit and the fire was not only crackling but booming with its sparkling logs, Benbow showed Morning Glory how to draw a rabbit and a crow. He also drew a fighting Freedom-Fighter for her — with the boots, gloves and the rifle. This was in pencil. Fastidiously, he went around the outline in Sally's letter-writing ink so as to make the drawing stand out on the page and look more real. He gave it a final touch by adding a cap at a rakish angle, like Rambling Jack's slanting cap. Only then did they get down the playing-cards for a game of *Old Maid* or *Match 'em* — or else they took out the shiny gramophone records, and as the record spun round and round, the new school-child had her nose almost buried in the speaker with the music of each song seeping firmly into her.

More often than not, Benbow (oh, the devil that is inside a man) spiced up the evening with his tales accompanied by a roomful of spitty-lipped pipe-smoke — entertaining stories for Morning Glory which were all outrageously untrue: tales of a gigantic goat in the nearby Yellowstone Quarry, tales of a black-bearded lion that marched in the dead of night from

Saddleback Village to the road at Sandy's Cross, tales of how this goat and this lion had between the two of them sent many a man leaping in over the ditch on his way home from Curl 'n' Stripes' drinking-shop. It was enough to give a child's brain indigestion. Sally would stop skinning her rabbit and would laugh her two sides off.

'The only goats and lions left in Ireland — the only goats seen in the dead of night — are fixed to the bottom of a drunken man's glass of stout,' she'd say. 'Benbow, avic, if you were squeezed just a little bit more, I could get a few better lies out of ye and yeer innocent eyes!' Such a complete storyteller was her lying-hound-of-a-husband. And then her peals of laughter would re-echo off of the walls.

There was another side to their lives, and in between their bouts of laughter, there was an air of calmness. And when the story of Gabriel's Annunciation to Mary was told at school, Morning Glory understood it almost better than the master himself. Young as she was, how often did she feel that an angel of one sort or another (maybe one of the lesser ones) would soon be coming into their lives. She told no-one except her father. The angel came alright: it came in the shape of her new baby brother (Donie), who suddenly appeared while Benbow was away on the roads and when Sally was filling the burner with the spuds for the hens and turkeys. Her waters burst at eight o'clock one Friday morning just as Morning Glory was about to run out the door and follow her school-friends down the hill. The child ran back into the welcoming room and stood beside her screaming mother whose face had turned the yellow of a quince. On her own (and she still only 9), she tended to her mother's agonising birth pains. With Sally's guidance, she delivered the baby boy, every bit as cautiously as though she were Doctor Glasses or Black Bess, the nurse.

It was the talk of the hills that year. The child washed and cleaned Donie and presented him to her mother. It was the first time she'd ever missed school. Hurrying home, Benbow almost died of the shock, for he hadn't expected to see this little spark-of-a-son entering the world for yet another month. With Morning Glory, he fussed and he fussed over his wife. The two of them fussed Donie too, almost to death, so affectionately did they mollycoddle him.

Next day, when Benbow left for work, his young daughter washed the bloody sheets out at the yard-stream till her childish knuckles were red-raw. She hung them on the bushes in the haggart to dry (like her mother used to do). Inside in the welcoming room (with a renewed bout of whispering advices from Sally), she learnt how to make the soda-bread and the yellow-meal cakes, keeping the fire heaped high with turf till the cabin walls glowed. She put further turf-coals on whatever side of the burner-lid her mother requested (turn this bit in nearer the fire . . . put more coals on this side of the lid). Then she took the bread from the burner and put it in a blanket and took it in to her mother for her inspection in the sick-room bed.

When her father came back from the ditch-trimming, he marvelled at the sight before his eyes — to think the way Morning Glory had safely delivered her baby brother and how she had dealt with the afterbirth, burning it at the back of the fire. It was all too much for him to take in — how, throughout the birth, his child had followed Sally's instructions to the letter just as she did with the washing of the sheets and the baking of the soda-cake. It made Benbow think that a small miracle had taken place in his house — that an angel had indeed come and visited them. The angel was, of course, none other than Morning Glory, his enchanting daughter. And as if that wasn't all: before going off to school each day the child continued to do her chores, to fetch water from the well, to bring in the logs, to collect the eggs from amid the nettles, and feed the hens and gabbling turkeys. Meanwhile, Sally was getting back enough strength to scrape a bit of black-currant jam onto a few cuts of bread — as well as the roasted spud and hard-boiled egg that Morning Glory would need to keep her brains active during her lessons. The child kissed her beautiful brother and ran down the hill towards the schoolhouse.

There were rewards for her labours: she had sweets from Benbow, sweets so rare that no other children knew what they were. By her 10th birthday, she had one pure black tooth — a marvel to other children who longed to have a tooth like it. The rest of her teeth were a double row of tiny white pearls, but it was the black tooth that gave her this special charm. She wore three hairclips whereas no other child knew what hairclips were. And, when other children had their hair cross-combed into plaits, she asked for her own hair to be cut in a pudding-basin style like the boys at school. She wanted (it was clear) to vie with the boys — be it in the robbing of orchards, the gathering of hazelnuts, the climbing of trees on the Two Goats Hill, the jumping of rivers, or the catching of fish with the bag of flour. Like them, she raided the turf-shed of any farmer who happened to be in the way of their journey and stole the daily sod of turf so that Dang-the-skin-of-it could warm his extensive bum in front of the blazing fire.

Some children carried a small knife with them to school. She did too. She used it to cut herself a fair-sized turnip in a nearby field before wild creatures like the rats got their teeth into it, and she spent the day wiping the clay from it onto her sleeve and eating it raw during recess time. Her teeth would be swimming about in her head at the thought of getting a few juicy mouthfuls of her stolen feast.

She wanted to vie with the boys in the use of her knuckles too. One morning, she was on her way past Chesty Noolah's house with her newly-snagged turnip when two brave boys leapt out from the ditch to steal the turnip-feast she was cleaning. Ah, the little highwaymen! — they who had done none of the work themselves. Away in flight she ran, her legs scarcely touching the ground. Then came misfortune when she found herself trapped in the inescapable depths of the Yellowstone Quarry, like the rat trapped in the henhouse and awaiting its fate at the hands of Man and his hurley-stick.

What on earth was she supposed to do? There was no answer but to give the rascals her turnip or have her eyes bruised and battered. That's when the angel came again, bringing her a moment of pure inspiration. She ran at the astonished boys, brandishing her knife aloft and screamed out the old war-cry (hoolah! hoolah!) at them as she came on. Without a knife to safeguard their own skins, they lost their bit of foolish schoolboy courage. Morning Glory did not desist from her attack till she had given the brave little warriors an unmerciful pasting with her fists and had turned them into a black and blue painting.

3

It was the week of confirmation. Bishop High-Hat was particularly interested in the presence of Morning Glory, it being most unusual for a child as young as ten to be selected for her confirmation. Little Nell had been the only other one heard tell of. But before her turn came for the question-and-answer, an almighty commotion rose up. Red Scissor's son (Jackaby) had been at home for the sowing of the potatoes and mangolds and had missed the preparations for this great day, missed also the opportunity of selecting a saint's name for his confirmation. When asked what name he'd chosen as his confirmation name, he could have gone straight through the ground in fright, not knowing what name he was supposed to offer up.

Seeing how flummoxed he was, the rascally boys in the row behind him whispered 'Henry-the-Eighth! Henry-the-Eighth!' That's the name now in the very height of fashion. Whereupon poor Jackaby gave the answer that these cruel pranksters were hoping for: 'Henry-the-Eighth, your honour.' Bishop High-Hat almost swooned in his chair and with a crash he dropped the crosier from his hand.

'Put him out! Put that young devil out,' he shouted, and the ushers carried the misfortunate boy out of the church and into sad posterity.

Dang-the-skin-of-it, however, was going to be saved further embarrassment, for next in line came his best scholar (Morning Glory herself). You could see that he was as proud as punch of her, and he whispered a message into the priest's ear.

The priest passed the message to the bishop, 'The school's finest scholar,' he smirked. This was the moment for his specially-chosen child to put on her best performance.

'And tell me, my child,' said the bishop, his eyes popping expectantly as he looked down at the downcast eyes of a trembling Morning Glory, 'when it's their turn to die, where will all those souls go, who are not of the true faith?' He knew it was a most difficult question — indeed, he hadn't quite worked out the answer to it himself.

Without a blink of an eye, Morning Glory gave him the school's standard reply: 'To Hell, sir.' There followed a deadly silence. Without knowing it, she had disgraced the entire school. In spite of himself, Dang-the-skin-of-it (for he was normally a gentle soul) sent her back to her place in the church-pew with a clout to her ear.

Morning Glory was not allowed to make her confirmation. It simply wouldn't do. It's true — the gentry were not members of what us Catholics called the True Persuasion. Yet, it was these people who had prevented most households from starving to death during the dark days of the famine. How on earth could any of them be going down to Hell?

Though Sally was the soul of kindliness and calmness, she was a dangerous woman when crossed. On hearing of her child's rejection, she was beside herself with rage. She could picture the wagging tongues and the disgrace her child would face opposite everyone once they found she hadn't passed the bishop's confirmation test, and her eyes filled with tears. The old gossips would rub their hands gleefully together and spread the news the length and breadth of the countryside. There was nothing for it but to stand and fight her daughter's corner as any mother should.

Up to the gates of the schoolhouse (a thing unheard of till then) she stamped her boots and burst in through the door. In front of the open-mouthed children, she made a mother's heartrending assault on the ears of Dang-the-skin-of-it: 'And if my child had told that smart-minded bishop in his fancy togs that those who are not of the true faith would have as much right as ourselves to enter the gates of Heaven — what would his high-and-mightiness have thought about that sort of answer? All our lives we've been taught and have believed that they were nothing but a pack of heathens!'

Of course, Dang-the-skin-of-it realised that such an alternative answer would have met with an equal rebuke from the bishop. The normally good-humoured master was somewhat ashamed of his previous anger and the clout he'd given to Morning Glory's jaw. He realised he'd been caught between two fires. But he couldn't help thinking of all the high-falutin' ceremony, the expensive suits, the cakes, the high tea. It had all been grand stuff, meticulously prepared for the bishop's arrival. Damn it — when all was said and done — he had been made a holy show of by Morning Glory in front of Bishop High-Hat and his attendants with their long black robes and their red buttons and crimson skullcaps. What was the bishop to think — only that the innocent child had given him the answer that the master had been teaching his scholars all year long. He'd be lucky if he still had a roof over his head this coming spring and not be sent to the back end of Clare. He had been handed no alternative but to give the child a clout to the jaw.

In spite of the way Sally had nobly defended her daughter, Morning Glory was to receive a penance and it came quite unexpectedly. She had her father's bag of sweets (the humbugs) and was secretly sharing them with Meg-the-Leg at the back of the classroom. The long schoolhouse had two parts to it: the lower end was normally under the tutelage of the master's wife (Biddy) and her musical piano, the upper end, backing away from it and in charge of Dang-the-skin-of-it. However, Biddy was laid up with a twisted ankle and in her place was a newly arrived substitute (Briary), a lady anxious to make a big name for herself.

Briary was teaching the younger children the virtues of the darning needles whilst Morning Glory and her companions were under the exposition of their master and enjoying their favourite book of poetry. The two girls dug their sticky fingers into the bag of sweets and silently began consuming them in the back row where they thought no one could see them.

Suddenly, from behind them, streaked a raging torrent in the form of Briary. The first (and the last) thing that Morning Glory knew was the mistress's red-and-white point-to-the-map stick dipping expertly into the mouth of the bag of sweets, which was sent sailing to the four corners of the room. The two little heads were clashed fiercely together and both girls fell to the ground — unconscious and, as far as the other children could see, stone dead! Seeing stars was a phrase that Morning Glory would later understand only too well.

Before next morning's cockerels had finished crowing, Sally found herself once more in a state of incensed rage. She drove her ass-and-car up to the gates of the schoolhouse, all the time framing the severest of curses in her mind. She startled the children once more with her whirlwind entrance as she raced across the room. She pushed Briary up against the wall and threatened to send her packing out of Tipperary.

'Back to the rocky county where ye have just come from,' she roared, 'back picking spuds, where ye have always belonged — that's where I'll have ye if ye ever again lay hands on mee child.'

4

It was the following Christmas. Everyone put on their thick coats and scarves. The lady in the big house was as busy as a gnat, taking little gifts to the children all over the hills. Family parcels from the Land of the Silver Dollar and the Land of John Bull had to be delivered and excitedly unwrapped. These parcels were so numerous that Herald-the-post came calling on Benbow to help him get the deliveries up to the more remote parts of the hill country. There'd be dozens of gifts

Christmas was a great time for postmen. The twelve-mile journey out beyond Keeper Hill and the bog — as far as the Last Lookout and Diggledy-doo — would leave their two old mares irritable and steaming. Herald and Benbow didn't mind a bit for, wherever they went, they'd be greeted more-than-friendly ('a happy Christmas to the pair of ye') with a bit of bacon, a few slices of Christmas cake, and a glass or two of the raw-gut potheen to take the chill out of their bones.

The first night that Benbow returned from his long journey, he had difficulty finding his way into the yard, and he stumbled about, almost falling into the stream. Tired, weary and befuddled, he finally made his way in the door to Sally and staggered across to the fire. He was as drunk as a mule. It was the first time he'd ever put the raw-gut whiskey past his lips. Sally made a grab at him and pelted him directly into the settle-bed. Like the rest of the women, she had an unnatural hatred of the dreaded drink. In her eyes, it was the greatest curse on earth.

Next time round — even though the twelve-mile journey was a tough one to travel — she felt bound to call on her young daughter to go with the chastened Benbow when he was making his list of postal deliveries. Her child would make sure there'd be no back-pedalling ever again on his part. Morning Glory (as always) followed her mother's instructions to the letter. Benbow (a lesson well-learnt, fair play to him) did not come home drunk that evening or any other evening for the rest of his life.

5

The following spring was the time for the flowers to return all over again and for Morning Glory to learn to cycle her new bike — a gift for her not being allowed to make her confirmation. Benbow was patience itself and soon the rest of us saw the bliss of a first morning's cycling when his young daughter and the hollow-sounding rattle of her mudguards came speeding exuberantly out passed our ears. We'd hear her tingaling-tingaling bell and her singing voice racing down High Straits and frightening everything in her way — goats, horses, pigs and turkeys alike.

'Clear the way, let ye! Here comes a woman from Tipperary!'

The accident which had occurred to Lofty years ago, on the day his brakes gave way when he went tearing around La-de-dah's bend and had half his ear torn off along the slates of the linhay lean-to, was a story all our children knew only too well.

'Remember what happened to poor Lofty,' their mothers would roar after them when they first took to the bike. And then they'd follow this bit of advice up with: 'Test the brakes before setting off towards Gret's Kill.'

Unfortunately, the brakes of Morning Glory failed to pass this elementary test, and she was halfway down the slope leading to the drinking-shop when she found herself zigzagging across the road. She knew it wasn't an angel this time but a ringing devil coming to visit her. Miraculously, she steered the bike (maybe her angel was still working for her) across the road at Abbey Cross. She managed somehow to avoid getting herself killed by the horses that were racing home from the creamery. She saw the green door of Merrymouth's drinking-shop in front of her. The door saw her. Her bike went in through the doorway at the speed of a bullet, knocking half-a-dozen pints of stout and several pipes of tobacco skyways from the startled gobs of the faithful drinkers. Another little miracle — she ended up in a bag of flour next to the Gawk and his good friend Gunpowder (a man with a weak backside) — her head ending up the size and shape of a snowman.

The cuts to her face told us she had been only half-killed. That evening, several of us came up the hill to visit her and see the results of the accident. The sweets given to her would take her a year-and-a-half to eat and would surely produce yet another fine black tooth.

Merrymouth was no fool and moved his shop-door a few feet further west so that such an accident to his bags of flour would never happen again and that neither his doorway nor his seasoned drinkers would ever again have the discomfort of a mad child and her even madder bike meeting them like a runaway train from Limerick. The next misfortunate child could break her goddamn skull off of the wall instead: the gospel according to St. Merrymouth!

6

The Platform-Dances were held again the following summer on the wooden boards laid out in the fields. Across from Morning Glory's windows stood one of these platforms amidst the wild goats and the even wilder asses, who must have been amused and intrigued by the wild music and the tidy dance-steps of the men in their clattering hobnail boots.

Morning Glory was now 14 and a damp heat often filled her body. She was what we called a half-child and half-woman — at a delicate age — a troublesome time of mood swings for her and girls of the same age. With her heart pounding, she'd spend her evenings kneeling on the stool in her bedroom, peeping forlornly out the moonlit window at the platform and the dancers as they went swinging their way round about on their skelping feet. She pictured the fun they were having and could hear the fiddles and squeeze-boxes rasping away. And as she gazed out over the darkening hillslope, she felt more and more like a prisoner locked in some fairyland tower and unable to reach out and participate in the joy of the heavenly music. The roars of laughter told her that a life of great beauty was out there — a place of mystery, a place of magic. No matter how many times she asked her mother if she'd let her go dancing, it was always the same answer.

'A child is a child and men are but men. They'll take advantage of ye and yeer innocent pink cheeks.' Morning Glory wondered what all this sort of nonsensical talk could mean.

The night of her daring escape came on. The hillside fairies tiptoed into her room and wriggled their way into her head.

They opened the latch of her bedroom window for her. Tiptoe. Tiptoe. She eased her way carefully out the window and stepped down onto the dewy grass that awaited her eager toes. She patted the dog (Sinister) into silence. With her heart in her mouth, she feared none of the nightly ghosts as she hurried across the field to the dance.

It was a heavenly night, and the flickering stars seemed to fall all round her. Soon she was having the time of her life, and she swore the older girls into silence. Later that evening — and long before the moon had gone back to sleep behind the clouds — she tiptoed home again and crawled in through her window and into bed. It hadn't been a dream. Her mother would never know what she'd been up to, and she was to repeat the joyful dancing every Saturday night throughout the summer till her feet were red-raw from it.

It had to happen. A lad called Jonjo (the son of By-Jimmy) found his way out onto the floor. He was a year older than Morning Glory, and it was his first year wearing the long britches. There was a swagger that ran throughout his body and a smile that would melt the heart of an innocent girl. Midway through all the fine dancing, he plucked up courage and took Morning Glory out behind the ditch. She was the picture (he thought) of a red apple waiting to be plucked. But — brave though he was — he didn't know what he was supposed to do once the two of them were alone in this unknown world. He stretched his arms out sideways as though he were about to stop a runaway calf. Morning Glory (the little innocent) repeated the gesture. It was a moment of tender intimate beauty when their two hearts rocked like a ship on the waves. Scarcely breathing, they wrapped their arms awkwardly round each other. They gave one another one or two shy little pecking kisses from lip to delicate lip.

On that enchanting night, Morning Glory was transfused with happiness and skipped swimmingly home through the silent grasses. She thought she was about to fly out across the chimney-tops and off into space. Breathlessly, she got into bed and pinned herself in, wrapping the sheets round her like a stuffed mummy in case she might truly fly off to heaven where (she knew) all the happy souls lived. The kisses of Jonjo had been as sweet as a jar of treacle.

7

Something happened. It happened without Morning Glory planning a bit of it. It was a sunny Monday morning when the angel she'd often dreamt of came into the house. Her mother was out in the haggart hanging the sheets out to dry on the bushes, content to leave her daughter alone in the house, coo-cooing over the chuckles of little Donie — popping her head now to this side and now to that side of his crib, much to his amusement.

Morning Glory felt an eerie silence entering the room. She was sure it was her angel — coming for her at last. At first, she heard nothing and then she seemed to see a luminous light. The welcoming room was humming with that strange humming noise that greenflies make round a heap of dung. The invisible messenger came closer and closer and whispered inside her ear. It told her that the kisses of Jonjo at the Platform-Dance were not meant for her, told her that she was being saved for a far nobler calling, told her that God in His Heaven (the angel's call now seemed deafening) was beckoning her to come and join Him in his heavenly task amongst the poor wretches living in the backstreets of cities far across the sea.

It would not be easy for Father Honesty to persuade her mother to let her go. But the angel was now firmly in control and told her what to say. A week later, though she was still young, she packed her small suitcase for her trip on the train and the cattle-boat across to the land of John Bull.

Poor Benbow — he who throughout her childhood had played those childish games of leg and a duck and can you see Dublin? — was grief-stricken beyond measure and kept trying to squint his tears away. He had nothing left now except the echoes of her girlish laughter.

'For the love of Christ — she's but a child,' he wept, spitting the words out with as much distain as he could muster. He thought his heart was about to burst inside his shirt.

He took Morning Glory to the railway station. Sally had cried throughout the whole night and was too heartbroken to leave her room. Benbow placed a slice of bread-and-jam and an apple in his daughter's fist and went off down the railway platform where he spent a long time in the lavatory. He couldn't bear to look his child in the eye.

'I've a cold in mee eyes,' he kept saying through the midst of his tears. But the tears kept swelling up and rolling down his jaws.

Sally and Benbow waited and waited — all the time praying for a return visit from their lovely daughter. She dusted the welcoming room as never before, and Benbow whitewashed the walls. Even the horse's tackling got a polishing where it lay in a heap on the side of the hob. There'd be no sense welcoming their daughter back to an untidy house and having her trip over the buckets, kettle and skillets, would there? The whole place shone like a church.

In the meantime, the nuns in the city had used the hedge-trimmers to sheer off Morning Glory's lovely long hair, as was the custom. It lay in a sad heap in a panier-basket in the convent corridor. Then they put a gold ring on her finger and told her she was now a bride of Christ.

In due course, the saintly damsel made several trips home on the cattle-boat. The nuns had pledged themselves to this so as to soften the sadness in the heart of Sally and Benbow and assure them of their daughter's happiness.

As soon as she arrived home, their spirited daughter showed she was still able to prove herself handy with her fists — the fists that had saved her turnip from the thieving boys those many years ago. And so, whenever a young man came calling at her door in a vain effort to persuade her to give up her

ridiculous holy notions (going back to the convent, I ask you!
— to marry Christ and a nun's ring on her finger), she was
seen spitting on her fists before leaving them flat on their back
and nursing a terrible toothache from the clouting she gave
them.

There was a new Guard below at Abbey Cross — a dashing
young fellow — what Dowager called a modish blade. He had
come over from Clare and with him he had brought a dazzling
new motorbike — a machine that was out of this world. Its
equal had never before been seen by us — what with our
simple ass-and-cars and our horse-and-carts.

The old folk ran out to get a look at it and marvelled at the
shine in it. The men fell into a shock at the speed of it. With its
red and its silver and its long mirrors and its intricate pipes
that weaved through its middle like waves in a river, it glowed
like the sun (said the young girls, the poetry coming out
through their ears) and they clasped their hands together. If
only they could get a ride on its saddle. Their mothers had
other thoughts. The handsome Guard with his wondrous
motorbike was the snake from Eden and left them scratching
their heads: had this fella come down to us from the moon?

It wasn't long before he called at Morning Glory's door in
the hope that he and his beautiful machine might pluck so fine
a flower and have her for himself. When he entered the half-
door, he saw her sitting by the fire — herself and her nun's
black veil. She was as stunningly beautiful as he'd been told
— even more so than his new bike.

But suddenly — he couldn't believe what his eyes were
looking at — he saw her pulling on a Woodbine fag together
with Benbow — the two of them sending hollow smoke-
signals up to the rafters. Father and daughter — and they as
happy as a king and queen: a nun and a fag in her fist — was
the likes of it ever heard tell of in all Ireland?

Without a blush, Morning Glory followed him out into the
yard. She felt a rush of excitement. What was her previous old
bike with its runaway brakes to her now? How had she ever

thought so much of it? She followed his beckoning finger and sat behind him on the saddle. Seconds later, her veil whipping back over her shoulder, her Woodbine fag cocked daintily in the heel of her fist, she found herself tearing round the windy bend — flying past the astonished drinkers who had raced out the shop-door to see the sight and hear the roar of the engine. From that day forth, Benbow and Sally were down on their bended knees most of the day — crossing their hearts and praying that their daughter wouldn't meet with an untimely death.

Each day the Guard came dallying and languishing. He and Morning Glory and the bike — they flew through the valleys and out over the hills and sped as far as the town. For the whole summer, our heroine smoked fag after fag with her new companion from Clare. She drank bottles of stout alongside him on the ditch whenever they took a break from riding his magical machine.

But what could this young man have known about the thoughts lying inside in her saintly head? She was merely acquiring the lower and lesser habits she'd need to learn if she was ever to work alongside the down-and-outs in the backstreet slums of big cities. She'd have to learn (and quickly) what it was like to take on the day-to-day manners of a downtrodden man. She knew that her endeavours to match the young Guard in his smoking and drinking would prove a useful weapon when the time came for her to reach inside the minds of those poor embittered men, none of whom had a hope in hell of making a better life for themselves on the rough streets of the city.

THE OLDTIMERS

1

The lonely old men and women who lived in along the grassy lanes a mile or so above Sheep's Cross would become alarmed and fidgety whenever they saw our children's bare flinty feet running in along the yard. They didn't know whether to laugh or cry, and they often did both alternatively since a visit (any visit) was a break from their natural loneliness. They'd hobble back in the half-door and cut their young visitors a few slices of soda-cake and a glass of milk.

Some Saturdays after they'd done their household jobs such as bringing back the buckets of water from the well, driving back the cows to the Rishy Field and filling the chest with armfuls of logs, an army of Moll-the-Man's children, led by Lippy, would scamper out the half-door. They'd scurry up the hillslope, their eyes all the time searching for the hills ahead of them and wishing that one day they'd reach the place they called fairyland. Once they'd rounded Fort Dangerous where the gold was said to have been buried by the ancient Danes, they'd find themselves well into the unknown world at the other side of The Valley-of-the-Pig and the Valley-of-the-Black-Cattle.

From there it was a short distance to the remote thatched cabins of these old men and women — the few who were left and had not taken the steamer to the Land of the Silver Dollar. The earlier inhabitants had mostly staggered away during the famine — droves of them like the Gog's uncle (Skycracker) and were never seen again.

It was as quiet as the Sahara Desert up here — as though time had forever stood still. A little further on, the children could hear the harsh rushing water where Growl River and

Brawl River flowed into one another at the Eagles' Nest. It was next to Obscurity (said Dowager) and a mile from the River Sticks (said Moll-the-Man) and that was the very end of the world (they both said).

The little cabins were smaller than our own — mere dolls' houses. The walls were thick, and the rooms were light and airy — cool in the summer and warm in the winter. They were built next to a natural spring-well so that the old ladies never ran short of a drop of water for boiling their spuds and washing their clothes. Sometimes there was the added gift of being at a bend in the river where the water ran slowly and was shallow enough for the women to wash their sheets and bolsters, the ass dragging a snow-white cartload of them across the ford and back to the yard. Clusters of trees hid these old people's world until the children learnt to find an opening where once there had been a gate. It'd be covered in briars and furze bushes, placed there as a safeguard in case the rest of the inhabited earth might come up the hill and run away with the old dears.

On sunny afternoons, once their work was done, they'd sit like demure cats on their chairs in the yard and look at the scorched trees in their haggart and the pink roses on their yard walls. They'd nothing else to do but watch the lovely sun and the copper clouds peeping in and out over the evening trees — wait for the meeting between day and night to come and take them away.

They had the ass-and-car in the yard to get them to the shops for their bags of flour and to bring back a few odds-and-ends like candles and matches to light their fire and a drop of paraffin to light the lamp in the evenings. Their ass had his own field behind the house where he could chew on the thistles.

Good neighbours from further down the slopes stacked their turf and logs for them in the shed next to the hen-house, and the sow had her own little nest at the other end of the living-house. They kept a cow or two for their milk and as many black cattle as they could muster abroad on the hill. They used their haggart as an orchard with a few spindly trees with small red apples on them in case they ever got hungry. There were some blackcurrant and gooseberry bushes for their jams and the odd pear and damson tree.

Once the children got through the complicated opening of the furze bushes, they found they were in the largest field they'd ever seen — a lush green meadow that made them imagine they really were entering fairyland.

Delighted to find the freedom of such a huge space, they did several cartwheels round the field, frightening every little rabbit back to the protective paws of their mothers in the ditch. They became as giddy and silly as the invisible fairies spying on them from the far side of the field. They could see in the distance the blue smoke spiralling out from an old couple's hitherto unseen chimney and ascending among the pine trees. They knew that in a minute, they would be safely hidden from the rest of the world — even from God (one or two of the younger ones felt). Then they merrily winged their feet on towards the river and the little thatched house below them.

One day (thought Gallantry, the young poet amongst them), I'm going to build myself a mud hut out here in the wilderness. I'm going to put a grass roof on it and a wooden gate for a door and without a latch to it and then everybody from down below can come up and visit me. And with my lovely Cherish by my side, we'll live out here as happy as the king with his queen in their big palace across the sea.

But imagination wasn't the gift of Gallantry alone. For some of the cabins had been long abandoned, just the ashes and leftover hedge-clippings in the fireplace and the dusty door and windows hanging off in flakes of green paint — grand places for the children to visit and explore.

On some Saturdays, the younger ones found time to walk through the cabin ruins, the bigger boys making up tall tales for the little ones — all about the people who had once lived there. They would play for an hour or so as though they were pretending to be adults in a new sort of cubby-shop. They'd sit down at a broken bit of table and have their pretend dinner.

'I'll be the father — let you be the mother and let this be the bedroom where all the children of the past once slept.' Then the bigger ones would settle the little ones across two old chairs and pretend to tuck them into bed, and they'd all join their hands and say a little prayer as though they were ready for sleep. Then they'd go behind the ruins and explore a bit further.

Is this the pig-house plot? 'And will you, Battlin' Sal, be the great big pig?'

And is this the stable? 'Let you, Leppity, be the mare'.

It went on and on — the echoes of the past and all its ghostly souls (humans and animals alike) getting honoured over and over again by this little group of adventurers.

2

In spite of eating the old folk's soda-bread and drinking their tea during these carefree hours, it was a far different story on the long summer evenings. By-Jiggery and Moll-the-Man would be out in the cowshed milking their cows, and the children would be left sitting with their feet in the fireside ashes. This was the last thing that would soothe their savage little minds when there were a few more hours to kill before going to bed. It was the time when Mister Boredom raised his ugly head. It didn't take them long to forget the sincere efforts they'd made to be good and holy children during the recent mission. Without a backward look and with the hills forever beckoning them, they went on tiptoe across the stream in case they'd be called back to do some more back-aching jobs — like making sure the gate was closed behind Short-Arse, their patient ass, or cleaning out his stable for him. The wanderlust of the goat was on them and as soon as they were up the hillslope, they became as talkative as chicks bursting out from the shell.

In the next few hours — and the further away from home they got — the more and more brazen did they become, the invisible spirits (not always the better ones) awakening in them a new set of adventures. They got up to all kinds of mischief, back-pedalling into their sad old ways — harmless at first but growing more and more dishonourable, though not quite as wicked as the little ones helping Slipperslapper drown an innocent puppy or Lippy belting the ears off of Mick-the-Walking-Hayshed.

It was as if these little scallywags felt a need to hurt or to laugh at anyone or anything other than themselves. They thought nothing of frightening to death the poor old men and women whose withered legs were no longer able to run after them and chastise them with the yard-brush. In the approaching twilight, and to avoid letting this new boredom creep up on them, they took up the amusing pastime of running the hens, geese and ducks round and round some poor old woman's haggart till the harmless creatures stopped flapping their wings and fell down almost dead with fright and exhaustion.

As the wildness of their sport increased, so did the children's unintentional cruelty gain further steam. They brought out the reins from the stable and tied the dog to the ass-and-car and roared with fiendish laughter, imitating the howls of the tormented creature. There was a list as long as your arm of their inventive and downright rascality, which would have alarmed the rest of us, did we ever get to hear of it.

A day or two later, Moll-the-Man heard the roar of Father Honesty's motorcar coming up the road. Without a handshake, the holy man leapt down from his car and marched into her welcoming room. He wasn't the same fatherly man that smiled at them most Sundays from the altar but had a face on him longer than a tinker's fiddle. He stormed up and down in front of the children. He felt like kicking the little arses off of them.

When he had calmed down a bit, he talked to them about Hell and he talked to them about damnation. He talked to them about shame and about guilt and how it would take time for these feelings to evaporate from them and how their behaviour had diminished their souls in the eyes of God. He told them they had each crossed the bridge between good and bad. He told them the savage beating that God would give them in the next world if they ever again tormented the old saints in the hills. Then he made them kneel down in the yard. After that, he brought out from his car a large bottle of holy water (it would have to be a large one) to re-baptise them and bring comfort and peace back into their souls. By now, they were full of self-loathing and felt very sorry in front of such a great man. They limply hung down their heads and genuinely flickered their eyelids and were chastened. He gave each of them a good dowsing of the holy water and at each turn of his heel, he called upon the devil that was hiding in their souls to come out of their bodies: 'Come on out, Satan! Come on out this minute, ye scarecrow!' Then he blessed each of their foreheads and told them that their contrite hearts and true sorrowfulness had restored them to an unblemished state in the eyes of God and that God had forgiven them — on this occasion. At this they felt a good deal better.

Only then did he turn aside and give himself a little self-satisfied smile and put his bottle of holy water away. He too had once been a child. He too had once been a rogue (but not as big a rogue as these little heathens).

'Go and sin no more,' said he. 'Far better for ye to go down to Ducks-and-Drakes and worry the life out of her old sow, who has been threatening to tear the legs off of little children going to the well.' Without so much as a salute, he hopped into his car and went roaring away down the hill.

By this time, Moll-the-Man was in a savage state of anger. She moved at lightning speed to the hen house to bring back her yard-brush and draw blood from her children's legs. By-Jiggery also proved himself unusually vengeful and was already arming his fist with his best sallyswitch. With feet that the best greyhounds in Ireland (Caruso too, had he been alive) would have been proud of, the little army raced into the Rishy Field in a great big frightened heap and easily jumped the three-foot wire fence that led into Old Stroller's orchard. They were safe — for now.

3

Dan and his sister (Judy) were two old-timers who lived in a little thatched house in Currywhibble at the far side of the bog. A Monday morning came when old Judy had washed her bed-sheets and hung them out to dry on the bushes.

Fat Noolah lived a little way down the hill with her husband (Sad Sam). She was always looking out the window like a nosy old crow to see what Dan and Judy were up to. An hour later, she saw the old pair setting off for the bog to plank a few rows of turf since the footings were well dried out by now.

They'd be working like blazes until the daylight would slip away from them and the charcoal sky take over. Fat Noolah and Sad Sam now spotted a chance to improve their lives at Dan and Judy's expense. They were desperate to get their hungry sow a good feed, and they raced up the hill and unclasped the latch of the old pair's door.

As soon as the door was opened, the heathens let in the starving sow to adorn the welcoming room with her presence. What a welcome was inside for her! Had you been there and peeping in the window, you'd soon have seen how this particular sow dealt with the simplicities of Dan and Judy's cabin. She rushed wildly about the floor, driving the ring of her nose at the chairs and the dishes on the table and almost landing herself in the fire. She was no longer a sow but a raving bull as she knocked over the pots and pans and anything else that stood in her way. It was (thought Fat Noolah) better than the Daffy-Duck Circus to see such pandemonium.

Then the precious creature knocked down the crockery and the pewter from off the dresser and went on to spill the milk and the spring-water from the two buckets. For a finish, she buried her head in the bag of flour. The Devil in his home in Hell was warming his hands to see such gallantry in a noble sow. What a miserable picture — a sow no longer pink but as white as Daddy Christmas as she pitched the flour all over the room. There was no greater sin than to destroy a man's flour, the flour that he'd be needing for his soda-cakes, the flour that had to last him for half a year's eating.

Mercy-on-us! When Dan and Judy returned to the cabin, they saw the state of the floor and their simple possessions, all ruined beyond belief. Their faces turned grey with hopeless grief. Then they took a look behind the hen house where they saw the happy face of the sow looking up at them — as contented as the missioner after the mission, and she covered from head to tail in their hard-earned flour.

'Ah-ha! A sow with the staggers!' yelled Judy, her sadness and her anger all rolled into one. For once, she had forgotten her normal holiness and saintliness.

Dan caught her anger and fanned it: 'Quick! Get the four-grained fork,' he roared.

'Stick it down the impudent sow's throat!' shouted Judy.

'Get its blood,' cried Dan. They were demented to think of their lost flour and the hunger that would now be upon them.

What happened next beggars all belief. To the everlasting horror on the faces of Fat Noolah and Sad Sam, Dan took the four-grained fork, and Judy took the hayfork, and they proceeded to try and kill the wicked sow who had ruined their house. The two ruffians were now terrified out of their wits, seeing that they were getting a bit of their own medicine back for their recent crime. They thought they might get sent to the Beyond with the pitchforks, and they hid behind the curtains of their sad little cabin. They watched their sow facing up to what surely would have been its last and fatal punishment, had it not had the good sense (when it felt the first dart of the fork up into its arse) to run and jump clean out over the wall. It was never seen again from that day to this (said our merry-faced drinkers) — except on a drunken man's way home at night.

4

Dan was working in his well-loved bit of bog under the clear blue sky and the reddened clouds where he'd gallivanted with his father (Hushabye) when he was a child. Growing tired, he tripped in the heather and hit his head on a sharp stone. Like a young calf searching for its mother, he tried to rise up but stumbled again. A man who had been as hardy as a snipe all the days of his life, was now scarcely breathing and he lay there in the sun, his saddest hour. He knew that Death wanted him.

Harrowed with grief, he wanted to cry out and bellow, 'I'll give three bawls of the hunger before I let ye take this land from me!' — for the Gadfly men had been pestering him for years to sell his bit of land to them for next to nothing. He would die as he always said he would, out in the open air, on the land that he loved so well, unwanted and unloved by all except his beloved sister, Judy.

When he didn't come back for his midday bowl of soup, Judy took the road to their bit of bog. Sorrow of sorrows, she found him there, stretched out like a useless old scarecrow, his glazed eyes looking up at her and she looking down at him like a frantic bird mourning its fledgling. He spoke not a word. Judy wasn't sure if he could hear her speak. But she knelt down and put her mouth into his ear, all the time searching for the right words to say to him. She told him of her love for him. She told him of the absolute love that God had for him. She told him that a better place was now being prepared for him in the kingdom. Her heart was breaking up inside in her chest with a love and an aching and a longing which hurt her ribs more than the punch of a man's fist.

Dan closed his eyes for the last time. Judy crossed his two arms across his chest and stayed a long time praying over him. She gave him the death prayer (The Act of Contrition) — gave it to this brother of hers who had never ever sinned in all his life. He had outlasted the greedy money-grabbers. He had indeed given the world his three bawls of the hunger before he died. The angels came floating down into the bog. They put their wings around him and carried him away with them from all the complexities of this life.

When the other turf-gatherers arrived on the scene, they found his beloved Judy whimpering softly to herself with her two arms round her brother's neck and the spindly bog-land trees looking down protectively on his body in their hoods of green.

Dan's soul was now very far away, and he looked down and blessed his sister, and he called out to her from the sunshine of eternity. And it wasn't many weeks (God rest her) before Judy and her piety heard his call and left the wastelands of life here on this Earth and came rushing through the skies to meet up with Dan.

\

TO THE RESCUE

1

It was now the winter sports and the sledgers and gliders were a stone-throw away up at Fort Dangerous preparing for the downhill slippery slide. It was the only field steep enough and long enough for the fine sliding and gliding they'd be doing.

The day was marked out as a bad one for the tallest lad imaginable (Mick-the-Walking-Hayshed). He should have been celebrating more than anyone else, having left the imprisonment of the Dang-the-skin-of-it's schoolhouse for good the previous week. He was not, it seems, full of the joys of the other boys and girls but as good as heartbroken — not only over the recent death of his sheepdog (Red Rose) but (far worse) over his beloved father's untimely death from long days feasting on raw-gut whiskey. His mother understood and forced him to take out his thick-latted belly-board to enjoy himself and give himself a bit of distraction on the snowy slopes. However, his recent sadness was nothing to what was now awaiting him for he was about to be introduced to the real meaning of childhood sorrow.

He was the last to come sailing down the slope. 'Here comes Mick-the-Walking-Hayshed!' roared the sporting hordes of sledgers as they encouraged him on his downhill slide. All eyes were glued on him.

'Keep the way clear, lads!' With an increasing rush he stormed on and on. Look at the sway of him (here he comes!), a-skidding, a-flying and a-leaping — his ruddy face ablaze with unspeakable joy, the look of a chased hare on him.

Suddenly, his face registered absolute terror when he realised that he and his belly-board were unable to halt. He hit the ditch with a tremendous rap and like a shot from a gun went sailing out over Free'n'Easy's crab tree and landed in the road at the side of Fingers-Jack's cart. The poor lad — you should have seen him. His face had the whiteness of death stamped on it, and he looked like an ancient leprechaun.

'Stand back! Stand back!' cried Fingers-Jack as he leapt down from his cart. He beckoned the children to his side and in a gentle whisper ordered them to run to Dowager and quickly bring out the blankets and bolsters. In the meantime, he knelt down and went on whispering in a strange and musical voice into the ears of the injured youth. At the same time, he kept on testing the limbs of the lad with his skilful fingers like a fiddler tuning his strings or rosining the horsehair of his bow. The children's eyes were all peeled on him.

The road ached with a moment's unbearable silence and not a single bird's song could be heard. Was Mick-the-Walking-Hayshed alive or was he dead? The crowd of children stood there wondering, and one or two of the girls said a silent prayer that Fingers-Jack and his magic would somehow turn the trick and revive the hapless lad.

The older boys had been closely watching the serious skills of Fingers-Jack at work. They knew that if anyone could now change the fate of Mick-the-Walking-Hayshed, it was this famed bonesetter of theirs and no-one else — a man of the purest tenderness whenever he was called to his work. These last few months had been an eventful time for him — what with Madge Roundabout's damaged shoulder and Little Dan's two shins — but nothing like this. The great man turned his eyes up to the sky as though he was asking the help of his father and grandfather. Then he gave a smile that lit up the road like a blast of orange sunlight.

The children now found themselves looking into the enlightened soul of Fingers-Jack and they knew it — even before Fingers-Jack said so himself — that before next year's Saint Patrick's Day was seen and gone, their young friend would have new wrists on him — that Fingers-Jack would have made them as strong as the handles of a plough, and Mick-the-Walking-Hayshed would be stepping out and helping his widowed mother sowing the spuds and twisting their stalks later on in the year.

2

Fingers Jack wasn't the only expert among us. Everyone remembered the harvest day when they saw Black Bess and her van — the van that was infamously labelled the truck, she not having a properly-shaped motorcar to call her own like the priest or the vet or the doctor. The children saw her clattering up the brow of the hill at the Kill next door to Galloping Gret's red roses. The smoke from the engine was rising to the heavens like a battered old tractor, and she and her cheeks were as red as the rosebushes in Fatty-Matty's garden.

Her chief claim to fame was the black soot-drop that she painted on her cheek each morning. It was pasted just below her left eye. The children had never seen her before, and they were awfully anxious to get a proper look at her soot-drop. Alas, from where they were helping My-son-Jack and Lofty to turn over the hay in the seventh field, there was little chance of that.

In her truck, Black Bess was carrying all the medicinaries (her word) that she'd require: the iodine, the smelling salts, the temperature gauges, the bandages and safety pins and so on. Had the children been able to join up with her, she'd be seen entering Sissy Hoppalong's half-door. The misfortunate Sissy was expecting her first child, the product of several brazen bouts of summertime tussling and tumbling when she'd initiated a brace of inexperienced adolescent boys into the sporting realms of pleasure above in her hayshed.

Black Bess was in an awful hurry to get to her as it was going to be a difficult birth, and maybe Sissy would be dead before she even arrived. Some of the haymakers in the fields were looking out over the ditch and left scratching their heads.

This was a new one on them — to see a nurse and her truck steaming up towards the crossroads where no-one in living memory had ever seen or heard tell of a nurse hurrying up their hill. The children stood on tippy-toe and watched the trail of smoke from her receding van. My-son-Jack left off tramming the hay, and Lofty left off gathering in the dried-out hay-rows towards the trams. Why on earth (they said) would a nurse and her van be coming up their quiet hillslope?

A day later, the old gossips brought back the reason for summoning Black Bess: Sissy was forty-five (although she always said she wasn't a day over forty), and she had never given birth before. A first birth at such an advanced stage of life was a thing unheard of and was thought to be impossible for any woman to achieve. How grateful we were that evening when we learnt of the wonderful skills of Black Bess and how, after a labour of only four hours, she had safely delivered the new baby (Tom-Tom) into the tearful arms of Sissy. We blessed and crossed ourselves for the skilful work the nurse had done. Maybe the Guards would leave Sissy alone and stop pestering her over her love of young lads. Maybe Father Honesty would let her keep little Tom-Tom and not carry the child away to the orphanage or snatch the poor woman off to the nunnery. Maybe next year, Sissy would forego the tussling and tumbling with her lively young lads. Maybe. Maybe.

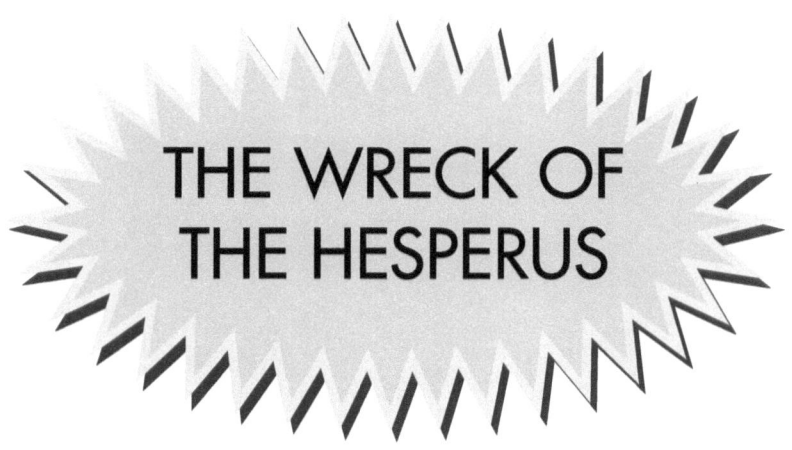

THE WRECK OF
THE HESPERUS

1

Daisy-Chains was a far-out cousin of Joe Solitary and his daughter, Kate. She was a day-dreamer if ever there was one. For, once the dawn came around, you'd fine her humming little snatches of songs to herself in competition with the cockerels and making those flowery bangles with the field daisies (if they were in season) and handing round her flowery necklaces later in the day to the schoolchildren as they met her on their way to and from school.

As she grew into womanhood and became ripe for the eyes of her future husband (Mee-Ould-Segocia) and the eighty acres of land he'd inherited from Dan-the-Lion, she became awfully heavy in the chest — so much so, that the weight almost threw her off balance and sometimes she began to have trouble catching her breath.

Instead of admiring her strength and amplitude, there were one or two jealous women who hadn't the gift of a fine big chest, and they'd snigger to one another: 'Will ye look at that eejit, Daisy-Chains with her two blown-up bladders wobbling this way and that way inside her blouse and struggling to get out.' Ah, the heathens, to be saying such things about the good woman when (if she'd heard them and hadn't been such a soft-natured creature) she could have knocked them down senseless with a belt of her fist.

Daisy-Chains was the daughter of Mercy-on-us (a mere morsel-of-a-woman), who was always ready for celebrations, be they hurling-matches, fairs or circuses. And Mercy had been married to God-be-with-the-times, a mild-mannered man who, as the years rolled by, had shown all the signs that hardship brought in its train — a stoop in his shoulders and a slight limp in his knee from the kick of an ass. As far back as Daisy could remember, he'd had a white beard on him with green and yellow streaks in it, and Mercy said (if you were to believe her) that he could swallow a goose with one gasp of his jaws, so hungry was he at every blessed hour of the day.

Whereas the women showed all these signs of impolite jealousy at the size of Daisy's chest, men were always kindly-spoken about her. She was sixteen stone in weight and, one and all, they wanted to slap her proudly on the back. They simply loved a big fat woman.

'That Daisy-Chains is a fine big paunch-of-a-woman,' they'd say, as if they were examining a pig they were fattening for the market. Of course, it was a handy thing for them to see her so strong. When it came to lifting a gateway pier or a boulder out of the ditch for a cornerstone to a new pig house or even for dragging a lifeless drunken man out of the ditch, Daisy-Chains was always the woman for the job.

Black Paddy (Warbling Will's uncle) was once sprawled out in the dyke, drunk beyond repair outside Red Scissors' father's place above at Sheep's Cross. That was the day when the father of Din-Din-Dinny was having his farewell funeral procession down the hill. The women and the keeners were all out in their best black finery and parading along respectably in front of the coffin as it started to make its way down the slope.

Bless the bit! — who was it but Daisy-Chains (on her way down to bring back the drop of oil for her lamp) who spotted the trouble Black Paddy might cause. As quick as a wink, she ran on ahead of the procession. She shouldered the misfortunate drunk onto the broad of her back before he had the chance to bring unforgivable disgrace on his family with his moans and his groans and the filthy bad language pouring out of him. Then she whirled him three times round her shoulders and, as though he were a javelin below at the Abbey Cross Sports, sent his two feathery heels flying in over the ditch just below Free 'n' Easy's stile. The good name of Black Paddy (and the rest of his people, thank God) was thus ensured, and the day was saved for the dead man's family too, and they were all able to sleep like lambs on the green that same night. Fair play to you, Daisy-Chains!

Now, whereas Daisy-Chains was on the heavy side, her husband (Mee-Ould-Segocia) was as thin as a bed-rail. Not a soul believed his lovely wife when she told anyone who'd listen to her that, as soon as he'd had a few pints of stout inside his belly, the little animal was wont to wave his trousers in the air as he came in the half-door and pelt her down on the bedroom floor in an undignified attempt to inject her with a small infant to go along with their first-born child, the future Wreck of the Hesperus.

Of course, you can't beat the canoodling and the frolicking inside in the bedroom. But (woe and alas) a second child for Daisy-Chains was not to be got from this sort of tumbling with Mee-Ould-Segocia. She got up one morning and said her few prayers as usual and headed out along the bog road. She was hard at work, footing the little tents of turf sods at the end of her bank, when the fairy-like mists suddenly came down around her.

Poor Daisy-Chains! She couldn't see further than her nose and a strange feeling of alarm and terror crept over her. Shivering with the cold and dampness, she strayed off the path and into a very deep bog hole. Like some of the wild horses in the years before her, she fell to the bottom and got drowned, and her spirit sailed off over the clouds to meet up with Mercy-on-us and God-be-with-times in the Beyond. The older women said that the wilderness fairies had come out from behind the rowan trees at the back of the bog and carried her off to a far better place than this Earth. Enough said.

2

When the whirlwind of his schooldays was over, no-one knew how the Wreck of the Hesperus might turn out. That was a great pity. For, if they'd known the way he'd make the lives of our children such a misery, they might well have tied him to a windy bush abroad in the bog and left him there for the carrion crows to do away with.

Of course, he wasn't the first one to frighten our children. There was an unending list of imaginary creatures that filled their nightly dreams with terror — a list that they kept to themselves so as not to let their parents think them faint-hearted and cowardly in the face of the unknown.

Remember Old Corkscrew, who was said to be a hundred years old. He'd a yellow tobacco-stained beard on him that reached down to his toes. His ghost sat on the ditch, ready to snatch the little ones into his grotto as they raced past him to get the buckets of water from the well.

Take the Boodeeman, who came mysteriously into the bedroom through the hen house wall without knocking a rock out of it and loomed over their terrified beds in the dead of night.

Then there was the Ghost-Thrasher that stood on top of the pig house with a silver axe in his hand whilst the thrashing-machine was in the haggart doing its work. 'The ghost fairies need a few tasty morsels for dinner tonight,' he'd whisper, 'I'll crush yeer bodies to grain-stones.'

There was another devil — the ghost of Malignity-the-Witch, who had once been seen below at Old Sam's stile, sucking on her clay pipe and chewing on a sod of turf. If she caught any children ('twas said), she'd gather up a snot-load of phlegm and spit it into their eyes and blind them for the rest of their lives. Hadn't she been seen doing this very thing beyond in Kerry?

Her brother's ghost was Veins-in-the-Nose, who had once threatened little boys with his army sword. 'Coom here, little boys, till I cut off yeer private bits,' he roared. Oh, the monster! And this demon might still be alive! And what would little boys do then? They'd have nothing left to piss with, and they'd surely die.

But none of these frightening ogres was able to compete with the Wreck of the Hesperus for he was not a made-up tale told by the conniving adults but a piece of real flesh-and-blood. You'd hear him stamping down the hill, always on the look-out for unsuspecting children — him and his raggity greatcoat flapping in the breeze and his fierce red eyes. He'd a nose on him red as a peony from all the hard drinking he did and could lift a bag of meal like Daisy-Chains used to do without drawing a bead of sweat. On his back, he carried a sack, and it held a huge jar big enough to hold a hen. It was full to the gills with hard drink.

The children never knew when he'd be traveling their way. They might be hurling their horse-chestnuts round the road when his fiendish laughter ('Ah-ha mee byze! What have we here!') would come upon them as he rose up out of the misty fields, waving his sack in the air, inside which (he told them) he was carrying his hammer and horse-nails. If he ever got hold of them, he'd nail their bodies to the nearest tree ('and ye'll never see yeer mammy again!') and leave them hanging there (like Jesus) for the fox to make bits of during the night.

If a mad dog had gotten hold of their britches, they'd not have felt such terror as they then did when he came thundering out on the road and tried to snatch them into his sack. Where now was their former bravery with the tinker's pup as they left a stream of poolie behind them and leapt clean over the far-side ditch, the wild man's laughter ringing behind their heels.

The silence that followed was far more frightening than all the fierce shouting as they raced across the fields and came crashing in through their mother's half-door. And then followed the outright list of their lies — how the Wreck of the Hesperus carried the Devil's whip with him, how he swore he'd kill every one of them, how he'd leapt down from the ditch and threatened to eat them alive — each lie getting bigger and bigger — as though the truth itself weren't bad enough for their mother to listen to.

That's when Moll-the-Man lost her temper, and her voice turned colder than a winter's yard. 'What's our life coming to, Jiggery? Our children won't be able to roll their bowlee-wheel down the road if we let this shitty-arsed tramp thrash the lives out of them. He'd fitter go home and clean his bogied nose.'

3

Once the hay was saved and brought in, it was time for the corn to be thrashed. The Wreck of the Hesperus found himself behind the sacks of Jim-the-Bear's thrashing-machine, and then he took himself up onto the thrasher's roof and started to fist the sheaves of straw down into the hole.

When the rest of the men were going down the haggart for their sup of tea, they left the engine running, it being the devil's own job to start it again. Suddenly, they heard a roar that could be heard above in Dublin. The Wreck's forearm had been sucked into the thrasher's flywheel as he was trying to put in the last few sheaves of corn. To see the gallons of blood that dyed the straw, you'd think a pig had been stuck. Not even Fingers Jack would have been able to repair the damage. It'd take a professor to do the trick before the poor fellow ended up a corpse. The Limerick Hospital (thank God) was finally able to repair half-a-dozen breakages to the wild man's arm, but he'd not be wielding his sack of hammer-and-nails for many a day to come! The doctor had given him an entire transfusion of blood, the gift from a poor young man killed by a falling tree that same week. It took several gallons of this youthful blood to keep him alive, and he needed every drop of it to get back his former strength and courage.

If only the children could see him the day he was transported back to our hospital in town — one leg to the south of him and the other leg to the north of him and not a hammer or bag of horse-nails in sight. Their mother's prayers had been listened to, and after this little episode, they lost their dastardly fear of him and were as merry as jaybirds.

But a strange thing now took place in the life of the Wreck of the Hesperus. The kidneys, which (none of us knew) had been an infernal trouble to him since his early childhood (the time his mother died) returned inexplicably to their proper working order. Better still, the new blood from the young man was seen to have the most alarming effects on his body, and it sent the women shrieking ('Go way to blazes, ye dirty devil!') when it became known that he had developed a new set of peculiarities from the blood squirted into him.

At first, he didn't know what to make of it and he became awfully anxious. The truth was that it had found its way down along his veins, down into his belly and into a lower and, ahem, cruder part of his manhood, namely his as-yet-untested private particles where it was unexpectedly and delightfully coursing the finest of streams that hadn't been felt since his wildest and most energetic schoolboy days. Had the world turned upside-down? If the rest of the men (particularly the byze in the drinking-shop) got to hear of such blood, they'd surely be selling all their horses and cattle and would go as far as Dublin to get some of its juices and become new men again like him.

In order to rid himself of the devilish liveliness that this new blood was causing him in his britches, the old heathen proposed to several fair damsels in the town (they blessed themselves twice over). Then he proposed to the married women as well as the unmarried ones. Even the holy nuns (you won't believe it) had the Devil's own work cut out for them to avoid the outcome that his lusty blood transfusion might cause them if he got hold of their robes. They ran like blazes, escaping from the town altogether and out through bushes and over stiles. Even the childish schoolgirls (and they no more than twelve years old) fled up the nearest tree-trunks and were seen high-jumping over ditches and gates when they saw him and his jug of whiskey running across the fields after them.

News of him spread like fire and there soon formed an earnest queue outside the gates of the hospital led by every hairy individual as old as nine and ninety. They all wanted a drop or two of the new blood in the hope of revivifying the reproductive particularities (Mee-Ould-Segocia's words) that had once been theirs.

4

But all this excitement to satisfy his needs was soon to take second place to yet another small incident. He got himself a terrible pain just below his left ear. Black Bess and a few other good nurses (those that weren't still running across ditches) came out and took him into the town hospital. It seemed that all the badness and wickedness in him had turned itself into an unnatural growth sticking out from his neck. As soon as he was settled in the hospital bed, Curl 'n' Stripes (he was a distant cousin) went in to see him and brought him a nosegay of fresh flowers and a naggin of whiskey to oil his throat.

For once in his life, the Wreck hadn't an ounce of energy in his body, and he left the nurses alone. They were as busy as fleas and started preparing a bath for him. The sight of his dirty naked body would be an illuminating spectacle for, like most of us, he'd never had a bath in all his life, and they were anxious to get him under the hot towels and tend to his unmentionables.

It was a black-looking morning when he realized that these women were going to strip him of all his clothing. He was suddenly awfully shy and refused to take off the hospital chemise he was wearing. If only he could sprout wings and fly away! If only he could die! Seemingly, the new blood had stopped working for him, and he had to put up with the nurses (all six of them) molesting him as no woman had ever before molested him and tickling him here and tickling him there (be nice for us, Wreck — go on, do!) where no woman in her right mind should have been allowed to dig at a man of his nobility. Ah, the dirty little savages that they were!

His terror reached such a pitch that he could stand it no longer. It was as though a river dam had suddenly been let loose in him. An avalanche in the shape of his hairy body came storming down the corridor and out through the hospital gates, sending Curl 'n' Stripes (he was coming in the gates at the time) and the flowers and the wasted whiskey to the four corners of the hospital gardens. Then came the nurses close behind their wild man, their arms flailing and full of the remains of his clothing, which they had snatched from off of his back.

As bone-naked as a newly-born child, the Wreck of the Hesperus made as tidy an exodus as a doomed pig before the butcher's knife. At an unheard-of speed, he vanished across the hospital flowerbeds and out onto the road. He headed in the direction of Jinnet Street and its astonished wayfarers and took the direction that would lead him home to Mee-Ould-Segocia. The nurses (fair play to them) continued their pursuit till they got as far as the railway bridge. But our hero was suddenly seen to make use of the blood transfusion inside in him and to keep his legs ahead of the pack. By then, these ladylike scholars were utterly exhausted and had to return to the hospital empty-handed. They were sure they'd be losing their jobs and would have no goose to eat next Christmas.

That same afternoon was a shivery one for our runaway. The rain was beating down on hill and valley, and there was no shelter for him as he struggled home by way of the Sheep Field a mile out of town. He reached Jiggity-Nan's farmyard and there (Lord be praised!) he found a pair of her satiny bloomers handily airing themselves inside her back door and waiting to be ironed — waiting also for his naked self to adorn himself in.

Togged out in this ridiculous garb (by this time the angels in Heaven were splitting their sides laughing), he made his way across five miles of fields before falling down, exhausted, near his home where the astonished Tom-the-Bee and Scooraloon Phil helped him out of his silk bloomers. This was a new one on them — a man in a pair of women's knickers. They took him home to Mee-Ould-Segocia and brought in an armful of furze bushes, which they lit around the fireplace. They kept his nose up close to the blaze to keep warm the last breath of life in his body. Very soon, they had such a mighty blaze going that the cat ran out the back door, steamed with the heat from it.

Next morning, the sun shone bright and gold. Arming him with a suit of clothes and his own best boots, they took him down to the river. With far less difficulty than the nurses had shown, they managed to strip him bare and pelted him, screeching, into the sally-hole. Then they jumped in after him. What fun and games these three merry fellows had as they washed him all over with the carbolic soap. He came out of the waters as though he'd been baptized in the Jordan River by John the Baptist's own good self. Then, dressed in the suit and wearing the big boots, he smelt as fresh as a new daisy. It could have been his wedding day! After all these heroics, they marched him back into hospital and informed the nurses that he was now as clean and crystal as a walking nun.

5

Matchmaking was part and parcel of our lives. Each year, Mee-ould-Segocia had held an auction of bachelors outside Din-Din-Dinny's stable. You know the long-winded way he always had with words.

'What am I proffered for this hairy old article and the fine specimen gaily resting between his thighs?' he'd whisper to the prospective brides, causing them to blush to the roots of their hair. He'd have the rest of us in stitches — he and his crafty impenetrable words.

The Wreck of the Hesperus had reached the comely age of 34 — a day or two more than when the tufts of downy fur first appeared on his cheeks, said Mee-Ould-Segocia, who realized that his beloved son was now old enough to catch a good roll-of-a-woman, a sorely-needed damsel for taking to his bedroom, and teasing with the love that had been warming itself in his britches. Yes (he thought), now was the hour for his son to stop chasing youngsters round the countryside and to put on the hard collar and necktie and go fetch back a woman to help him plough the eighty acres and give himself a houseful of children to gaze up at him and call him Daddy and in later years molly-coddle him to death with their smiles and laughter.

September was the month when matchmaking was in full vogue in the rattling towns of Clare and Galway. Mee-ould-Segocia got out the butter and lard for the brown boots. He got out the hedge-trimmer for his son's hair-cutting. He shaved him with his own cut-throat razor — nothing else was sharp enough for so great an occasion.

Next morning, the Wreck of the Hesperus was up early like the larks in the dewy grass and ready to go cast his magic wand on the waters of Love herself. He donned his pea-green flannelette shirt, which Mee-ould-Segocia had worn on his own wedding day. He put on the smart new sports-jacket and the grey flannel trousers. His father filled his pocket with sovereigns from the sale of three cows and two pigs. His son eyed himself in the glass — the larded hair, the buttered boots and he almost jumped out of his skin with the fright and delight. He was a pure glitter-of-a-man!

Mee-Ould-Segocia looked at him proudly. 'Ah-ha, mee charmer, doesn't the love-making flog all!' said he with a smile. He got his son further into trim by fixing a bit of shamrock in his coat, and with the rack, he carefully combed down those long forelocks of his, to cover the hole round his ear after his operation in the hospital. He gave him the sheep's red rodden to put his customary mark on the woman of his choice when he reached the matchmaking town.

It was almost time to set off. Mee-Ould-Segocia brought into the yard his finest white stallion (Swanny). Nothing less would do for this charming son of his. He polished and oiled the stallion's hooves as though he was taking him to the Show Fair. He tightened up the saddle-girth. Everything was now in ship-shape, and his son leapt up onto the saddle like a trooper. His father drenched him with holy water and gave the stallion a scapular and medal to twist in its mane. He brought out the Sacred Heart picture and a couple of religious medals and his son kissed each of them devoutly.

'Ah-ha, mee bucko, aren't you the rale dazzle-of-a-man!' he said as he looked at his son with his new double-sized hat that hid the hole next to his ear.

The Wreck of the Hesperus was ready for the road that would lead him to the mighty Shannon River and the Clare mountains. He'd been thinking about this day a good while — ever since that wondrous blood transfusion in the hospital and the alarming effects it had caused in his lower body. As he left the yard, he was like a lad who'd sold his first cow with the coins jingling in his pockets and his father's loving eyes on him. What joys he'd be having!

The sun was high in the sky and not even a few ribbed clouds seen anywhere. We could hear the clattering tattoo of Swanny's hooves coming down towards us from Sheep's Cross where the children were playing with their jackstones. Then into their view came the man himself, proudly riding his swan-necked stallion — the man they had recently feared would leap out at them and nail them to a tree.

They marvelled at the change in him for he was in the best of spirits and singing his father's old song: 'She's down from the mountains, her stockings are white and I'd like to be tying her garters tonight', and this time the children didn't jump into the nettles. He'd a smile on his lips tugging away at the corner of his mouth. He had his father's best suit on him, and he look-ed as good and new as a sweet-smelling rosebush and with fists of good money jingling in his pockets, and riding the best of his father's stallions, the white one.

The children were not to know that he was off to the matchmaking town to attack the young women and breed from one of them. He himself wasn't too sure how it would all turn out. If the worst came to the worst, and he failed in his quest, he'd be sure to get a good soak in one of the hot baths, and it'd do his body a power of good (his father had told him so). There'd be dancing and singing where he could give the floor the heel-and-toe and render a verse or two of the old songs. Besides all that, he would drink Clare dry (said he to himself), and if that wasn't enough, he would go on from there and drink Galway dry too.

By now he had reached Old Sam's stile and his heart continued to whoop with joyful feelings, unlike one or two of his sad forebears who had travelled down this same road and gone on to foreign shores — themselves and their look-back tears.

The inquisitive children ran down the road some ways behind him. They got as far as Gret's Kill and the waterfall and then he was gone from their sight — just the echo of Swanny's hooves as he stampeded on towards town and the unknown world ahead. They returned and sat in Old Stroller's orchard where they continued to wonder if they'd ever set eyes on him again. But their thoughts didn't last long, and they scurried up the slopes to continue their game of jackstones at the crossroads.

As the rest of us sat round our fires, we imagined his journey. He'd have crossed the Shannon (we knew that) before nightfall and maybe be out across the stone-walled fields of Clare and on through those mysterious towns of Match'em and Marrying-Fields. If Swanny proved good, he'd be near the Rattling Town itself and the drinking-shops with their merry crisp fires and the bright faces and the hot rum and whiskey. We'd heard it all before, and we sighed. Oh, how we wished we'd all thrown life aside like him and gone down the road to join him.

THE SHY WOMAN

1

The Wreck of the Hesperus had a lot on his mind as he sailed on towards Clare. His father had given him strict instructions. When he got to that far country, he was to sell his stallion at a fair price — that is, if he was able to agree on a wife to bring back with him. He was to purchase a horse-and-cart and two robust Clydesdale mares for the road home — the first horse to drag his beloved woman in the processional cart and the other one to follow along behind with the reins and blinkers and take over from time to time in the pulling of the good woman towards Tipperary.

He was in no mood for failure. Gone was the simpleton of yore that had pissed his trousers in the schoolyard from a pair of weak kidneys the time his mother drowned. Wasn't he the grandson of the dandified Dan-the-lion and no longer fit to be called the Wreck of the Hesperus? Wasn't he now a pure dandy himself? He knew he looked a treat — himself and Swanny, his big stallion. Before the day was gone, he'd have given both of them the finest of adventures across fields and farmyards, would have scattered several turkeys and geese and alarmed several herds of cattle and wild ponies as they went on their merry way — all taking flight at the sight of a man and a white horse on a mission of marriage.

2

He was there at last — at the watering-hole in the Rattling Town — and just in time for the opening ceremonies. On the journey, his mind had been racing round in his head, recalling how he and his father had had to put up with the salacious laughter of the jolly-boys in Curl 'n' Stripes' drinking-shop during his evenings of preparation — how the old gossips went round the countryside, mimicking the way he'd be screaming his way through Clare and then see them nodding their wicked old heads at what they believed ('we told you so') would be his abject failure to secure himself a wife.

'Be damned to the lot of them' (thought the Wreck of the Hesperus) — 'I'm mee father's son, and I'll make fools and horses' tails out of them all before I'm finished with them!'

He pushed his way boldly up to the centre of the Market Square where sundry farmers were busily exchanging accounts of their bank-money and (above all) proof of their land and its boundaries. The noise was tremendous — enough to wobble a poor fellow's stomach.

'Clear the way, lads!' roared one prospective farmer — as if to say here comes a fellow of some importance (namely his own good self), a brave man, who had taken to the map to take his chance in life and seal his dealings for a wife.

The fact that the Wreck of the Hesperus had a hole in the side of his head was going to mean little if anything to the young damsels. All that mattered (we all knew it) was that he owned land. Blasht it all! — hadn't he (though nobody in Clare yet knew it) eighty acres of the finest land — double the size of most farmers' apportioned divides? He also (being but 34) had the youth stamped on him since many of the prospectors were men in their forties and fifties, though they were still called a fine catch because of this very thing — the land. The more he thought about it, the more confident he grew that he'd beat the best of them when it came to bargaining — what with his charming boyish years (if he were to believe his father) and this double-sized land. What would a damsel say to a few broken teeth in a man's mouth?

And then there was another side to his thoughts on the bargaining — the makings of a suitable wife. What had his father said? Unless she'd be able to plough and bear him a houseful of children, what good would a damsel's rosy cheeks be to him? What good would her ruby lips and heavy chest be to him? They'd be gone into powder and dust within a decade whereas the land and he would be there to warm her purse and her bed for years and years to come.

He found himself a lodging-house above one of the countless drinking-shops where there were half-a-dozen other wishful farmers already stationed — some of them in their father's hand-me-down clothes. They were crowded like flies into a room behind wooden partitions where the reeking smell from their drinking, coughing, pissing and farting (a neat little combination) was strong enough to knock down a Dublin train. One or two of them talked incessantly in their dreams.

'Oh-ho, mee damsel, if I could get a hold of ye and get a little squeeze out of ye and mark mee claim on ye with the red sheep-rodden! cried one fellow.

'Oh-ho, mee damsel, if I could only get a few jostles from yeer pretty limbs — give ye the pleasure of a small injection now and then on a cold winter's night,' said another fellow.

On and on went their quaint phrasings and a few less salubrious compositions thrown into the bargain, against which a confession-box priest would have to block up his ears in case his soul might catch fire. How could the Wreck of the Hesperus get himself a blessed wink of sleep?

3

At this stage of the proceedings, the Wreck of the Hesperus hadn't an inkling of his intended bride's existence. The Shy Woman (as she was called) was whiling away the first morning of the matchmaking season in the kitchen of her mother (the Queen Bee) in Rindy-View on the outskirts of town. Before returning to the knitting of a particularly long stocking (a gift for her father), she was busying herself making half-a-dozen apple and rhubarb tarts to take down to the Market-Square and sell to the farmers. She had prepared a dozen doorstep-sandwiches of ham and mutton to help keep the drinkers in good spirits and line her mother's purse with those extra few shillings from the sale.

In the preceding years, her two older brothers had bought an early ticket for the steam-train to Dublin and on to London, the city we called Pandemonium, leaving their father (Patsy) weeping on the station platform for the loss of them. There'd be nobody left to tend their 18 acres now. You couldn't blame them for running away. They couldn't go on waiting till dooms-day when they might finally hear stubborn old Patsy making up his mind on his deathbed (if at all) as to how much land he'd give each of them. It was always the same sad tale.

And what of the Shy Woman's older sisters? These two (Gabby and Snooty) were twice as well off now and were the envy of the town — able to put on fancy black hats and black lace across their faces on Sundays when they were at Mass and wrap scarves around their throats and ears. They had grey double-breasted suits and (would you credit it!) they had shoes with four-inch high heels — they, who had been seen in the bare feet only the day before yesterday. They were (their mother, the Queen Bee, sighed) as good as any queen on a throne and would never look back to the stony hills around Clare. They were settled in style for the rest of their lives, living on the fine clay-fields of fertile Tipperary.

Like today — it was at the Matchmaker's Fair that these two lucky girls had met their future husbands, accompanied in the dealings by the middle-man and the go-between. God be praised! — after the fuss and the wedding bells they soon became endowed with new refinements — attending to their hens, ducks and geese, learning how to take their place in the marketplace for the springtime sales of lambs and calves, getting to know the delicacies surrounding their noble sow and her piglets. It would be the same (God willing) for the Shy Woman, who still had nothing better to do than spend her nights looking out the window at the stars clustering above the streets. She'd better hurry on. For, though still a few months short of 20, she was beginning to feel like some small bird trapped in a cage and longing to get free. She knew that the universe elsewhere was a very big place indeed.

There were other things she also knew — that when it came to the match-making, there'd be no mention of that strange word, romancing, which she had read about. It simply belonged to the realms of fairyland. Like all her young friends, she knew that these old farmers were all made up from the same package when it came to their dealings with a young damsel. They liked the drop-of-drink, liked to be working out of doors, liked the fresh air of the hills and the woods and the rivers, and were as shy as a pack of wild asses when it came to that little bit of romancing that a young girl's heart craved for. There'd be no holding of hands, no amorous blandishments (blasht these savage old farmers!) whispered into her ear. The hugging and the kissing may as well have been written in Bog-Latin for all these hairy old lads cared. None of them would be bothering a wife too often in the four-poster bed unless they had a fair share of drink in their bellies to give them that bit of a lift. Indeed, all the intimacies that the Shy Woman and the other convent-girls had dreamt of a year or two back while strolling in the school gardens — all their dreaminess about some charming prince coming to them on his white stallion and waiting with his foot on the stirrup for them at the convent gates — was just hot air in a pig's bladder. However, a prospective bride was always prepared to bear this miserable cross upon her back for the sake of the bit of land and a lifetime of security from poverty and spinsterhood.

She had two younger sisters left with her at home, not yet thought ready to enter the marriage stakes. These two now set out to view the excitement of the matchmaking. They were as skittish as young mares and as eager as girls going to their first Platform-Dance, parading with feigned disinterest amidst the fun going on at Goosy-Goosy-Gander's drinking-shop up at the Market Square. And (damn the bit!), whom should they first cast their eyes on? Why, the Tipperary man himself, the Wreck of the Hesperus, and he just leaping down from his stallion. They eyed him from his boots to his poll. He was not exactly a charmer-of-a-knight-in-armour out of their dreamy school-books. And yet, he was a dasher-of-a-man. Having tied his horse at the ostler's gate, he went in the doorway of the drinking-shop.

They had brought along with them their ten-year-old brother (the Gossoon) with a job for him to do.

'Find out all that ye can about the man from Tipperary,' they nudged him. 'Keep yeer ears cocked when ye're inside in the drinking-shop. Bring us back all the news ye can get.'

But they were already having their own thoughts. They could see he had the fine white stallion — a sign, perhaps, that he'd come into money or owned a fair-sized farm. Also, he had a face well-reddened by the sun, and this (they believed) was not a man who sat lazily by the fire the livelong day. And he had a belly on him like a harvest frog. This showed them a man well-fed with a fine table full of the best food. Whether he knew the delicacies of how to handle a knife and fork was not of great importance. Nor was it assumed a setback that he has a few bad teeth in his mouth.

The Gossoon came running back breathlessly to give them the news they had wanted to hear. The Tipperary man was the owner of land — land in plenty (said their brother), having two divides and not one, namely eighty acres of fine grassland and hardy black cattle and horses to go with it.

4

Patsy sent the Gossoon to fetch back the matchmaker and the go-between with him and left instructions for these experienced fixers of matrimony to find out all they could and bring back the news to him that evening. Of course, none of them could set sail for Tipperary and walk the land of this prospective catch. But the daughters had seen how he had brought with him the papers and indentures, and it would be a simple matter of confirming his ownership in the coming days. When the cunning matchmaker arrived (for there was a reward of money in it for him), he failed to mention that the Wreck of the Hesperus had a small hole on the side of his head and a lost ear to go with it.

'No,' said the Queen Bee, 'he's not such a bad catch, and he's only 34.' The deal could be settled that evening. The land would do it.

Patsy was warming to the idea, having had a sad little thought to prompt and encourage him. He could picture his daughter sitting like a sick lemon at the side of his fire for the rest of her days — growing into ripe old spinsterhood and knitting an everlasting stocking that would fit a giant. He had to agree with the Queen Bee: the Tipperary man was the best offer she was ever likely to get. She'd be safe and secure for the rest of her days.

As always with parents, both he and his wife were far too uncomfortable to talk to their shy daughter about those more intimate husband-and-wife matters. They hoped that that she would cope (like all women before her had had to do) with the bedroom arrangements, for she had assisted both the bull and the stallion at the time of procreation — not to mention the billy-goat. And besides (they thought), her priest would be only too glad to advise her what to do. One way or another, she would get herself enough fat babies to support her during the latter stages of her life, thank God.

5

The Shy Woman gave a little shudder. The thought of it all —
a future husband and he was only 34, and she still an almost-
child and just three years out of her ankle-socks. Gabby's
husband had been 52 and Snooty's man 46, and yet both
of them appeared happy enough souls. No (she thought), the
age of a man wasn't what led to the altar steps. After a little
persuasion from her young sisters, she decided to go downtown
herself and cast an eye on this fine specimen of a man and see
was he the rale shilling. If things went according to plan, she'd
be hopping up on the Tipperary man's cart and setting sail for
the new county within a day or two.

She arrived at Goosy-Goosy-Gander's drinking-shop where
the Wreck of the Hesperus was busily carousing. She took a
good look at him from outside the window. The shop's lamp-
light illuminated the faces of all the sturdy farmers, shining
on their jerseys and the cock of their hats thrown back on
their polls. They were putting pipe-smoke to the heavens and
drinking their drink hot-and-fast as though it were the last
drop on earth.

And then she beheld this new ornament-of-a-man with his
buttered toecaps — a man with high cheekbones and his hair
down the middle of his back like a long distemper brush. It
was a sight not seen every day in the Rattling Town — like a
horse's mane (she thought) and the colour of a sweet nut. He
had a huge felt hat gingerly slung over his right ear — a
charming effect in itself, and it gave him a strangely noble
look. She noted the way he cocked his elbow as he ladled his
glass of stout down his throat, the way he gently wiped the
beer-froth from his upper lip, the way he sat contentedly on

the high stool next to an old fellow itching his backside, the way he flared the match and lit his cigarette in his cupped hands and shook the match in a gay little flourish. He'd do entirely (she thought to herself).

She was now inside the shop-door and had the chance to take stock of the other farmers looking for a woman to be the mother of their future children. Unlike this man from Tipperary, some of them (she saw) had a scrofulous look about them — some of them painstakingly picking their nose and inspecting the findings, others holding their nostrils in a pinch and expertly blowing out the well-aimed snotty contents into the fireplace and wiping their hands daintily on their trousers or spitting gobfuls of phlegm into the fire and watching it sizzle. They'd never get a woman that way.

The Tipperary man seemed a nobler specimen with none of these ungainly habits. No young foal had ever cocked its tail so high (she thought) as this fine fellow sitting on his stool and engaging himself in carefree conversation with the other farmers as though he'd been here all his life. And (best of all — she couldn't get it out of her head) this was a man with a double-sized farm — eighty acres of land to his name.

For his part, the Wreck of the Hesperus couldn't help noticing the way the Shy Woman kept staring at him, the way she was holding her own bit of red sheep-rodden in her awkward little fist. He felt the sweaty drops of shyness hanging on his brow as he thought what he'd have to do to ensnare a young woman as fine as this. Then he thought of his father back home and, in spite of his awkwardness, he managed to hop down from his perch and shove up close towards her. Stammeringly (a mannerism she also well liked), he introduced himself to her.

She could see his uneasiness, and she gave him a little nod and followed it up with, 'I am very glad to meet you, kind sir.'

This damsel (said he to himself) was the fairest creature he'd seen in a long while and a tenderness crept over him. He couldn't take his eyes off her and the vivacity that he saw in her. She reminded him of his gentle mother (poor Daisy-Chains) and the waxy curls of her hair, black as a cat. He could see she came from sturdy stock — who'd help him milk his cows and tend his wheat-field whilst he handled the heavier tasks with the pickaxe and long-handled shovel. If he could find a way to mark her with his sheep-rodden, he'd be the happiest man the length and breadth of Ireland. He'd be Samson and Solomon rolled into a ball, should he bring back this innocent young woman as his wife — and do so at his very first attempt at match-making.

He said a silent little prayer and took out several sovereigns from his coat-pocket and threw them nonchalantly on the counter. He bought the Shy Woman a thimbleful of hot rum-punch and a platter of the best ham and spuds, and soon the two of them were having a rale good time of it as they shovelled down these relishes. He continued to give the Shy Woman the glad eye, and she in turn, it must be said, was every bit as good at giving it back to him. By now — what with all this carousing and the ham and the spuds and the rest of the tomfoolery — he had won over a small portion of her heart and, if he hadn't already quite succeeded in winning all of it, he had won over the brains inside in her head, what with the fine 80 acres of Tipperary land that he and his father shared. And there and then they gave each other a small smear-marker of the sheep-rodden.

6

'Twas the evening for the match to be made. The matchmaker and the go-between were called to the house. Patsy was seated inside the half-door to welcome the Wreck of The Hesperus. The Queen Bee rested herself regally on the settle-bed. They had saved the best chair in the house for the Tipperary man (brought out from the parlour). There followed a small bout of pretend coquetry and artless affectation on the part of the shy couple.

A respectable silence then took over, marred only by the ticking of the clock. And then there came the spit on the fists and the sweaty grip of the hands of Patsy and the Wreck of the Hesperus to cement the bargain. Patsy could see how happy and unruffled his young daughter was. A merry heart started to beat under his coat at the sight of the shy and pensive Tipperary man and he took to him (and his land, I hear you say) as a shine to a plate.

There were further handshakes all round and there was no need for any intervention from the go-between or the middleman. After that bit of cordiality, there followed the luck penny in the form of five golden sovereigns from the Shy Woman's father as a dowry and good fortune proposal. The Wreck of the Hesperus gave the Queen Bee and Patsy the two red apples he'd kept in his pocket for this special occasion. Then there followed a further dose of good luck as a few solid pints of stout apiece were manfully ladled down into the stomachs of the partakers sitting round the fireside before the handsome pair were allowed to depart for the parlour and to converse privately in their own good time.

In the meantime, the Queen Bee had dragged the table out into the middle of the floor and had covered it with her best white tablecloth. The celebration that followed was nothing short of a small banquet and no economy was spared for such an occasion. She brought down her best cups, saucers and plates from the press. She jingled her Sheffield-steel knives and forks onto the tablecloth. She placed the sougan-chairs round the table and invited her guest to get ready for the feast.

She cut up the yalla-meal bread and curranty cake into huge slices and layered them with thick butter. Such a bustle — would she ever stop fussing? She then got busy with the tea-caddy and kept the teapot going. In less than a minute, she had a heap of sausages and onions sizzling and spluttering on the pan in the middle of the blazing fire and the savoury steam rose up to the rafters. And soon no one was behind-hand in tearing their knives and forks into the fine fare (there'd be no leavings left over for the cat or the dog). Then the good woman brought forth from the burner a great big apple-batter cake for all their eyes to feast on. It was a dish as good as a pigeon-and-ham pie (thought Patsy), and they'd need the stomachs of a wild rhinoceros to eat all that his wife had laid out for them on this evening-of-all-evenings. It wouldn't be long (thought Patsy again) before they'd have to unbuckle their britches, one and all.

Finally, the Queen Bee brought out her pink wine glasses from her own wedding-day. She poured out the fiery potato-whiskey (the potheen), and they all quickly pounced on the drink with their noses dipped down into the glass. Sweet indeed was the drink as it worked its way down inside their throats. It began to get the better of them, and it loosened their tongues. Laughter and merriment egged them on to spin a yarn or two and all that was missing (it was Patsy yet again) was a bit-of-a-dance and a chance for the heel-tapping of the Clare-batter to be hammered on the flagged floor.

The Wreck of the Hesperus shook hands once more with the Shy Woman's father and mother. Then (as was proper) he knelt before Patsy and asked him his blessing, which was now royally given.

'We are decent people,' said Patsy with a bit of a stammer. The Wreck of the Hesperus then shook hands with the go-between and the matchmaker. He shook hands with the Gossoon and with the sisters. He was speechless with joy, and there were tears in his eyes as he smothered the Shy Woman's hair with his innocent kiss. The match was complete.

From now on, both he and she had their fame and fortune. With God's help, a brood of children would follow and bless them in their old age. They'd be taken to the early-morning Mass next day for the priest to strengthen their spiritual resolve and get the priest's consent before courting in earnest could commence. Finally, the holy water came to the fore and the two of them were showered with it. The Queen Bee (her eyes full of dreaminess) brought out the grandfather clock from the bedroom — this, to be her daughter's dowry and a wedding present for her future sound man.

7

A day or two later, it was time to hit the road for Tipperary and start their new life. With the help of the Gossoon and her two sisters, the Shy Woman was ladled up onto The Wreck of the Hesperus's new horse-and-cart. True to his father's bidding, he had also replaced the white stallion with two good Clydesdale mares, which were both given a good soaking of the Cindy-foot powders to prepare their legs for the long journey ahead and rubbed down with the potato-sacks to dry them off.

Patsy had to shade his eyes as he performed this task so as to hide the fat tears dripping down his jaws. He gave the sacks to the Wreck of the Hesperus so that he could wipe the mud from the mares' legs and scrape it off before they reached Tipperary. He ran back in the door and came out with the bottle of holy water from the press. He showered the happy couple with it and blessed the two mares with a liberal dose of it.

After that, they loaded the grandfather clock up onto the back of the cart, and Patsy (an additional surprise) roped onto it a big bed he had been hiding from them — to enable them (he said) to get merry when they got to Tipperary. Then the Wreck of the Hesperus wrapped a thick tartan rug round the Shy Woman's feet and gave her a shawl for her head and shoulders in case the rain came on. He seated her on the lat board and the sacking stuffed with straw. There she sat — ladylike and with her head higher than usual and clasping the shawl tightly round her calico skirts.

Her eyes were glistening. She couldn't help looking down at her sad parents and a rich flow of mixed blood was coursing through her heart. She felt those twin feelings that all who had ever left the homestead before her must have felt — pain at leaving her parents and the loss of them, joy for the long road ahead and the merry new life she'd be starting out when she got to Tipperary.

The Wreck of the Hesperus looked back at his Shy Woman and thought to himself what excitement there'd be in a day or two when the two of them would see the smoke rising up from Mee-Ould-Segocia's chimney and the hillside full of people rushing down the lane to welcome them and run their eyes up and down this fine young woman coming to live among us. The thoughts of others wouldn't worry the Wreck of the Hesperus a bit, for he knew that the sunlight would rise up and shine forever between him and his Shy Woman. Enough said.

After all the fussing and the blessing and loading the dowry gifts up onto the cart, it was already afternoon and the little swifts were beckoning the happy pair to follow them up the lane that would lead them out of Rindy-View and eventually out of Clare.

The whole neighbourhood had gathered in the yard and out onto the lane, their nervous handkerchiefs ready to wave over their heads. Though some of them were already crying, the Wreck of the Hesperus felt like a cat full of morning cream, and his thoughts were feathery light when he thought of his future ahead. He pulled out his father's Sacred Heart scapular and his mother's religious medals and kissed them ceremoniously.

Then he raised his eyes to the heavens and cried out, 'Praise be! Praise be! At mee first attempt I have found meeself a wife, the grandest damsel in all the world.' And everybody cheered and clapped their hands. No wonder he felt so happy; for Din-Din-Dinny had been coming out west for 17 years before he was able to get himself a young woman ('to throw mee leg over,' he'd said, the rascal).

The Wreck of the Hesperus pulled the cart out jerkily from the yard and away they set towards the peace and quiet of the Tipperary hills. With the gift of the grandfather clock and the big bed, he felt like his granduncle (Old Turtle) who had once packed up all his sea-stores and headed off for the green fields of Canada.

They were soon out of sight and gone forever, and it was a very sad and faint-hearted Queen Bee that stood looking up the lane at the ghost of her daughter and her man in the cart. She knew it wouldn't be long before they'd be swallowed up in the sun's afterglow and the shivery night across the mighty Shannon River. The Wreck of the Hesperus (no tears in him) had managed to hold onto a good few of his father's shiny sovereigns and had kept them locked in his hip-pocket. There'd be time for yet another big celebration when he and his Shy Woman reached home.

8

After two days hard travelling, the horse-and-cart reached Echo Bridge. On the bridge, the Wreck of the Hesperus saw the children's ass-and-car and their unfilled tar-barrels for their mother's water. He pulled up in the middle of the bridge above the heads of Moll-the-Man's children. He held back the reins tightly in his fists and leaned back in his cart.

Blasht it and blasht it all over again! The children had never expected to see him again in this mortal life. He'd now know where they were hiding in the bushes and none of them had the courage to come up from their hiding-place. The tar-barrels could go hang!

'We'll fill them when he gets a piece further up the slope — or else he'll kill us all if he finds us here.'

Then Lippy, Philly and Gallantry took stock of the situation. There was no sign of the wild man's hammer and nails, and his once-distorted face had a far different hue to it. Where had their ogre-of-old disappeared to? Had they forgotten how cheerfully he had left them only the week before last? And somehow the sky seemed bluer and the sun seemed to have turned as white as a daisy and appeared to grow out of the back of the Wreck of the Hesperus's head, turning him full of its brightness.

He sensed that the children were hiding in the bushes, and he raised himself nobly into the air. From under the lat board of the cart he took out his sack. By now Young Jim, Leppity, and Battlin' Sal had started to peep their little snub noses out from behind their big brothers' backs. They were ready to run their legs off between here and Dublin should he get down from the cart and chase after them.

'Stay, little children, stay!' cried the wild man and his smile was as broad as Galway Bay and his voice as soft as sugar. He then did a mighty strange thing and waved the sack three times round his hat before pelting it away from the cart where it landed beside the children in the bushes. This once-terrifying taskmaster then looked down into their frightened eyes from above on his cart, and he had the ruby light of love in him, which at once banished all their fears.

'There'll be no more sacks,' said he. 'There'll be no more hammer and nails. Never again will a child be nailed to a tree. I give ye mee solemn oath.'

An even stranger thing then happened. This former vagrant — this serene new man — drew out from his pockets two handfuls of golden sovereigns and without so much as a frown, flung them to the four winds and let out a roar from inside in his belly, a roar like no bull had ever roared before.

'I have coom home! I have coom home! I have brought ye home mee fortune!'

The children were left scratching their heads and wondering if the Wreck of the Hesperus had turned into a hobgoblin. For they could see that what he had just said was nothing but a damned lie — he had thrown away his entire fortune, hadn't he? If they'd looked a bit closer they'd have seen, however, the wistful eye-of-romance in him. He had his fortune safe and sound in the shape of the young woman sitting beside him, to whom his outstretched arms were now pointing — his own lovely Shy Woman.

9

As soon as the cart went on up the road, Lippy, Philly, and Gallantry were seen scrambling out of the bushes. They took an hour and a half, but they collected all the sovereigns. They followed the Wreck of the Hesperus all the way back to his yard — to give them back to him. By then they could see how much he was in love with life and with this innocent young woman from Clare.

It was getting on towards evening, and the sun would soon be going down. Mee-Ould-Segocia thought he heard the rattling wheels of a cart buffeting its way up the windy lane. He rushed to the half-door stretching out his neck like some hungry crane. A procession of neighbours had gathered down the lane to follow the Wreck of the Hesperus and his dainty new woman in the lane. Solemnly, they led the cart and her across the stream and into the yard. All the time they were eyeing her up and down. Her charms were beginning to beguile them all. They could see she was a hearty young woman that would bear the Wreck of the Hesperus a host of beautiful babies in the years to come. Her children (though this and much more they were not yet to know) would prove to be sweet-natured like herself. She would knit her sound man fine pairs of socks to keep his feet warm in winter. She would be his companion at the closing of each day. She would warm his cold arse in the five-fat-blanket bed. She would help him with the sowing and the ploughing. She would help him with the milking and the harvesting. Like a goat that finds itself willingly tied to another goat (a goat that cannot free itself from the chains and the post), the Wreck of the Hesperus would stay as delighted as could be to be entwined to his Shy Woman from Clare.

The Shy Woman kept staring at all the new wonders — the house in front of her, newly-whitewashed as if in her honour, the surrounding pine trees that had forever graced the hills, the chickens and the geese in the yard (seemingly there to greet her).

The father and son shivered with joy when they finally laid eyes on each other. Mee-Ould-Segocia shook himself several times. Was this his prodigal son returning from Clare and with such a fine young woman as this? Could this vision truly be his beloved boy and he still wearing his grandfather's wide-brimmed hat? He raced across the yard to greet the hero and marvelled at the sight of the Shy Woman (she was indeed a catch amongst many). A sheen of moisture covered the poor man's eyes as his son hopped down from the cart and fell into his arms. Mee-Ould-Segocia could see that he had turned from a snail to a busy bee at the matchmaking scene beyond in Clare — that together with his new woman he would indeed prove himself a new man in the days and nights ahead. Not forgetting his manners, his son went back to the cart and gently lifted his Shy Woman down from the lat board. He led her in through the half-door, and then the crowd of neighbours went away home respectfully, knowing that all would be well. He took the two mares by the blinkers and led them into the shed and gave them each enough hay to feed a famine for the way they'd behaved themselves on the long journey home.

Everything inside the welcoming room was in the best of shape. Mee-Ould-Segocia had scrubbed the floor and had swept the hearth clean. He had decked the walls with green bushes and red rowan-berries in anticipation of this happy day. He had polished the table and dresser as good as his dead wife (poor Daisy-Chains) had ever done in the past, and they shone like a haystack in a snowy haggart. Indeed, everything shone with a bright light, and he'd completed the arrangement with a raging fire blazing up the chimney.

10

The following day, Mee-Ould-Segocia (and you remember the way he loved using those great big words of his) sent out a host of intricately-worded invitations all over the hills — as far as Diggledy-doo and the Lackadaisicals and the High 'n' Dry Men — to celebrate the occasion of his son's prodigious home-coming with his esteemed young ladylove from the confines of Clare.

All the local celebrities (indeed half the countryside) would come scurrying up the hill bringing their inquisitiveness along with them, so as to get a close look at the new woman, and to see if the women from Clare were any bit different from our own women. They'd be sure to take a polite little tour of the yard and the outhouses and inspect the flowers along the walls as well as take a look in at the two new pigs. Among them would be those crazy characters: Slipperslapper and Clever Jack, the Yellow-Boy and Old Stroller, By-Jiggery and Moll-the-Man, Rambling Jack, Red Scissors and My-son-Jack, Taedspaddy, Bunnyfoot and Tommy's Tim, Din-Din-Dinny and Ducks-and-Drakes, Galloping Gret and Cackles, Curl 'n' Stripes and Leggins — all these and countless others (not to mention a few of our more venturesome cats and dogs), as well as a host of children ranging from Lippy and Philly downwards, Gallantry with his youthful charmer, Cherish, together with Young Joe, Leppity and Battling Sal.

Mee-Ould-Segocia was wet-eyed at the thought of what would happen next. The Shy Woman and her dignified beauty would make each of her guests a graceful little bow of welcome. And then (he could see it all) it'd be as fine a night as was ever seen in the hills of Tipperary — what with the homemade songs (many of us had that small bit of silver in our throats) and a few recitations that would bring back a memory or two. And for once in her life, the little song-thrush drying her feathers in the nearby bushes would find herself out-glittered as she looked on at the harmlessness of Man and the innocence of Woman.

There'd be a good bit of dancing with one or two youngsters giving each other the odd little love-glance. He himself would be seated in his armchair, puffing on his pipe by the fire and watching the merry-go-round with his happy leaky eyes. We would each bring enough foodstuff to feed a famine, filling our bellies with lashings of roast goose, hams and sausages, fletches of bacon, hare-soup and pig's cruibeens. There'd be chicken and rabbit delicacies (as good as a priest's supper) and gallons of milk to wash the whole thing down until the lot of us would have a slab of grease from ear to ear. For the men, there'd be jars of raw-gut potheen as had never before washed the insides of a man's stomach. There'd be three big barrels of stout so that everyone would be like gaunt corpses for days on end and find themselves on Doctor Glasses' sick-list for at least a week-and-a-half. What on earth would the Shy Woman make of this great big welcome for her? Were we all pure mad?

And then the day came on — late September before autumn crept in, and the summer crept away from us. With such a crowd there was only one barn big enough to house such a gathering — the Big Balloon's barn. The whole pack of us (humming with excitement and all scrubbed and cleaned to death, even behind our ears and the back of our necks) hurried across the hills in our best britches and colourful Sunday dresses, not forgetting our well-cleeted boots ready for a bit-of-a-dance.

We soon reached the Big Balloon's barn with its huge red doors (yes — she had been a monstrously fat woman that was dead and buried these last 80 years). The woodland fairies now followed the ghost-of-us through the blackened pine trees, leaving the slopes far behind and as bare and bald as an egg. And then everyone was there in the barn.

See the merry faces of the well-wishers, swollen from all the fine cheer laid out before them. Listen to the wondrous rushets of fiddle-playing music from Fiddler Jim as well as the concertina and squeeze-box of Gus Gilton and Hammer-the-Smith bouncing off of the walls and thrashing the rafters. Hear the deafening shouts. Such rich red laughter (was it a fair day?). Such a flittering of half-sets and spinning of polkas, all as light and tidy as a buttercup. Such unclouded glory in the eyes of the dreamy waltzers wheeling their toes out into the dark recesses of the cobbled yard. By now you'd think the flagstones were on fire, so frisky were the young sparrow-farts in our midst. Even the old ones (though they hadn't had a drop of the newly-transfused blood given to the Wreck of the Hesperus) were trying desperately to get back the youth that had long run away from them as they busily flexed their leg-muscles. And another thing — no cow, ass, horse or hen would get an ounce of sleep this blessed night.

But finally, we were all left as tired as a turkey with a cramp in her jaw — beaten into utter exhaustion from the magic and royal style of this great night in the Big Balloon's barn. There wasn't a soul that didn't feel better than they'd ever felt before from the reaping of it all — especially the wide-eyed children. It had put an end to the sorrow they had felt for poor Sammy the night of the Wran-Byze Dance. But oh, and alas — and before you could blink an eye — the misty moon departed, gobbled up in the charcoal haze of lessening night, and the dawn came in far too quickly, and the downy owl and the woolly bat flew silently home and disappeared into their hidey-holes. A little speck of pink and orange showed softly in the darkness and came creeping into the yard. We heard the early-morning cuirlew achingly calling us from the depths of the bog. And then the Big Balloon's barn was slashed with harsh slits of daylight coming hot and foxy through the doorway and onto the turf-floor and blinding the eyes out of us all. The sky above the pine trees grew rusty-red all the way down as far as the river. It had been a rattling good time that none of us would have wished to miss.

'A great bit of a night,' said Rambling Jack, and Mee-Ould-Segocia had to laugh at such a pure understatement.

As the daylight finally scudded in over Corcoran's well, our dark silhouettes shambled home in dribs and drabs, our heads full of dreams — to get back to the stern reality of chopping the daily logs for the morning's fire. The grainy-eyed children too — it was high time for them to disperse and get back to their innocent playgrounds — the fields, the woods and the rolling rivers and the fairy spirits that were forever calling out to these little scallywags of ours. And in the days that followed this wondrous bout of revelry, Clever Jack would tell us how he had turned himself into two new men before the end of this night-of-all-nights — into a fellow called Half-Drunk and another lad called Dead-Drunk, after he had traced his drinking-glass along a stick so as to guide the beautiful booze into the back of his mouth and down his throat. And the men from Diggledy-doo (a number of them not too good at the written words), to whom he had once told his wicked lies when reading them the daily news from the newspaper, now had to laugh out loud. They'd have their own news from the Big Balloon's barn – the best news ever - to tell the old folk as soon as they got home.

www.ingramcontent.com/pod-product-compliance
Lightning Source LLC
Chambersburg PA
CBHW030243200626
46816CB00002BA/481